36
RIGHTEOUS
MEN

36
RIGHTEOUS
MEN

Steven Pressfield

W. W. NORTON & COMPANY
Independent Publishers Since 1923

Copyright © 2020 by Steven Pressfield

Printed in the United States of America
First Edition

For information about permission to reproduce selections from this book, write to Permissions, W. W. Norton & Company, Inc., 500 Fifth Avenue, New York, NY 10110

For information about special discounts for bulk purchases, please contact W. W. Norton Special Sales at specialsales@wwnorton.com or 800-233-4830

Manufacturing by Lake Book
Book design by Ellen Cipriano
Production manager: Anna Oler

Library of Congress Cataloging-in-Publication Data

Names: Pressfield, Steven, author.
Title: 36 righteous men : a novel / Steven Pressfield.
Description: First edition. | New York : W. W. Norton & Company, Inc., 2019.
Identifiers: LCCN 2019014779 | ISBN 9781324002895 (hardcover)
Subjects: | GSAFD: Mystery fiction. | Suspense fiction.
Classification: LCC PS3566.R3944 A614 2019 | DDC 813/.54—dc23
LC record available at https://lccn.loc.gov/2019014779

W. W. Norton & Company, Inc., 500 Fifth Avenue, New York, N.Y. 10110
www.wwnorton.com

W. W. Norton & Company Ltd., 15 Carlisle Street, London W1D 3BS

1 2 3 4 5 6 7 8 9 0

FOR STERLING LORD

And God saw that the wickedness of man was great in the earth, and that every imagination of the thoughts of his heart was only evil continually . . . And the Lord said, I will destroy man whom I have created from the face of the earth; both man, and beast, and the creeping thing, and the fowls of the air; for it repenteth me that I have made them.

GENESIS 6:5–7, BEFORE THE FLOOD

If it don't splatter, it don't matter.

SAYING AMONG LAW ENFORCEMENT OFFICERS

BOOK ONE

DIVSIX

1

A MURDER IN GEORGETOWN

MRS. PERRY COULD HEAR the dog barking. She thought immediately, *Something's wrong.*

Mrs. Perry [Madelyn R., 47] stepped out onto the rear landing of her townhouse. From there she could see the animal below in the adjoining courtyard of the townhouse belonging to Michael A. Justman. It was Dr. Justman's dog [didn't get name of animal]—a ninety-pound Rhodesian ridgeback, a special breed bred in Africa to hunt lions.

The dog, Mrs. Perry stated, was normally very well behaved. It was now, however, "acting completely crazy," making "violent rushes" from the ground-level courtyard halfway up the flight of steps that ascended to the rear landing and back door of Dr. Justman's townhouse, barking furiously, then running back down, still barking, then charging back up again.

A characteristic of Rhodesian ridgebacks, Mrs. Perry said she had learned earlier from Dr. Justman, is that they don't bark, or only a little.

Mrs. Perry was now seriously alarmed. She called to her husband, Ernest V. Perry, 51, who was inside their townhouse. "I told him to come out right this second and bring his phone."

Mrs. Perry descended the flight of steps into her own rear court. She could see the ridgeback dog up close now, on the far side of the common wall between her yard and Dr. Justman's. The animal's ears were lying flat and saliva was dripping "in long strings" from its jaws. Mrs. Perry noted neighbors appearing on other landings above the common court behind the row of townhouses. She recognized one friend, Ms. Luterinaitis [Alicia C., 67], whose residence was on the far side of Dr. Justman's. Mrs. Perry shouted to Ms. Luterinaitis to call 911.

[I have all this, by the way, from the local PD incident report (Georgetown V-663-61724) and from the detectives' written statements. I have verified its accuracy by reviewing the townhouse association's security video, Dr. Justman's personal in-home security video, and my own notes. I interviewed Mrs. Perry and her husband, and three neighbors, including Ms. Luterinaitis, the following day, 18 April 2034.]

Mrs. Perry had now advanced to a point halfway up the rear stairway of Dr. Justman's townhouse. She called Dr. Justman's name but received no response. Mrs. Perry heard a "terrible sound" and, straining to see into the kitchen of the townhouse [the rearmost room], thought she saw a body, which she assumed to be Dr. Justman's, "flung through the air as if it had been kicked by a mule" and crash into the wall, against which were a Wolf stove and a double-door Sub-Zero refrigerator. Mrs. Perry could hear the body "collide violently" with these objects.

Suddenly, Mrs. Perry stated, the ridgeback dog bolted past her up Dr. Justman's steps. The animal burst through the rear [kitchen] door, which apparently was partially ajar, and charged into the house. Mrs. Perry took one more step but, she stated, was too frightened to advance farther. She heard a man's cry from inside the kitchen and another "smashing sound of flesh against flesh." The ridgeback dog was now fully inside the house, barking even more furiously than before. At this point Mrs. Perry's husband arrived from next door, joining Mrs. Perry on the stairwell, as did Ms. Luterinaitis from the townhouse on the opposite side. In a group the three climbed the final steps and peered through the open rear door into the kitchen.

Dr. Justman's body lay at the base of the refrigerator. No other individual was present or visible from the witnesses' vantage point. The ridgeback dog had advanced all the way into the living room now. This room was adjacent to and visible in its entirety from the kitchen. The dog was barking and making the same furious up-and-back rushes. None of the witnesses could see what the dog was rushing at. All three stated that they had an unobstructed view of the full length and breadth of the interior of the front room as well as of the foyer, but could see nothing in any of these but the dog.

Suddenly the animal stopped barking. A sound like the closing of the house's front door was heard. Mr. Perry crossed the kitchen from the back door to where Dr. Justman lay motionless. "Are you all right?" he said, calling Dr. Justman's name. He repeated this several times, then knelt and attempted to find a pulse. Dr. Justman lay still. His throat was "bruised and discolored" and his neck was twisted, Mr. Perry stated, at "an unnatural angle."

The house had become deathly quiet. The neighbors stood in a group above Dr. Justman's body. The ridgeback dog came back from the front room into the kitchen. The hair was standing straight up on its dorsal spine. The dog took two steps into the kitchen, then sank to the floor and collapsed in death. A necropsy [veterinary autopsy] performed the following morning determined that the animal's heart had burst.

2

MIDTOWN ATHLETIC CLUB

MANNING [DETECTIVE JAMES T.] wrestles every morning for exercise. It's part of his fitness routine. He enters the wrestling gym in the basement of the Midtown Athletic Club in Manhattan at five forty-five sharp. He has two friends, both former college wrestlers, as he was. They work out together.

Manning leaves his cell phone in a secure locker while he wrestles. He will not respond to any communication or text during that hour or the shower and towel-off time immediately after.

I have been present in the wrestling gym on several occasions when departmental emergencies have compelled me to collect Manning in person from the club. He never speaks. He doesn't even grunt. He immerses himself completely in the competition and the exertion.

The Midtown Athletic Club [216 W. Sixty-Eighth Street] is the downscale cousin of the Metropolitan Athletic Club [East Side House, 236 Madison Avenue]. Until a few years ago, the Met AC accepted no blacks, Jews, Hispanics, or, God forbid, Filipinos. The club has been sued repeatedly over the decades and only ameliorated its policy, when it did, grudgingly and belatedly. In contrast, the Midtown AC takes everybody.

Manning, if he had read these last sentences, would order me to strike them as "editorializing" and "unprofessional." He would not, in truth, order me. He would simply give me a look.

My name is Detective Third Grade Covina Duwai. I am called "Dewey." Third Grade means I'm a grunt. The ranks above me are Second Grade and First Grade. In pay I make more than a patrol officer but less than a sergeant. Manning's rank is First Grade. He gets the salary of a lieutenant, though in his case he's got so much seniority, being a twenty-seven-year veteran, the final tally would probably almost double that.

I am one of three women in Division Six of the NYPD's Detective Bureau. DivSix is the special homicide investigative arm of the seven mid- and uptown Manhattan precincts as well as Precincts 12 and 13 in South Harlem. In 2027, responsibility for the investigation of all cases involving sensitive and high-profile homicides—terrorism, hate crimes, killings of police officers, politically motivated murder, etc.—was taken from the individual precincts and consolidated under Division Six. (Investigation of federal crimes committed in Manhattan is the responsibility of the FBI, reporting to the U.S. Attorney's Office for the Southern District of New York.) DivSix reports to the New York County District Attorney's Office. The division's responsibility, as with that of a conventional homicide bureau, is not only to investigate crimes and make arrests but also to prepare cases for prosecution by the district attorney.

I am twenty-eight years old, the youngest female in DivSix by nine years. My degree is a bachelor of science in criminal justice from St. John's, plus three years as a patrol officer. I served in the Marine Corps for three years before that. I speak fluent Spanish and can get along in Portuguese and Tagalog. Like every other woman/minority in the division, I am presumed by the detectives hired before me to have slept my way into the job. That, or of being the beneficiary of the department's antique and universally reviled affirmative action program. The second allegation may be partially true. There is no one in the division, however, who outworks or outhustles me. For this I receive, as expected, zero props and bupkis for credit. "Bupkis" is Yiddish for "nothing."

DivSix's reason for being is, as I said, the investigation of special-case and high-profile homicides. The division was set up because the department wanted to take potentially dangerous (for the department) cases out of the hands of precinct detectives, who could not be counted upon either to resolve the cases with sufficient dispatch (read: get convictions) or to comport themselves in a politically sensitive manner (read: keep the department out of the press), and to hold these sensitive cases in-house, under control of the Manhattan DA and the mayor.

To establish credibility for this new division, an "all-star team," as the *Daily News* phrased it, of homicide investigators was assembled under the command of Lieutenant Francis T. "Frank" Gleason. Gleason had been the lead investigator in the mayor's Anti-Terrorism Task Force from '21 to '27. He is regarded as a rising star not only in the department but in city and state politics as well. Gleason is a lawyer (NYU, '14) and the husband of former Mayor D'Antoni's daughter Miranda.

DivSix was given technical resources and advanced investigative tools that no single precinct could support. Each Third Grader like myself must complete a six-month course at the Academy Annex in College Point, Queens, learning to use these resources before he or she is cleared to join the division. Most of the senior detectives, in contrast, are traditional shoe-leather cops who either scorn or are intimidated by this new tech arsenal. The upshot for the young detectives is that, even though we are junior to all in experience and seniority, we play a disproportionately influential role in investigative work, empowered as we are by the new technology.

Manning finishes his shower at 6:57 on this date. He shaves and dresses in one of his three identical gray suits, then climbs the grimy, unlit stairway from the basement of the athletic club to the grill room on the ground floor. The club's kitchen doesn't open till seven but the cooks put out an urn of coffee and a spread of bagels, bialys, and Danishes. Manning takes his coffee black with four sugars. He snatches two Danishes—one cherry and one prune. He wraps the prune Danish in a double-folded paper napkin and slips it into the right-hand pocket of his suit jacket. The cherry Danish he eats as he crosses the lobby toward the front double doors.

At this time Manning turns on his phone and begins receiving messages and texts. He glances down now and reads:

> TO: MANNING
> FROM: DEWEY
> RE: CASE 426-37S

Manning stops reading when, through the club's glass front doors, he spots me waiting at the curb beside our unmarked unit, a '34 Ford Crown Vic Electric AV (self-driver). I would not have been sent to collect him unless there had been another murder.

Manning pushes through the doors and starts down the steps.

"Where?" he says.

3

ACELA CORRIDOR

THE TERM ACELA CORRIDOR refers to the run of states, cities, and municipalities between Boston and Washington, D.C., that lie along the route of the high-speed train service, the Amtrak Acela. The term is often employed in the demographic sense as well, as in, "Presidential candidate X can count on votes in the Northeast suburbs and along the Acela Corridor."

The Acela used to be a decent train. I remember riding it as a kid. It hit 150 per and was operated by its crews with care and pride.

"Christ Almighty!" says Manning now as a bottle bomb explodes against the armor grille outside our window. The flash of the gasoline wicking off barely makes a dent in the steel-slat deflector, but the gel charge leaves a gooey yellow mess across the armorglass. It splats like a thrown egg.

We're not even to Baltimore and the train has already been fléchetted and firebombed four times. The army should clean out these nests of squatters and the dispossessed.

Manning is reading the third of the seven files I have prepared for him this a.m. I've been up since two-thirty working on this. Manning refuses to read reports off any kind of screen. He insists on paper. He sits across from me now in the facing seat. I'm riding backward. Two businessmen commuters, buried in their (paper) copies of the *Times* and the *WSJ*, fill out our four-seat packet.

My notes are in typescript, following the form that Manning insists upon.

VICTIM #2

Justman, Michael A. 57, married (separated), 2 children.

George Washington Univ., Pol. Sci. '05; London School of
Economics, Intl. Relations, '07; Kennedy School, Harvard,
Asian Studies, Ph.D., '10.

Deputy Assistant Undersecretary for Economic Growth,
Energy, and the Environment, 26 months.

State Dept., SLS Grade 2 (Senior Level Service = pay levels
above GS-15) = $273,000/year.

Michael Justman, Ph.D., is the victim whose murder Manning and I are being sent now to investigate.

"What was the last project Justman was working on?" Manning asks me now. "What the hell does a deputy assistant undersecretary do anyway?"

I tell him I haven't been able to get a definitive answer to either question. No one in the State Department will go on record, except to say that Justman's last assignment was classified. His most recent overseas trip on official business, according to the *Washington Post*, was to Tbilisi, Georgia, with additional stops in Ingushetia and Azerbaijan.

"Russia?"

"Backyard. I'll follow up."

Manning absorbs this. "Victim Number One . . . Davis . . . was involved in what? The oil pipeline from—"

"Baku to Ceyhan. Georgia, Turkey, southern Caucasus."

Nathan Davis is the first homicide victim in this file jacket, murdered in Manhattan nine days ago, killer's MO identical to the Michael Justman homicide.

VICTIM #1

Davis, Nathan J. 47, married, 4 children.

Born "Natan Orlovsky" in Russian Crimea.

NYU, Philosophy, Asian Studies, '07; Duke Law, '10.

CEO, The Davis Group, investment banker. Hedge fund.
   17 years.

Davis Building, 63 Broad Street, NY, NY 10004.

Net worth $9.7 billion. 64th richest American. Philanthropist,
   conservationist. Founded "Street Smarts" educ. trust,
   sponsors 6 academies for poor kids in NE, budgets $670M/
   yr. Founded Aegis Maritime Wildlife Conservancy, budget
   $260M/yr.

Manning's military service was as an infantry sergeant, E-5/0311, in Operation Iraqi Freedom, 2004–5. He served with 3/7 [Third Battalion, Seventh Marine Regiment] in Fallujah and Ramadi. His methodology for police work mirrors the Marine Corps' protocol for operational orders, meaning that at the top of the page, above "objective," comes "commander's intent."

Manning's objective now is:

IDENTIFY ALL CDs BETWEEN VICTIMS 1 AND 2

His *intent* is different—and of a superior order:

ESTABLISH A MOTIVE. WHY WOULD KILLER
SPECIFICALLY SELECT VICTIM 1 AND VICTIM 2?

CD means common denominator. In Manning's lexicon this connotes not just social, political, or religious links but *any* association, however remote, that could conceivably tie the two men together. "Did they know each other in college, the army, postgrad? Did they compete in sports? Did they sleep with the same woman (or man)? Were they sued by the same litigant? Did their wives know each other? Did their goldfish know each other? Are they brothers, for Christ's sake?"

There are old-school detectives, and then there is Manning. He's a troglodyte, a Neanderthal. I know next to nothing about his personal history, other than the fact that he came out of a twelve-month leave of absence following a family tragedy two weeks before I was assigned to work with him.

Rival officers regularly attempt to engage me in behind-Manning's-back rat-fuck convos on this subject. I shut them down. I don't want to know Manning's past. I accept his moods. I live with his irascibility. He's Old Corps. Serving under a salt like Manning is the ideal way to be trained, even if you yourself don't want to wind up as that kind of cop or that kind of person.

Manning's standards are levels loftier than those of any other detective in DivSix. My job is by far the hardest of any junior detective. But every task Manning assigns me contains an element of instruction.

He's teaching me.

He's my mentor.

Manning instructs by means of mantras. His first is, "Never discount the obvious." Manning believes that clues and evidentiary breakthroughs hide in plain sight. Look for what's staring you in the face. The obvious things are the ones you miss.

Manning almost never talks to me, or to anyone else for that matter. The closest he comes to conversation is thinking out loud. My job is to listen. Entering the scene of the Davis murder nine days ago—a private dining room at the Century Association on 43rd between Fifth and Sixth—I hear him mutter to himself, "What would the dumbest sonofabitch in the world think in this situation?"

Manning's second maxim is, "Never assume."

Cadets at the academy are taught to be wary of assumption. Manning takes this two levels further. Flawed investigations, he says, are almost always "towers of speculation built upon foundations of assumptions."

"When you enter a crime scene or begin an interrogation, you arrive with assumptions. You assume a suspect with needle tracks up and down his arm is a junkie or that the guy holding a smoking nine-millimeter is the killer. Stop thinking like that. Flush that shit out of your brain."

An investigator's responsibility before anything else, Manning believes, is to achieve and maintain awareness of his own unconscious assumptions—and to banish these from his thinking. "A little kid sees clearly because she is unburdened by assumptions. 'The emperor has no clothes.'"

We're approaching the new Baltimore Harbor Tunnel. The largest and most desperate homeless encampment on the East Coast squats here, almost three hundred thousand souls displaced by the rising water and funneled into camps above the rebuilt seawall. The train slows nearing the tunnel entrance, not so much for attacks, as the police and army have routed most of that, but for suicides, even mass suicides, of people hurling themselves in the dark onto the tracks.

Our businessmen seatmates come alert as the train decelerates. But we're good today. Other than a broadside of obscene signs and graffiti, we pass through without incident.

Thirty-six minutes outside of D.C., Manning excuses himself and makes his way to the men's room. When he steps over the legs of Businessman #1 and into the aisle, I note in his jacket pocket the Imitrex STATdose kit. It's gone when he returns, so I know he has used and discarded the injector.

The only time Manning speaks on the whole trip other than giving me my instructions is when he gets on the phone to the Georgetown PD supervisor whose jurisdiction we are encroaching upon as part of a TJTF, Temporary Joint Task Force. Manning thanks the officer in advance [Detective Sergeant Stellabotte, Rubirosa A. "Ruby"] for letting us work the room, i.e., the crime scene, and for permitting us to employ our proprietary DCSR, Digital Crime Scene Reconstruction, technology. We have brought from New York (actually summoned from his family vacation in Rehoboth Beach, Delaware) our own forensic reconstruction expert, Dr. Jesse A. Uribe.

Before Manning and I boarded the train two hours ago he had me forward to Detective Stellabotte all our files and background about the first New York murder victim, Nathan Davis, and the two others in Russia who share the same profile (about whom we have tantalizing but so far incomplete parallels.)

From Baltimore south, I work this angle on my phone and my laptop.

Manning has a migraine. I can tell his level of pain by what it does to his eyes. He hides them now behind dark glasses, turning his face toward the bulkhead and feigning a snooze. He's in agony, I know.

4

CRIME SCENE RECONSTRUCTION

Another of Manning's mantras: "Nothing ever goes down the way you think it will."

The case, we are informed upon arrival at the scene, has been taken away from the Georgetown PD and kicked upstairs to the next superior jurisdiction, Metro D.C. According to Detective Stellabotte, who apparently has extensive experience in the politics of law enforcement in and around the capital, the case will almost certainly be snatched away from Metro by the FBI, if not the CIA, DIA, or NSA. As a consequence our Crime Scene Unit and Digital Reconstruction guys are working furiously to gather as much evidence as they can before the window of opportunity closes.

Apparently the post occupied by the victim, Michael Justman, is higher on the political food chain than any of the investigating officers had originally realized. His responsibilities, Manning is informed by Detective Stellabotte as we arrive, fall just short of Cabinet level.

Dr. Justman's recent work is of critical import, Manning is told, to several classified international negotiations, one or more of which may have a bearing upon his murder. Our boss at DivSix, Lieutenant Gleason, has been on the phone with the Feds all morning, apparently. Gleason has clout. DivSix has not only been cleared to participate in both the autopsy of the victim and the crime scene analysis, but has been specifically requested to do so.

How do we know this case is big? By the concentration of network and cable press lining the lane outside Dr. Justman's townhouse, even eighteen hours after the murder. An ABC satellite van is parked directly opposite the entry. Up and down the block sit others from CNN, Al Jazeera, and RT, Russia Today.

"Which one of you is Manning?"

"Are you guys DivSix?"

Correspondents call out aggressively as our group dismounts from its vehicles and starts up the sidewalk. Reporters are scanning Manning and Uribe with the new FaceRec apps that'll pull up your name, shield number, and base pay in less than ten seconds. Judging from their shouted questions, the newshounds have somehow put U.S. Victims #2 and #1 together. The prominence of the decedents has the journos betting this story holds national or even international significance.

> YOUNG WOMAN AMONG CROWD
> Detective Manning! Is this victim
> imprinted with the "LV" sign? Does he
> have the "LV" like the other victims?

Manning's eyes swing instantly to this female. I see his anger even behind his dark glasses. His glance to me says, *ID this woman right now! Find out how she knows about "LV."*

Before I can take two steps toward the woman, who is dressed more like a street person than a journalist, she has ducked away into the rear of the crowd. When she sees me pressing after her, she glances back momentarily, then turns and breaks into a run. I get an on-the-move video of her with my phone. But she screens her face skillfully.

She vanishes.

Manning pushes ahead, up the steps and into the townhouse. Uribe, Stellabotte, and I follow. Amid the professional introductions and expressions of gratitude and cooperation, Manning grills his colleagues. "Who let the word out about the 'LV' mark?"

Denials all around.

> MANNING
> How did that woman outside know?

No one has an answer.

As for the video I shot, it turns out to be too low-resolution to support a FaceRec search. The mystery woman is smoke. All attempts at ID come up goose eggs.

We're in the townhouse now. The place, like every other elite crib from Alexandria to Anacostia, is decorated in faux-Colonial style. West Wing–type curtains, antique sofa and chairs, Alexander Hamilton wallpaper. The oil painting above the mantel is of the sea fight between the *Serapis* and the *Bonnehomme Richard*.

The kitchen is modern, however. A Wolf stove, open and blood-striped. A stainless-steel Sub-Zero with a dent that looks like a body was flung against it.

Stellabotte hands Manning CSU photos of the room in its crime scene state.

> DETECTIVE STELLABOTTE
> Dog was a ninety-pounder. Army-trained.

> MANNING
>
> What killed it?

> DETECTIVE STELLABOTTE
>
> Heart stopped.

Stellabotte hands Manning the necropsy report.

> MANNING
>
> What killed Justman?

> DETECTIVE STELLABOTTE
>
> Let's find out.

The office of the chief medical examiner is at 401 E Street SW, three blocks south of the Mall and within sight of the Capitol. We ride in Stellabotte's patrol car, a non-AV (Autonomous Vehicle) that he drives himself, way cooler than our NYPD self-drivers.

The forensic pathologist from Metro D.C. is Dr. Ernestine Carter. She performs the autopsy. Two detectives from Metro are in attendance, along with Stellabotte from Georgetown. Two doctors and an administrator of OCME attend initially, the former pair departing twenty minutes into the examination, called by other duties.

Our own Digital Crime Scene Reconstruction chief, Jesse Uribe, is also an ME, meaning he's a medical doctor. I met him this morning for the first time. He and Manning go back years, apparently. Manning clearly likes him, which is strange to see. I've never seen Manning like anybody.

Uribe is Manning's age, about fifty. He collected me and Manning at Union Station this morning, driving his '29 Buick Enclave, another non-AV, coming from Rehoboth Beach, Delaware, where he was on vacation with his family.

The body of the murder victim, Michael A. Justman, lies under the lights on the stainless steel examination table. Dr. Uribe has requested of Dr. Carter that she perform a specific incision and peel-back on the area between the eyebrows. She has agreed.

I've got two recorders going, phone and lapel, while taking pencil notes feverishly. Dr. Carter will also, after she finishes the initial incision, examine the "strap muscles" of the neck to determine if cause of death is strangulation, as it was on U.S. Victim #1, Nathan Davis, and the two parallel cases in Russia. An autopsy tech, operating a bone saw, will make a perimeter cut around the skull. This, Dr. Carter explains, will cause drainage of the blood from above the subject's neck, so that the lower areas to be examined can be seen cleanly.

As she works, Dr. Carter dictates notes into a mike suspended from a ceiling pod. Uribe leans in at her left shoulder. Over his eyes he wears a DOM, a digital optical maximizer, which looks like a tiny pair of binoculars affixed to an eyeglass frame. Dr. Carter wears her own DOM. Hers delivers a magnified 3-D image to a TV screen above the examination table. She makes the cut between the eyebrows and peels back the skin. All of us except Uribe are craning our necks at the screen.

                         URIBE
              (looking through his own DOM)
          There it is.

                  DETECTIVE STELLABOTTE
          What?

                         URIBE
          Just like on New York.

Uribe indicates on the screen a dime-sized contusion between the decedent's eyes. The area stands out prominently from the surrounding tissue, looking exactly like the letters "LV." It's as clear as a brand on a Texas steer. The mark, Dr. Carter dictates in her notes, is a "subdural capillary hematoma." Ruptured blood vessels.

                    MANNING
    "LV."

                    URIBE
    Bigger than shit.

Uribe calls up onto his own laptop the video from his examination of Nathan Davis, the New York victim. Sure enough, the identical "LV" appears in the identical location, equally prominent and unmistakable. Even to a non-medically-trained observer like me, it's clear that this mark has not occurred naturally.

                    URIBE
    And on the Russian corpses too.

Twenty minutes later Michael Justman's skull has been cut, the blood has drained. We can see the killer's finger marks on the strap muscles of the throat.

                    URIBE
    Cause of death: asphyxia due to tracheal
    compression. Crushed windpipe. Same as
    New York. Same as the two in Russia.

The discussion continues for several moments, including both Stellabotte and the two Metro D.C. detectives. All of them cite the skull fracture (or what they believe will be proven to be a skull fracture) on the victim. Couldn't that be the COD?

Dr. Carter says no. She directs the group's attention to several figures in a statistical column on the screen. Not only was the larynx crushed, she says, 7.9 seconds before the skull fracture, as indicated by tissue oxygen depletion, but, judging by the angle of collapse, the victim was lifted off the ground vertically by the throat. She points out the killer's finger marks—thumb and four fingers, which somehow have left no prints. These indicate with 99.9 percent certainty that the lift was accomplished with one hand.

> DETECTIVE STELLABOTTE
> Then the "LV" is just bruises. The killer
> bounced this bastard off the stainless
> steel fridge, for Pete's sake!

Uribe indicates the matching "LV" sign on his laptop—beneath the skin on the forehead of Victim #1, Nathan Davis.

> DETECTIVE STELLABOTTE
> What are you saying? Somebody "branded"
> them both by rupturing specific
> capillaries? How could anyone do that?
> And why?

> URIBE
> I don't know.

Forty-five minutes later, Manning, Uribe, and I are back at the town-house watching Uribe's techs wrap up the digital reconstruction of the crime scene. Conventional CSU has completed its workup. It has drawn a blank. For the assailant: no prints, no foot tracks, no DNA. Even more extraordinary is the video evidence. CSU has examined the community security cameras and Dr. Justman's own in-home security video. Both show Justman. Both show the Rhodesian ridgeback.

But no assailant.

Uribe cues up his team's preliminary profile on his laptop. Manning stands at his shoulder.

Uribe is explaining about respiration. DCSR detection gear can pick up presences as minuscule as ten parts per billion. Not just breath but epidermal and follicular exudations.

> URIBE
>
> For this crime scene today—and for Davis's
> in New York—we got nothing. Other than
> the victims', and here the dog's, the
> sheet is blank.

Uribe indicates a column of figures on his laptop screen.

> URIBE
>
> See this stack? That's the dog's breath.
> Exhalation from lungs, ventriculus,
> gastric mill. Here's the victim's—Dr.
> Justman's. This third column here?
> That's pollen from the geranium on the
> windowsill.

Uribe's gesture takes in the full screen.

> URIBE
>
> We got nothing from any other human or
> animal source. Zip. Zero.

Manning's glance to me says, *Make sure you're recording every word of this.*

> MANNING
> (to Uribe)
> What, the killer wore a face mask? Some
> kind of respiration device?

> URIBE
>
> Even that would show. It has to vent.
> Particle respirometry will pick it up.

> MANNING
>
> So the killer didn't breathe? What, he
> held his breath?

> URIBE
>
> Jimmy, all I know is what the instruments
> tell me. And they say the same thing for
> both victims—Davis and Justman.

Manning glances to me, to make sure I'm writing all this down, then turns back to Uribe.

                    MANNING

Lemme get this straight, Jesse. For both
homicides, the killer flew in the window.
He didn't breathe. His feet never touched
the floor. He murdered the hedge fund CEO
in New York and the State Department guy
in D.C. by picking them up with one hand,
crushing their windpipes, and hurling
them bodily across the room. He then
made his escape, again without taking a
step or exhaling a breath. That's what
the instruments say, and the instruments
don't lie.

                     URIBE

Exactly.

5

THE BROTHERHOOD

GLEASON

Bullshit. I don't believe a word of it.

We're back in Manhattan, 0830 the next morning, April 19, 2034, in the sweltering (City of NY climate policy: no A/C before 1100) conference facility at DivSix called "the Bunker."

Four DivSix teams totaling nine detectives have been assembled in this meeting space. We're watching video from Russia—a secure-link convo between our boss, Lieutenant Gleason, assisted by his second-in-command Lieutenant Silver [Lionel T.], and the supervising officer of the first of two Russian teams investigating what are coming to be called within the division "the LV murders," a pair in Russia and now the same number in the States.

The translation software is seamless. Our guys speak in English, the Russians get it instantly in Russian, and vice versa. It's like there's no language barrier at all.

The first Russian murder, eleven days ago, took place in a prosperous suburb of Saint Petersburg called Tsarskoye Selo. The victim, Alexei Marinovich Tcheckousky, fifty-seven, was a prominent official in the Ministry of Agriculture, not unlike our own Victim #2, Michael Justman. The investigating officer is identified on the video monitor as Inspector Anatoly Y. B. Koverchenko. He's on-camera, in his office, with two associates whose identities are not revealed.

Koverchenko is a voluble guy, about forty, with a shaved skull and a salt-and-pepper beard complete with soul patch—a triangular brush of gray between the lower lip and the chin. He is happy to share intelligence with his American friends. On the video Koverchenko tells Gleason and Silver that "his" victim and the other murdered Russian (Dr. Alexsandr T. V. Golokoff, an author and speaker, killed in his apartment in the affluent neighborhood of Filyovsky Park in Moscow) have been determined to have known each other personally; both were members of a dissident organization called the November Group, which advocated for freedom of the press, for action on climate change, and for the rights of political prisoners.

The inspector seems to have no problem with this politically. In fact, he appears to admire the two victims' courage. He confesses his astonishment at the "anomalies and aberrations" of the Tcheckousky crime scene, for which he declares he can discover no precedent—a violent murder, producing abundant evidence of a physical struggle (what is called in the Eastern European underworld, he observes, a "crime of the hand," meaning a homicide enacted without a weapon) resulting in the fatal crushing of the victim's airway as well as a fracturing of the skull, and yet the inspector's best forensics experts can discover no sign of entry, forced or otherwise; no fingerprints other than the victim's; no assailant's DNA, no foot tracks, no nothing.

As the inspector is testifying to this on-camera, a side door to his office can be heard to open offscreen. Koverchenko turns toward this entry, as do his two associates. Immediately all sound ceases on the video. A discussion ensues between those on-screen and off, but we, at the other end of the transmission, can hear none of it.

When sound returns, which it does after an interval of about thirty seconds, Inspector Koverchenko explains to the camera, i.e., to Gleason and Silver, that he was perhaps premature in certain of his conclusions, which should not, he declares, be taken as the official position of his department. He is, he says, not at liberty to discuss the details of this homicide further until he has spoken with and received clearance from some entity that he names but that the software refuses to translate.

Gleason lets the video run but mutes the sound.

> GLEASON
>
> We got the same horseshit from Rooskies #2—the Moscow cops investigating their other murder.

Gleason kills the video and turns up the lights in the room. Our boss is about ten years younger than Manning, forty or so, with a shock of Kennedy-esque hair and a sturdy Auld Sod jaw. It's impossible to be in his presence and not project him as a future mayor-slash-governor-slash-senator.

Gleason has his own theory, he tells his teams now, on these "LV" cases.

He believes that all four homicides were planned, financed, and carried out, either through contract operatives or outsourced assets, by the FSB, the Federal Security Service, i.e., the Russian secret police, the successor to the KGB of Soviet days.

Why has DivSix been permitted to continue to participate in what is obviously a multi-jurisdictional, in fact federal/international, investigation?

                    GLEASON
Because the first U.S. body dropped on our
turf. Because we got the tools and we got
the chops. And because if these murders
ain't "special case," I don't know what
the fuck is.

What Gleason doesn't say is that he and the New York County DA, not to mention the mayor, smell a big one here, and they've called in all markers to keep DivSix in the game.

I've only been in the division for five months, but one thing I've learned: anytime there's a task-force-style investigation like this one (four of the division's nine teams have been assigned to these murders as Priority One), every team conspires nonstop against every other and competes without scruple to make its own theory come out on top.

From the meeting room's wings, Gleason's tech sergeant brings forward a quartet of easel-mounted whiteboards. The first is headed "LV SIGN." Bullet points hand-scrawled in grease pencil read:

LV = ?
Terrorist signature? Political? Satanic?
Why does killer leave sign? To communicate what?
Why subcutaneous? Why between eyes?

I snap pix of all the whiteboards, but take notes by hand as well. Another Manning mandate.

Gleason begins by addressing the significance of the "LV" sign. It's just weird enough, he says, and creepy enough to point in a very specific direction and at a very specific criminal entity.

He spells out his working hypothesis.

Gleason believes, he says, that our two U.S. murders were subcontracted by the FSB to homegrown operators, specifically professional assassins of the Russian Mafia, also known as the Solntsevskaya Bratva, "the Brotherhood," based here in our own five boroughs. These were the killers, Gleason believes, who took out Nathan Davis and Michael Justman.

It goes without saying that Gleason would like nothing better than to be the law enforcement official responsible for taking this notorious outfit down, not just for the points he would score within the NYPD but because it would ace the Feds, the CIA, even the NSA.

The second thing I've learned in my months at DivSix is that when the skipper puts forth his own theory on a case, you the individual investigator have two choices—ride along or ride into the sunset.

Up front Gleason has stepped to a second whiteboard, this one headed "RUSSIAN CONNECTION."

Victims #3 and #4 killed in Russia. Both anti-Kremlin activists.
U.S. Victim #1—Russian-born, did biz w/Russia
U.S. Victim #2—State Dept (Russian affairs)
"LV" = Roman numeral 55 = FSB code for political murder

Gleason circles this in red.

> GLEASON
>
> LV is the Roman numeral for fifty-five.
> "Fifty-five" is FSB code for political
> murder. Not only that, but FSB protocol is
> to cite codes not in numbers but in Roman
> numerals.

This stirs a murmur.

Even Manning reacts.

Gleason notes that the FSB has been notorious since the end of the Cold War for the brazenness of its assassinations of foes of the Kremlin, both in Russia and on foreign soil. It has hit civilian targets including journalists, politicians, businessmen, even religious leaders, in England, France, Germany, and the States. It has poisoned them, asphyxiated them, caused them to die in car crashes, tumble from rooftops, expire of heart attacks, all in highly public ways and all clearly intended to send a message.

Gleason, up front, steps to a third whiteboard. This one holds mug shots, arrayed in the form of an organizational chart, of about a dozen Slavic-looking individuals, with names, aliases, etc. Board title:

RUSSIAN MAFIA—"BRATVA"

Atop the chart Gleason pins an MTA map of South Brooklyn with the neighborhood of Brighton Beach, the territorial province of the Brotherhood, circled in black grease pencil. He adds three photos—one NYPD drone surveillance shot and two Google Earth pix—of an urban compound, about a block square.

This, he tells his teams, is Bratva's home field and its starting lineup.

A fourth board is headed:

MAP PROXIMITY

This board includes MS's, movement scenarios, for various known Bratva gunmen in relation to the New York decedent Davis and the D.C. victim Justman. Charts trace the whereabouts, determined by cell GPS, street-corner surveillance cameras, and so forth, of three specific operators, including the notorious Alemany "Yoo-hoo" Petracek (nicknamed for the soft drink he favors), the American-born hit artist reputedly responsible for twenty-seven murders, six with his bare hands. Petracek's profile is so high he has his own Wikipedia page.

Gleason reviews the map intersects for Petracek. They put him practically in the lap of the New York victim, Nathan Davis, on two of the nine days preceding the murder.

I find myself writing "WOW" on my notepad.

Gleason wraps his presentation. His tech sergeant distributes assignment envelopes to the four teams. The detectives stand, tucking their packets under their arms. The mob migrates to the Nespresso machine and the departmental kitchen. I fall in at the rear with the other Third Graders. Up front Lieutenant Kiriakin [Donat C., "Don"], one of the up-and-comers in the division, is saying something to Manning about the "LV" sign—that it indicates that the killer "is fucking with us."

> DETECTIVE KIRIAKIN
> A special-case murderer wants to be
> caught. That's what you always say, ain't
> it, Manning?

Kiriakin is about thirty—twenty years younger than Manning. Manning draws up amid the group.

> MANNING
> No, that's not what I say, Kiriakin.

Outside the Bunker we're allowed to turn our phones on.

> MANNING
> A special-case killer wants to be known.
> He wants to be understood. He wants his

suffering to be appreciated and his point
of view to be granted respect.

At this moment my cell pings with an incoming text. It's for Manning. (All his calls are routed through me.) Caller ID: UNKNOWN. A burner, no doubt. I tap the message icon:

LV is Hebrew. The letters "lamed" and "vav."
Google it.

I think instantly, *The woman. The one who shouted to Manning outside the townhouse in Georgetown.*

I text back:

Who R U?

No response.

I show Manning the screen. A stranger watching him would notice zero change of expression. But I see.

Manning's glance to me says, *Trace this ASAP.*

Gleason emerges from the Bunker. He comes up to the group. He has seen me show the phone to Manning.

GLEASON

What's this grab-ass?

I'm thinking, *A drop phone is untraceable. But I can back-link to the cell tower. I can find the neighborhood where the text was sent from.*

As I'm thinking this, a second ping comes in.

Don't believe me? Note victims. All 4 R Jews.

Gleason makes me show him the phone.

> GLEASON
>
> More bullshit.

But Manning's look to me says, *Trace this too. Same sender?*

Silver, Kiriakin, and the others all note this wordless clash between Manning and Gleason. Gleason notes that they note it.

> GLEASON
> (to Silver)
>
> Ready to roll?

Gleason's second-in-command confirms. Gleason turns to Manning and me.

> GLEASON
>
> You two. Take a ride.

6

CAESAR'S SANCTUARY

THE CAESAR'S SANCTUARY STEAM BATHS sit at the corner of Surf Avenue and West Twenty-Seventh Street in Brighton Beach, Brooklyn.

Brighton Beach, aka "Little Russia."

Gleason has ordered Manning and me to accompany him and Silver, in Gleason's car, with our own AV deadheading behind, trailed by a backup team in a blue-and-white. It's 1330, less than forty minutes after the meeting in the Bunker.

I haven't had one second to trace text #1 or #2, to run an info search on "lamed" and "vav," or to shoot Manning the even bigger questions:

Why did the sender send these to Manning?
And how did he (or she) get the address?

The only thing I've been able to accomplish, feigning a trip to the loo before we left, is to ID the phone that sent the two texts.

It is indeed a throwaway. Text #2 was the last message the phone sent. The caller no doubt chucked it in the trash the instant he or she hit SEND.

The phone's final message was relayed by cell tower 18706, Canarsie (actually an antenna array mounted on the top-floor facing of a tenement building), meaning the caller was somewhere within a block or two when the call was placed.

Our DivSix group, led by Gleason, dismounts now from its vehicles onto a sweltering Brighton Beach sidewalk, one long block from the beach, and troops up to the warped and paint-peeling doors of the steam emporium.

Gleason leads us in. Manning takes off his dark glasses, squinting into the gloom. I follow. Is it my imagination, or did some species of glossy rodent just scamper along the entryway floorboard? I feel a noxious drop of liquid strike my forehead, as if falling from a ceiling stalactite.

Caesar's Sanctuary? The place is the skeeviest, most unsanitary hellhole I've ever seen. I wouldn't touch a wall or a doorknob without rubber gloves.

Gleason, flashing his gold shield, blows past the reception desk, if such a term may be applied to a trio of pseudo-Roman columns glistening with condensation, topped by a faux-marble slab that looks like it was stolen from a Hollywood prop house, and manned by a white-haired Slavic gentleman, clad in a terry-cloth toga, who looks exactly like Charles Laughton as the Roman senator in *Spartacus*.

I look up and we're entering a locker room.

A men's locker room.

MANNING

(to me)

Wait outside.

GLEASON

No. She goes in.

I smell steam and male sweat. From a cloud of vapor emerge two burly pink humanoids, both bald as cue balls, shod in flip-flops, with towels wrapped around their bellies. One looks like Winston Churchill, the other like Nikita Khrushchev.

MANNING

Dewey's a woman, Gleason.

GLEASON

She's a law enforcement professional.

Gleason leads our party through the changing area and down a dingy tile-walled runway that opens into a slightly brighter (from a sky-light) steam room.

Half a dozen Roosky-looking gentlemen sit naked in various postures on multileveled, mold-infested tile platforms. One rises immediately to confront us.

RUSSIAN MAN #1

What the fuck is this?

The man clearly recognizes Gleason.

GLEASON

How's it hanging, Yoo-hoo?

I'm cringing. Manning has stepped in front to shield me from this sight that, once seen, can never be unseen. The denizens of the steam room, realizing a female has entered their sanctum, without haste tug towels over their privates.

"Yoo-hoo" is Alemany Petracek, the assassin with his own Wikipedia page.

We have invaded the Russian Mafia at lunchtime.

> YOO-HOO
> What bullshit are you pulling, Gleason?
> If you ain't got a warrant, take a
> fucking hike.

Gleason orders Yoo-hoo to sit. The Russian in no hurry pulls a towel around himself. He nods in my direction.

> YOO-HOO
> Get this bitch outta here. This is a men's
> steam!

Manning strides a step closer to the assassin, still shielding me. I understand now why I have been brought along—to humiliate the mafiosi in their most occult sanctuary.

As for Yoo-hoo, he is not particularly tall or muscular. But his Volga-boatman shoulders look like they could out-pull a pair of oxen, and his forearms, what I can see of them beneath a solid scrim of Iron Curtain tattoos, are as big around as most men's calves.

Clearly Yoo-hoo is capable of the physical mayhem performed in Michael Justman's Georgetown kitchen.

He sits. The other Russians glare at our party. Gleason sets a folded towel down onto the seating surface next to Yoo-hoo. He lowers himself, in his suit, onto it.

GLEASON

Brought you something.

Gleason hands Yoo-hoo a square flat package, wrapped in brown paper. Yoo-hoo stares.

GLEASON

Open it.

The Russian glances to his compatriots.
He unbinds the wrapping paper without enthusiasm.
The package holds a framed photo of Evgeny Karkov, the Russian president.

YOO-HOO

What the fuck is this?

GLEASON

For your wall. Like at the post office. To
remind you who you work for.

Yoo-hoo looks at Gleason the way a lion looks at a wolf. Strike that. Yoo-hoo is scarier. I'm eyeing Manning throughout this. He is clearly ready for anything.

Gleason now tugs a photo—an eight-by-twelve glossy tucked in a manila folder—from beneath his jacket. He hands the photo to Yoo-hoo. I can't see the picture, but I will learn later that it's a chalk-outline shot of "LV" Victim #1, Nathan Davis, dead on the floor of the dining room of the Century Association in Manhattan.

> GLEASON

Whaddaya know about this guy?

Yoo-hoo drops the glossy onto the slimy seating surface.

> YOO-HOO

I know he's dead.

> GLEASON

I bet you do.

Gleason asks the assassin how he left the "LV" mark.

> YOO-HOO

The what?

> GLEASON

What's the trick? How did you make the
blood vessels rupture in just that shape?

> YOO-HOO

I dunno what the fuck you're talking
about.

Gleason tells the killer he's got Verizon Wireless records of two phone calls from him, Yoo-hoo, to the home of U.S. Homicide Victim #1, Nathan Davis, from nine and six days prior to the murder. He says he knows that Yoo-hoo murdered Davis.

> YOO-HOO

Then arrest me.

                         GLEASON
      Don't worry.
                  (stands)
      I will.

Gleason leads our party two steps toward the exit. The Russians glower after him. I see Yoo-hoo meet Manning's eye, then look away.

                         YOO-HOO
                  (to Gleason)
      Whaddaya gotta come around here for, ruin
      our fucking day?

I follow Manning out. The sun hits us. I realize I'm drenched.

                         MANNING
      You okay?

Gleason speaks apart with Silver as our driverless vehicles, which had parked themselves at the end of the block, pull up at the curb and stop. Gleason tells Manning he'll speak to him back at the office. Gleason and Silver board their vehicle.

Manning starts toward ours, but not before flashing me a look that says we're not going back to DivSix just yet. Gleason and Silver's vehicle pulls out into traffic.

Manning boards ours. I follow. The engine is already on. The nav screen lights up.

                         MANNING
                  (to me)
      The cell tower. Where is it?

7

CANARSIE

THE SKIMMERS are all black and young—fifteen at the oldest; many look eleven, ten, even younger. Plainly this is their racket. Their uniform is porkpie hats perched on outrageously oversized Afros, no shirt, torso (almost always gaunt) solid with tats, beneath which droop cargo pants lapped atop unlaced Doc Martens. Dangling from their belts are stevedore-type hooks, which the skimmers use to pop open subway and sidewalk grates.

They're hunting for junked phones.

Here is how Manning teaches me "the street." We drive to Canarsie, just east of Rockaway Parkway, a few miles west of JFK. We park. Manning says nothing. We watch. At least that's what I think we're doing. I adhere to Manning's baseline directive, valid under all circumstances:

Watch me. Do what I do.

The neighborhood is South Brooklyn. We have come straight from the steam baths. Manning is scoping the skimmers. When these scavengers find thrown-away burner phones, which they do in quantities I could never have imagined, from dumpsters, trash cans, gutters, storm drains, etc., they collect them into black plastic trash bags. (Every skimmer carries one.)

We're tracking one particular kid, about thirteen, with a bag as stuffed as Santa Claus. It's not all burners. He's got soda cans, wire hangers, metal and plastic of all kinds. Finally he hoists his bounty. Time to cash in.

Ten minutes later I'm scrambling in Manning's wake across the flat, litter-strewn roof of a building that feels like it's swaying with each footfall we set down. Howard Beach/East New York/Canarsie was destroyed by Superstorm Lorelei in September '21. Entire blocks were leveled, building foundations undermined in the fourteen-foot storm surge. What derelict structures remain have been taken over as shooting galleries, or by squatters as "sit-downs" or "lay-bys." Unpermitted sweatshops and pop-up junk stores fill in the voids.

Manning has recruited two uniformed patrol officers, twenty-two-year-old beat cops whom we have run into randomly on the street. They're our backup. As with me, he tells them nothing, doesn't ask their names or volunteer his. "Hey," he says, tipping his gold shield and waving them to his side. "Learn something."

Manning crosses the rooftop in easy, unhurried strides. He jimmies an access door. We grope down a flight of steps, Manning in the lead, me second, the uniforms in the caboose, into an unlit, debris-choked stairwell. Manning hasn't told any of us what we're doing or what role we're supposed to play.

We have followed the young skimmer. He entered Building #1 via a side alley. To trail him directly would apparently give us away, so . . . up a five-story fire escape of the adjacent derelict, Building #2, across the roof, and now down.

A door.

We stop.

Voices and machinery can be heard on the far side.

Manning sets his gold detective's shield in its black leather case in his left hand, badge exposed. In his right appears his service weapon. I ape him. So do the beat cops. My heart is starting to fibrillate. Manning turns toward us displaying his weapon with its three safeties on—slide, grip, and trigger. We juniors follow.

"You," he whispers to the beat cops. "Disarm and cuff whoever is behind this door."

The next thing I know, all four of us are through the door, past a snoozing, shaved-skull bruiser packing a shotgun, and striding—Manning and me—holding badges high, down the central walkway of an abandoned factory, made over into a Tech Age sweatshop.

> MANNING
> (shouts to all)
> Police officers! Everyone remain calm!
> Stay where you are!

The work floor is wall-to-wall with cramped, doorless cubicles, each manned by an Asian or African female. The women are rebuilding and recharging throwaway phones. In the center of the floor, on a platform raised several feet above the ladies' carrels, squats a boss's station. Manning stalks straight to it.

A white man in shirtsleeves wearing a yarmulke springs to his feet. He holds up both hands, calling out something to the factory women in a language I don't recognize. Half of the ladies had bolted upright as well, wild-eyed, two seconds away from stampeding for the exits.

They calm down.

Manning has holstered his weapon. I can't hear what he's saying to the sweatshop boss. (He has motioned me to cover a side door.) Plainly the workspace is unlicensed, uninsured, in violation no doubt of scores of fire and safety regs.

Manning without a word has communicated to the yarmulke-wearing owner or manager or whatever he is that he, Manning, doesn't give a shit about any of this.

He's asking questions.

The boss is answering.

The boss calls again to the women on the floor. Again I have no idea what language he's speaking.

In response, one of the ladies raises her hand.

Manning and the boss cross immediately to this female.

I can't stand to stay in the dark any longer. I step to the cubicle too.

The factory woman is Laotian or Cambodian, I can't tell which. She wears a smock and a hairnet. Her workstation holds a dozen disassembled burner phones, with SIM cards, screens, memory units, and lithium-ion batteries spread across an assembly table. She wears magnifying lenses. Atop her work surface is an additional lighted magnifier. Two computer consoles flank the workspace.

> MANNING
> (to boss and factory woman)
> Eleven thirty-six oh six oh nine.

The woman looks scared to death. She glances helplessly to the boss, but cannot make her eyes rise to look at Manning. For some reason I find myself putting a hand gently on her shoulder. She peers up into my face. She can't believe an Asian female is a cop.

> SWEATSHOP BOSS
> (to Manning)
> You're certain that's the last call?

Manning shows him the record sheet. The boss takes the phone from the factory woman. He inserts the memory-component end into a slot on one of her consoles. A screen lights up, displaying the phone's record of calls.

Only two.

The first one matches, to the thousandths of a second, the time when the "lamed vav" text came in to Manning's phone.

The second is spot-on to the follow-up text.

> MANNING
>
> Where did the other texts or calls go?
> The ones made before these final two.

> SWEATSHOP BOSS
>
> Scrubbed.

The boss scrolls down the record sheet for Manning to see. Blank.

> MANNING
>
> How could someone do that?

Two items, the boss explains, make these burners different from legal phones—a password randomizer and a trace mimic. "The phones 'pretend' to be real," he says. "They piggyback digitally onto existing numbers."

> SWEATSHOP BOSS
>
> Scrub the number and you delete all
> record of the call. But to do that, you'd
> need tech gear that even we don't have.

> MANNING
> But whoever erased the main body of the
> outgoing texts left a record of the final
> two—the last ones made before they threw
> the phone away. Why would they do that?

The question is rhetorical. Manning is asking himself.

Because they were lazy?

Because they screwed up?

Or because they wanted us to know about the final two texts—and that this was the phone that made them?

> SWEATSHOP BOSS
> I have no idea. But I'll tell you one
> thing. Whoever tricked out this burner
> knows their shit.

Manning walks the boss outside into the hall. He signs to the uniforms that they can release the shotgun sentry and return to their regular duty. They do.

From his wallet Manning tugs a twenty. He hands it to the boss. "For the woman inside," he says. He pulls out a hundred and slips it into the chief's shirt pocket.

Manning indicates the skullcap atop the boss's head.

> MANNING
> "Lamed" and "vav" are Hebrew letters,
> right?

> SWEATSHOP BOSS
> Thirty-six. The Thirty-Six Righteous Men.

Manning's look says, *What's that?*

> SWEATSHOP BOSS
> It's a legend. God protects the world for
> the sake of the Thirty-Six. When they're
> gone, all bets are off.

> MANNING
> Meaning what?

> SWEATSHOP BOSS
> God destroys everything.

This stops Manning.

> MANNING
> Righteous Men? What does the legend mean
> by that? What makes someone "righteous"?

> SWEATSHOP BOSS
> You're asking me?

Ten minutes later Manning has the address of the kiosk that sold the phone and we're on our way.

8

LITTLE HONG KONG

Manning punches the dealer so hard in the chest that his (the dealer's) lower denture pops out and goes sailing across the display case.

CONTRABAND DEALER
What the fuck!

The dealer's choppers clatter onto the grimy steel floor. We're in a phone seller's kiosk, a converted shipping container on Jamaica Bay, in the floating mall the locals call Little Hong Kong.

The dealer is some kind of Bahamian or Trinidadian. He's got dreads and that charming Calypso accent. Not now, of course, as he spits and attempts to lunge past Manning to retrieve his lowers.

With a sweep of his leg, so fast I don't even see it, Manning takes the dealer's legs out from under him. The poor guy face-plants, full weight, into the deck. I hear a scream. The dealer's wife appears from a living section at the stern of the container. A boy and a girl, no older than four, cling to her skirts.

With one hand Manning hauls the dealer upright.

MANNING

I asked you nicely, didn't I?

Manning lifts the guy six inches off the floor. "No, no!" the dealer is bawling. "Not the merch!"

Manning flings him into the display case. Clearly this artifact is the man's pride and joy. It shatters into a million shards. The dealer crashes among splintered glass and featured sale items—counterfeit bags from Hermes, Kate Spade, and Bottega Veneta, a set of knockoff Craftsman socket wrenches, and, displayed impeccably on the now-demolished top shelf, throwaway iPhones and Galaxies.

CONTRABAND DEALER

Have a heart, man! I spill who bought the
burner and who will buy another from me?

Manning is getting a migraine. I can see it in his eyes. He reaches down with both hands and seizes the dealer. From the echo-chamber rear, wife and kids pump up the volume of wailing and squealing.

Manning takes aim on a second display of breakable merchandise.

CONTRABAND DEALER

Okay, okay! Stop!

Human faces, at least a dozen, all Asian, Arab, or African, have appeared on the walkway outside the container door. Other merchants and shoppers. Manning shoots a glance to me. I raise my shield and advance menacingly.

The lookie-loos vaporize.

Manning has retrieved the dreadlocked dealer's lower denture from the container floor. He wipes the appliance with a tissue from a box that had been on top of the display case. He hands it back to its owner.

The dealer accepts the device tentatively, examining it for fractures.

> CONTRABAND DEALER
> She was white. Thirty, maybe. Dressed
> like shit. She paid in reds.

Reds is local scrip. Good in South Brooklyn and nowhere else.

Manning has me cue up on my phone the fuzzy video I shot of the woman outside the Georgetown townhouse.

He takes the phone and shows it to the dealer.

> CONTRABAND DEALER
> Why the fuck didn't you show me this
> before you wrecked my place?

You exit Little Hong Kong on foot along a series of suspended walkways, like rain forest bridges, swaying dubiously about eight inches above the petro-scum surface of Jamaica Bay. These catwalks have no handrails. They're about as wide as a lawn mower. This constriction, however, does nothing to retard the bumper-to-bumper, two-way traffic of pushcarts, mopeds, deliverymen and -women using Chinese coolie carrying poles, tea and coffee hawkers with their dispenser tanks on their backs, not to mention hookers, skimmers, incense peddlers, acrobats, jugglers, three-card monte dealers, political orators, one-legged guys selling wild Siberian chaga, bhang, khosh, naswar, and half a hundred types of aphrodisiacs, psychedelics, soporifics, and herbal intoxicants that I've never heard of and neither have you. Canvas sheets overhead shield the floating city from the sun. Beneath these, shops founded on houseboats, moored water taxis, Asiatic junks, float-suspended freight containers, and Navy surplus Zodiacs peddle cures for baldness, impotence, incontinence, sleep apnea, herpes, and chronic bad breath. You can buy roasted duck, grilled yak, barbecued char. The only thing you can't get is a hamburger.

Every fourth catwalk holds a directory, which invariably is so faded from diesel fumes and the acid effluence of the bay that you can't read it. Besides, it's in Chinese. The city itself is a maze. How Manning got in is a mystery; how he's navigating out is equally incomprehensible. We pass shops selling phone cards, fake Rolexes, I ♥ NY T-shirts, WORLD'S GREAT-EST DAD coffee mugs, and plastic models of the Statue of Liberty.

My text window meanwhile keeps pinging with messages from Gleason's tech sergeant:

WHERE THE HELL R U?

GET MANNING TO PICK UP!

HAUL UR ASSES BACK HERE ASAP!

One of the things I love about detective work is you get to see the Hidden World, the spawn and species that normal people spend every resource to avoid. You see the human condition with all the bullshit stripped away, the secret lives people live and the extremes they'll go to to protect what they've got or to grab for some dream of pride or love or money, or just another twenty-four hours to keep drawing breath. You, the cop, tread in this hell without being part of it. Your shield protects you. At least you think it does. I tell myself, tramping out of Little Hong Kong, *Look around you, Dewey. Every poor bastard in this place is fucked, and you, without your badge, could and probably would be one of them.*

Back out finally into the blistering sun, I tap the Find Me app on my phone and Manning and I are reeled in digitally, across a fifty-acre parking lot, to our AV.

What have we learned from this morning's expedition?

1. Our mystery woman sent the lamed-vav text and made the follow-up call.
2. We don't know who she is or where she lives, if she in fact lives anywhere, except that . . .
3. She is off the grid, invisible, and . . .
4. She's tech-savvy.

We have also learned, incidentally, that "lamed vav" has something to do with the Jewish legend of the Thirty-Six Righteous Men, whatever the hell that is.

Is this Manning's assessment? What is he thinking? I turn to him as his gaze settles on the Bank of New York time-and-temp display across the neck of the bay in Canarsie.

                    MANNING
          April nineteenth and it's a hundred and
          fourteen in the shade.

BOOK TWO

LAMED VAV

9

THE DAKOTA

I DON'T KNOW WHY I worry so much about Manning. Technically he's not even my boss. Like everyone else in DivSix, I work for Gleason. Gleason is the one I should be sucking up to.

Manning doesn't even particularly like me. Sometimes when he's phrasing an order or an instruction to me, I can tell he's forgotten my name. He's running some mnemonic in his head; I can practically see the wheels turning behind his eyes.

Do I like him? Does it matter? I respect him. By miles he's the savviest detective in the division. Any junior with ambition would kill to be in my place. You want to be around Manning just to see how his mind works.

Driving back from Little Hong Kong, Manning gives me an assignment—what he calls an "interpretive." I'm to find out everything I can about the legend of the Thirty-Six Righteous Men. Where does it come from? What does it mean? What did the sweatshop boss mean when he said, "When they're gone, God destroys everything"?

And I'm to dig into the backgrounds of the four victims, including the two from Russia, with this question in mind:

Could they in any sense be considered "righteous"?

What Manning wants to know in legend terms is, *What does "righteous" mean?*

                    MANNING
        Is it religious? Ethical? What qualities,
        specifically <u>moral</u> qualities, do the
        victims have in common?

Manning instructs me to keep my mind open. Don't "pre-load." Follow where the facts, and your instincts, lead you.

Another of Manning's mantras is, "Pay attention to your unconscious."

My first week working with him, only a few days after he had rejoined the division, he said, "Let's go to a movie." I couldn't believe he was serious. We went in the middle of the day to the Beacon at Forty-Second and Eighth, a revival house. The film was *Double Indemnity*. I'd heard of it but never seen it. It was damn good. On the sidewalk afterward (no sit-down dinners or tête-à-têtes with Manning) he asks me what I took from the picture. I stammer something moronic.

                    MANNING
        The "little man."

In the movie Edward G. Robinson plays an insurance investigator. He refers repeatedly to the "little man in the center of my chest," who always knows more than he himself about any investigation he's conducting.

Manning's inner world, if my own little man is any judge, is about nothing but pain. He's buried in it. It lives in his cells twenty-four hours a day. I don't know the source and I don't want to know.

But I do worry.

The day ends. Manning exits without a word to anyone. I stay at my desk, finishing notes and reports for the day.

Manning is walking home from the office now. I know his route exactly because I've had to track him down half a dozen times on orders from Gleason or Silver, when Manning has walked out early or just bolted at day's end when there were still division meetings on the calendar.

DivSix's headquarters are at West Sixty-Eighth and Amsterdam Avenue, in the new city-owned complex two long blocks from the Hudson. Leaving there, Manning walks up to Seventy-Second and hikes east in all weathers. He never takes a bus or a cab, never calls for an Uber or a self-driver, and won't ride the subway even in a blizzard. He stops for an Old-Fashioned at Crosby's on Seventy-Second and Columbus Avenue, early, six or six-thirty, when the sun is still high in the summer.

Crosby's is a down-at-the-heels Irish haunt with linoleum floors and backless stools with chrome legs and red vinyl seats and little hand-lettered signs above the bar listing the prices of the ridiculously dated drinks they serve there. Manhattans, Rob Roys, Rusty Nails. Who ever heard of these concoctions? Crosby's is the most depressing joint I've ever been in. It's not even dark like a bar. It reeks of urine and old men. But Manning hits it every night.

His drinking is another character anomaly. Ask him any other time of day and he'll order a club soda like he's in AA (which he's not). But after work he downs an Old-Fashioned like clockwork and many nights more than one. I don't even know what an Old-Fashioned is.

Leaving Crosby's, Manning resumes his trek east along Seventy-Second till he reaches the Dakota on the park. He takes this same route every night. The Dakota was bombed in '27 during the Migrant Riots, when 1.7 million flooded into the States from Southeast Asia and sub-Saharan Africa, made refugees by crop failures, famine, and intertribal genocide. The Americans they displaced still haven't been resettled and they're all armed to the teeth. The forecourt of the Dakota remains charred black. The place still hasn't been reoccupied. The massive wrought-iron gates that were the Dakota's trademark when John Lennon was assassinated there back in 1980 have been replaced by concrete barriers topped with concertina wire. You can still smell the cordite as you walk past. What this means to Manning I have no idea.

He passes the Dakota and turns south, in other words backtracking, and walks down Central Park West, always on the west side of the avenue, away from the park where the tent cities of the displaced used to be and still sometimes are.

One time, about three months ago, Gleason sent me to fetch Manning when he had bolted from a conference without a word to anybody. I found Manning here, south of the Dakota, on the park side, standing just inside the stone wall that runs along the sidewalk of Central Park West.

A religious revival of some kind was in progress. A speaker, an African-American man, stood on an elevated platform spouting fire and brimstone to a flamboyantly responsive throng of women, middle-aged or older, conservatively dressed, mostly black. The preacher was declaiming about the sins of the race of mankind. The man-made eco-disasters of recent decades were proof that humanity was inherently evil and unworthy of its Creator's love. The Almighty, the speaker declared, had lost patience with us, as He had before in the time of Noah. Buses, a dozen or more—big interstate motor coaches—were parked at the curb along CPW. I couldn't help myself. I snapped a few pix with my phone.

FREE WILL BAPTIST CHURCH, Lee, MA

FOURSQUARE BIBLE FELLOWSHIP, Eufala, AL

CHRIST THE REDEEMER CHURCH, Marblehead, MA

NEW HOPE ASSEMBLY, Whitney, DE

I asked a man in the crowd if this kind of rally happened here often. He said gatherings like this had been taking place on this spot for years.

Manning stood at the rear of the crush. He was so engrossed that I held back for long moments, reluctant to break in on his absorption. The women of the congregations were apparently en route to the Holy Land. New York was their staging place. From here the buses would take them to Atlanta, where they would board charter flights crossing first to North Africa and from there to Israel. "Why are they going?" I asked the man who had told me about the gatherings.

"For the end of the world," he said.

Why Manning was so held by the speaker, I have no clue.

From here each evening, from this site by the park, Manning turns west on Sixty-Eighth. He enters the Midtown Athletic Club, his residence, not via the lobby, from which I pick him up on the mornings when I'm sent for, but through the kitchen, which has a delivery entrance off an alley just east of Amsterdam Avenue. Manning's mail is waiting for him at the front desk but he doesn't check it till morning. I've never seen him respond to postal correspondence. He scans the return addresses and chucks everything in the trash.

From the kitchen, Manning rides the service elevator (he never takes the passenger lift) up to his room on the fourth floor. I've been in this room. Manning sent me once to pick up a file he had forgotten. His instructions were to have the desk clerk retrieve the papers while I waited in the lobby, but when I got there the guy was so busy he gave me the keys (old-time brass implements that you insert into the lock and twist) and sent me up. When I opened the door I thought I had stepped through a time portal.

Manning's room is like a cell, a chamber for a monk.

From the bed, which is so narrow it looks like you couldn't turn over in it without falling out onto the floor, a person can touch three of the four walls. The fourth is only a few steps away. There's no closet, only an armoire that looks like it came from the Goodwill store, a single straight-backed armchair, and a rickety half desk/half bedside table.

On the wall beside the bed is a crucifix, one of those creepy three-dimensional relics with Jesus wearing a diaper and bleeding from a wound in his side. I have no idea if the thing came with the room or if Manning brought it himself. A single framed photo sits on the night-stand, of a woman and a young boy. The bed looks like the one from *Psycho*. I mean it. It's fucking scary.

I refuse, as I said, to probe into Manning's past. I don't wanna know where he used to live when his wife and kid were alive. But I worry. There's not even a radio in that room.

10

CHINATOWN

MY OWN PLACE is on Howard Street in Chinatown. I catch the Broadway–Seventh Avenue Line at Seventy-Second; I'm home in six stops with a change to the local at Fourteenth Street. My block, between Broadway and Mercer, was a hellhole till the '20s, when hipsters discovered it. The Flood of '29 and then construction on the Lower Manhattan Seawall drove them out. Now it's a hellhole again. Rents are cheap; I wouldn't live anywhere else. I'm in a second-story loft that's so big I could park a truck in it, with eighteen-foot ceilings and windows on two sides. I'm directly above a Korean greengrocer. My place smells like jicama and bok choy.

There's no such thing as off-line in DivSix. You keep your locator on around the clock and your earbud in 24/7. Mine chimes now, as I'm surfacing from the subway at Canal Street, with a voice mail from Gleason's tech sergeant instructing me for the third time not to waste any more time following up on that "crazy Jewish shit" that came in yesterday via text. The sergeant makes it clear that Gleason knows that Manning, with me in tow, has today hit the sweatshop in Canarsie and the contraband dealer in Little Hong Kong.

This note is succeeded immediately by a text from Manning.

BULLSHIT. DO WHAT I TOLD YOU.

Manning pretends not to like or to understand tech. But I've noticed that very few messages, even those with his in-box blacked out, get past him.

I grab a slice and a Diet Coke at the stand-up Ray's next to the greengrocer's. Ethnic prejudice is interesting in Chinatown. The Chinese hate the Koreans and the Vietnamese, whom they call gooks, dinks, slants, and slopes; the Vietnamese and the Koreans hate the Filipinos, whom they call flips. Laotians and Cambodians are beneath the notice of any civilized human. And everybody hates the Japanese. Whites are a joke to the Asians downtown. In my neighborhood the man or woman on the street literally can't tell an Irishman from an Italian. The quirk in intra-Asian bigotry is that money and social class override all. I'll be shopping in my greengrocer's; she'll catch my arm and start bitching about the gooks and slopes pouring into the States by millions, fleeing the rising seas and year-round monsoons in Southeast Asia. "See those two flips over there? They steal something every time they come in."

To her I'm not a flip because I'm a cop.

Two great things about my loft. One, it's elevated enough to catch the breezes between the rivers and off the Battery. The temperature sign on the Bowery Bank reads 112° tonight as I hike past, but with my big windows open and four industrial fans cranking, my place will be down to ninety-five by midnight. I can sleep in that. Two, I can work better from home than I do from the office. I've set up a standard consumer-grade VPN with basic encryption so my digital identity looks normal from the outside. Beyond that I'm pretty much invisible. I've masked my actual IP address, and with a sequence of homemade firewall hacks I can tap into all the databases at headquarters. Yeah, I would get into big trouble at work for accessing from off-site, except the only peeps at DivSix geeky enough to glom onto this subterfuge are the ones who would not only not turn me in but would actively abet me in continuing my depredations. In ninety minutes I've got enough background on the Righteous Man legend, not to mention apocalyptic coding, Hebrew language gematria, and End of Days eschatology, to print a dozen pages for Manning.

Just before midnight two more texts come in from Gleason's assistant. Both are team alerts for the upcoming SWAT raid on Russian Mafia headquarters in Brighton Beach. The date of the action is Saturday, April 22, seventy-two hours from now, but I am instructed to be present without fail, with Manning, tomorrow p.m. for weapons and body armor issue (the teams will carry assault rifles and possibly shotguns), test firing, and comm channel setup, at which each team member will receive his or her headset and frequencies will be tested and locked.

A SWAT raid.

What the fuck am I doing with my life? Every time my job forces me to confront the violent reality of this city, not to mention the male-dominated grab-your-bitch-ass culture within the department (including elite units like DivSix), I find myself asking these questions. What the fuck was I thinking when I signed up for this shit? What's wrong with me? Why can't I be normal?

I take my pizza crust and the last of my Diet Coke and perch by the northeast corner window. The industrial fans are wailing; temp will be down to the high nineties soon.

Should I be married?

Why don't I have children?

I'm twenty-fucking-eight, for God's sake.

But how can a responsible adult bring kids into this world? I mean seriously. I remember in second grade the teacher sitting us down, like every other class of seven-year-olds on the planet, and showing us videos of the vanishing Greenland ice cap and the death of coral reefs across the entire southern hemisphere. I've seen ten thousand worse since then. Or if you really want to scare the shit out of yourself, take a look at the sky at noon. I'm no scientist, but that shade of viridian ain't natural.

Sure, I'd love to have a baby. But how much time has the human race got? Fifty years? Thirty? Every report says the planet is past the point of no return.

I try not to think about it. Why bring innocent life into this world? So they can choke on CO_2 or go under in a tsunami of refugee gooks, dinks, and slopes?

11

THE DOROT LIBRARY

MANNING COMES ONLINE the next morning at 0650. "Well?" he says.

He has finished his wrestling regimen and powered up his phone. The GPS pin on my screen locates him on foot, having departed the Midtown Athletic Club, trekking down Broadway toward Columbus Circle.

I tell Manning I've got twelve pages for him. They're waiting on his desk right now.

I'm in the office already, ostensibly running research on Russian murder victim #2, Dr. Alexsandr Golokoff of Filvovsky Park, Moscow, per Manning's (and Gleason's) instructions, but actually bouncing back and forth between monitoring Manning as he moves and sneaking peeks at a '28 TED talk on climate change given by the Israeli anthropologist and Rabin Prize winner, Amos Ben-David.

Moscow, the news says this a.m., is roasting at 111° in the hottest April on record. Wildfires are scorching the suburbs. Civilian brigades are being recruited to fight wind-driven blazes that by nightfall could be threatening the city center.

On my screen Dr. Ben-David paces a stage in Cambridge, Massachusetts. His talk, I remind myself, is from six years ago, so any impending climate calamities are likely to be considerably more imminent today.

> BEN-DAVID
>
> ```
> What would have to happen for the Earth
> to turn back from the brink? What would
> mankind need to do? First the race
> would have to reduce global population,
> currently 8.7 billion, to 4.1 billion,
> with the intention of decreasing it over
> time to a maximum planetary carrying
> capacity of 2.3 billion. Fifty to
> seventy percent of the land currently
> in use for agriculture would have to be
> taken out of cultivation and replaced
> either by reforestation or restored to
> native grasslands for CO₂ recapture and
> sequestration. Use of fossil fuels (and
> every other energy source producing
> greenhouse gases, including methane from
> livestock) would have to decrease to no
> more than fifteen percent of the current
> rate and preferably to zero.
> ```

Swell. I hit pause and toggle over to Manning's lapel cam. It's 0743. He's digging into a plate of eggs with hash browns and wheat toast at Donovan's on Fifty-Seventh and Sixth.

I go back to Golokoff, our Russian Victim #2. Could he be called "righteous"? He served four and a half years at Dostoenko Prison outside Saint Petersburg for publishing works by dissident writers. His wife and eldest daughter were killed by a runaway panel van that jumped the sidewalk outside the GUM department store in the Kitay-gorod section of Moscow, facing onto Red Square. The driver fled and was never apprehended.

Back to the TED talk.

> BEN-DAVID
>
> Is this possible? Technologically, yes.
> Politically? My view is considerably more
> pessimistic. Forecast: global ecological
> catastrophe on a biblical scale within
> our lifetime. Everything in the Book of
> Revelation about the Four Horseman of the
> Apocalypse—famine, pestilence, war, and
> death—is on course to take place. I see
> nothing to stop it. The end of human life
> on Earth within a generation and possibly
> considerably sooner.

Wow, that's cheery. I work on Golokoff for another ninety minutes, then click back to Manning.

He has exited Donovan's, schlepped across to Fifth, then hiked south another fifteen blocks. He is just now entering the Public Library, the main branch with the stone lions out front at Fifth between Fortieth and Forty-Second. I monitor his progress via his lapel cam, past the security station, jog to the right and up the stairwell to the third floor. Manning emerges into a broad, marble-floored hallway and turns left. A clutch of Orthodox students passes him, speaking in Hebrew, or maybe it's Yiddish, I can't tell. A sign appears ahead:

DOROT LIBRARY

Manning turns left and enters. I google "Dorot." It's a research library of Judaica, funded by various Jewish individuals and philanthropic agencies.

The library's physical plant is laid out in the three sections—the main reading room, the librarian's station, and an inner reading room adjacent.

A few minutes later Manning has taken a seat in this latter chamber.

He's at one end of a lamplit oaken table. Three or four students or scholars sit in chairs at this same table. All are immersed in arcane volumes.

Manning's glance scans the scholars (all male). He takes in the beards, the *payot* side curls, the black jackets, and the knotted strings extending from the hems of the tzitzit vests under their white shirts.

The research librarian enters from the adjacent station. He's an academic-looking fellow about forty, wearing a *kippah* skullcap. He crosses to Manning, carrying three oversized, occult-looking volumes.

                         LIBRARIAN
                  (to Manning, in a whisper)
            These are the books you asked for on the
            lamed-vav-niks . . .

Manning thanks the librarian and clears a space on the table. "I'd suggest you start with this one," the librarian says. "It's the most accessible." He opens one of the books and sets it on the table before Manning.

                         MANNING
            This is in Hebrew.

LIBRARIAN

This is the Jewish library.

Manning's lapel cam switches focus to his knees and the floor. Audio sounds like snickering from several scholars at the table.

The librarian asks Manning if he wishes to keep the three volumes. Manning lets his silence answer. The librarian reclaims the books, excuses himself, and withdraws.

Two chairs down, a different scholar—apparently one who did not giggle—turns toward Manning.

SCHOLAR

You're researching the *tzadikim*. The
Thirty-Six Righteous Men.

Manning acknowledges this.

SCHOLAR

What have you learned so far?

MANNING

Damn little.

With a gesture the scholar asks Manning's permission to join him. Manning nods. The young man crosses to the chair next to Manning.

The scholar looks about thirty—tall, clean-shaven, athletic—dressed in jeans, T-shirt, and hoodie. He extends his hand.

SCHOLAR

Jake Instancer. I'm an associate professor

at Columbia in Judaic studies. I know a
little about this stuff.

Fifteen minutes later, Manning and the professor have relocated to
the café on the ground floor of the library. Plates and coffee cups sit on
the table before them. The younger man is leaning forward, scribbling on
a notepad, which he positions so that Manning can see it.

> JAKE INSTANCER
> Every letter in the Hebrew alphabet is
> associated with a number. *"Lamed"* [LAH-
> med] is *L*. It's associated with the number
> thirty. *"Vav"* is *V*. It's associated with
> six.

Lamed vav, Instancer says, is obviously thirty-six.

> JAKE INSTANCER
> Any Jew would connect this immediately
> to the legend of the Thirty-Six Righteous
> Men.

As Manning leans forward listening, the professor's eye chances
upon the SIG Sauer P226 in the shoulder holster beneath Manning's
jacket.

If this surprises Instancer, his expression doesn't show it.

> JAKE INSTANCER
> Remember the story of Noah and the Flood?
> God resolved to destroy the human race
> because people had turned out to be so

evil. The Almighty repented that He had
even created men and women. He sent the
Deluge to wipe us out.

The human race survived, as we know, Instancer continues, thanks
to Noah and his Ark.

> JAKE INSTANCER
> Since that time, God has promised: so long
> as there are Thirty-Six Righteous Men
> somewhere on Earth, He will never again
> take action to destroy the human race.

Manning absorbs this.

> MANNING
> Do we know who the Thirty-Six are? Is
> there a list?

> JAKE INSTANCER
> The Righteous Men are "hidden." In Hebrew,
> *nistarim*. Even the Thirty-Six themselves
> supposedly don't know that they're among
> that number.

> MANNING
> Who does know?

> JAKE INSTANCER
> Only God.

The younger man regards Manning thoughtfully.

                    JAKE INSTANCER
          Someone is killing the Righteous Men,
          isn't he?

                    MANNING
          Why would you ask that?

                    JAKE INSTANCER
          You're a police officer. That's why you're
          here. It's why you're researching this
          subject.

Manning makes no reply for long moments.

                    MANNING
          Why would anyone want to kill the
          Righteous Men? What possible motive could
          they have?

                    INSTANCER
          To create the conditions under which
          God is obligated, by His own promise, to
          bring about the End Times. That's what
          the Orthodox believe. They're terrified.

Instancer's eyes meet Manning's.

                    JAKE INSTANCER
          Have you heard of the Lubavitcher Rebbe?

                    MANNING
I thought he died years ago.

                    JAKE INSTANCER
The Great Rebbe, the seventh, passed
on without a successor in 1994. But the
Merkaz, the Council of Elders, appointed
an eighth Rebbe in 2024—a renowned
scholar of the same ancient line.

Instancer tells Manning that the new Rebbe has achieved in just ten years a stature nearly equal to that of his beloved predecessor.

                    JAKE INSTANCER
The Rebbe is a true sage. A "Righteous
Man" if there ever was one. He's the
spiritual leader of the largest Orthodox
community in the United States.

A trio of black-clad Chasidim happen to pass at this moment. Manning's glance tracks them.

                    JAKE INSTANCER
There are over a hundred and fifty
thousand Chasidic Jews in the city.
Most live in the neighborhoods of Crown
Heights and Borough Park, Brooklyn. For
the past month, both communities have
been buzzing with rumors about something
terrible happening to the tzadikim. But
the police won't take our fears seriously,

and there's not a mention of the story
anywhere in the press.

The professor sees that he has struck a nerve with Manning.

> JAKE INSTANCER
> The Rebbe is speaking tomorrow night in
> Borough Park. I'll take you if you want.

Instancer explains that this is a regular event called a *farbrengen*, a
Chasidic gathering.

> JAKE INSTANCER
> The Rebbe gives a talk called a *sicha*
> before an invited audience, then
> afterward he may speak privately, offer
> spiritual counsel to individuals or
> families. It's quite interesting actually.
> Sometimes these events go on all night.

> MANNING
> Would the Rebbe speak to me? A non-Jew? A
> cop?

> JAKE INSTANCER
> I'll see what I can do. But you can't
> bring a weapon—or a cell phone.

Manning and Instancer exit the café. In the hall the professor pauses.
"If you can tell me," he says, "how many murders is your department
investigating?"

Manning answers four.

                    JAKE INSTANCER
The community says six. Some say as many
as twenty. The Rebbe will speak about it,
I'm sure, tomorrow night.

BOOK THREE

THE REBBE

12

THE REBBE

THE REBBE STARTS SPEAKING before we even see him. There's a podium on the east side of the auditorium but the sage hasn't mounted to it yet. Where is he? We hear his microphone-augmented voice, but can't locate him yet among the throng.

Our party is Manning, me, and Jake Instancer, the young professor Manning met at the Dorot Library.

Instancer has rendezvoused with us at Columbus Circle in Manhattan, having taken the C train down from Cathedral Parkway–110th Street, a few blocks from his apartment in Morningside Heights, he tells us. He has guided us via our self-driver here to Borough Park in Brooklyn, gotten us past security into the community hall, and navigated us through the flock inside to an elevated station from which we can observe the full scene.

It's quite a sight. At least three hundred black-clad, fedora- and yarmulke-wearing Chasidim—men and boys (with a separate section for women and girls)—pack the converted private school that serves as the Rebbe's residence, house of worship, and community center.

Besides me, Manning and the professor, who wears jeans and a sports jacket over a black high-neck T-shirt, are the only ones in the room not dressed in Orthodox garb.

I know three things about the Brooklyn Chasidic community. One, their cell phones (the non-business ones anyway) are internet-disabled. It's an article of piety among the Orthodox to shun the modern world. Two, they love to buy old police cars. My uncle Eugene runs the NYPD's Equipment Recycling Division. "The Chasidim buy worn-out blue-and-whites for five hundred bucks and drive 'em for twenty years." Sure enough, when we arrive outside the Rebbe's, I note three antique cruisers parked at the curb, repainted black.

The final thing I know about the Borough Park community (which I learned two hours ago from research) is that the Orthodox have their own security force, called the Shomrim. Apparently one does not mess with these dudes. They patrol the streets, share radio frequencies not just with the Six-Six Precinct but across the full band of the NYPD. Borough Park is one of the safest neighborhoods in the five boroughs.

The event tonight, Jake Instancer is telling Manning as we settle into our viewing spot, is something of a special occasion. Normally the Rebbe's audience would be all-male due to the patriarchal nature of the community. One evening a month, however, women and girls are welcomed as well. The Rebbe will speak tonight for an hour or two, Instancer tells Manning, then receive visitors upstairs in his residence for individual or family consultations.

In fact, Manning has already shared a few words with the Rebbe, immediately after our arrival. The Shomrim security team had ushered us in. They secured our weapons and phones. At that moment the Rebbe happened to pass. He drew up to welcome Manning.

The Rebbe appears to be in his eighties, dressed in black from top to toe, with a bushy white beard and eyes of striking blue, set wide within a kindly face. Here's the exchange, verbatim, from my lapel cam:

                    REBBE
          (in Yiddish to Manning)
        Welcome! You are a Jew?

The younger of the two elders translates.

                   MANNING
        I'm Catholic, Rebbe.

                    REBBE
            (hard of hearing)
        Eh?

                   ELDER
        He says he's a Catholic, Rebbe.

The Rebbe switches to English.

                    REBBE
        No. He is a Jew.

Manning flinches slightly. The sage smiles and places a hand warmly on the detective's shoulder.

                    REBBE
        Don't look so stricken, my friend. It is
        your Jewish soul that will save you.

The Rebbe smiles and moves off. Instancer guides Manning and me to the place where we will stand. I hear Manning, who does in fact look a bit stricken, ask Instancer what the Rebbe meant when he said Manning "is a Jew."

> INSTANCER
>
> The Rebbe sees things that others don't.
> Perhaps he meant that you struck him as
> a soul in exile. That is a very Jewish
> thing to be.

Where has the Rebbe gone? The central well of the auditorium is wall-to-wall with a welter of foot-stomping, head-bobbing Orthodox humanity. The space is filled with a press of beards and black fedoras, black jackets, black trousers, black socks, black shoes. A song in Yiddish or Hebrew, more like a chant, actually, is being sung by the rocking, swaying congregation. Everyone seems to be having a great time.

Ah, there he is!

The young professor nudges Manning's elbow and points across the cavern. The Rebbe is picking his way among the flock. He's already giving his talk, his voice projected via a clip-on microphone.

> MANNING
>
> What's the difference between a rabbi and
> a Rebbe?

> INSTANCER
>
> There are a million rabbis but only one
> Rebbe. He's like the Pope but without the
> apparatus of the Vatican.

Manning's eyes track the Rebbe's path through the throng. The congregation is simultaneously ecstatic at their leader's apparition (my notes begin with a single word: "Elvis") and merrily oblivious to his presence.

ME

Is he speaking Hebrew?

INSTANCER

Yiddish. The Chasidic movement originated
in Eastern Europe in the 1700s. I'll
translate for you.

The Rebbe continues to cross toward the speaker's platform. Instancer is explaining to Manning that the Orthodox community is notoriously impoverished. All time and passion go into studying Torah.

One of Manning's standing instructions to me is to take notes on any individual I encounter in the course of an investigation, whether that person is "of interest" or not. "Don't think," he says. "Just record your impressions."

My impression of Jake Instancer is I desperately want to fuck him. I don't dictate this into my notes, however. Instancer is lean and charismatic, with dark eyes set deep beside a hawkish nose. He looks simultaneously scholarly and athletic. The male of the species, I confess, has never been my thing. But if anybody could pull me back across the line, it's this dude. Standing a body-width away from him, I have to call on all my resources to keep my voice even and professional. His shoulders. His hands. But the most powerful thing about him is his smell. At first I'm not even sure the scent is coming from him. Is it some kind of cologne or musk? I find myself actually edging closer just to get a noseful. Whatever this hombre is radiating, it is high-octane male mojo.

The Rebbe has mounted to the speaker's platform. He is expounding on a portion of the Torah. Instancer tells Manning that such study progresses through the five books of Moses—Genesis, Exodus, Leviticus, Numbers, Deuteronomy—taking sections of each in sequence throughout the Jewish calendar year. Tonight's talk is on the subject of "manipulation by evil."

The Rebbe speaks for twenty minutes, thirty, forty. The audience listens with total immersion. Many nod in concurrence, others appear to be praying silently. The tone of the Rebbe's speech is cerebral but also intensely personal. At least that's what I'm getting from the snatches of translation I catch from Instancer. The Rebbe's concern is not only for the souls of his congregation but also for the wider world, for whom in his faith the devotion of these pious Jews carries the hope of salvation for all mankind.

                    INSTANCER

              (to Manning)

        Are you getting a sense of how the Rebbe
        teaches? He calls upon every Jew to live
        as if the preservation of the entire
        world depends upon his godliness alone.
        Can you feel it?

The Rebbe is telling a tale of the founder of Chasidism, the beloved Rabbi Yisrael ben Eliezer, commonly called the Baal Shem Tov—the "Master of the Good Name." In the story the young Baal Shem Tov, an orphan, travels from town to town studying under various masters. He is learning the mysteries of the spirit, becoming closer each year to attaining the status of *tzadik*, a Righteous Man.

Now the Rebbe introduces a new character, a personage of evil.

This character's name is HaSatan.

                    REBBE
HaSatan means "the Satan." He is called
"the Adversary." HaSatan is the master
manipulator. He may assume any shape
or appearance. He plays with our minds,
seeking to seduce us from our virtue.
HaSatan's object is more diabolical than
to steal our souls. His aim is to make us
donate them of our own free will.

The Rebbe, for the first time, alludes to the current murders. He
mentions no names and cites no specifics.

                    REBBE
I know many of you are aware of the
recent rumors of *tzadikim* meeting violent
ends. Remember, the Righteous Men are
nistarim, "hidden." No one, not even the
individuals themselves, knows whom God
has chosen. I don't know. We cannot know.
What we sense is that wickedness is loose
in the world on a scale, perhaps, that we
have never seen.

The congregation has become totally silent, held spellbound by the
Rebbe's words.

                    REBBE
How does the Almighty communicate with
His children, the human race? He does

```
not call us together into a great hall
and address us from a high platform.
Rather, He chooses a solitary individual,
often obscure, and employs this soul
as a stand-in for all of humanity. Job
whom He afflicted, Jacob who wrestled
with an angel. Not to mention Noah,
Abraham, Moses. The Almighty tests these
individuals. He sets them trials.
```

Something makes me glance toward Manning. To my astonishment, his eyes are welling.

```
                    REBBE
How this solitary individual responds
affects the entire nation of Israel—in
metaphorical terms, all of humanity. The
instrument God uses to test this man is
HaSatan, the Adversary. HaSatan's role is
to force him to choose. To embrace the
Almighty or to reject Him.
```

Forty-five minutes in, the Rebbe breaks off his discourse. "Intermission," says Jake Instancer.

The Rebbe retires up a rear stairway, accompanied by three women, apparently his wife and daughters, to his living quarters, where he will rest for a few minutes, perhaps have a cup of tea and a bite to eat. Several of the broad-shouldered Shomrim men follow. The Rebbe will be back to finish his talk, Instancer tells Manning, in about a quarter of an hour.

"You guys want something to eat or drink? Use the bathroom?"

The professor excuses himself and moves off. He'll meet us, he says, back here in fifteen minutes.

Tea and wine, pastries, and little cheese pies are being served in a partitioned section, the women's, apparently, off to the side of the auditorium. I've been in this place for less than ninety minutes, yet already I feel like I've lived here my entire life. The Chasidic garb that had appeared so alien when we first entered now seems completely normal. I half expect to look down and see myself dressed like an Orthodox woman.

A glance from Manning snaps me out of this. His expression says, *Go circulate.*

I watch Manning move off to do the same. He crosses to a table serving tea and cakes. Within thirty seconds he has attracted a trio of Orthodox matrons. He won't interrogate them overtly, I know. He'll charm them. I can see him working already.

My style is different. As a young female and clearly a guest, I can be more direct, particularly with my peers. My notes from the next ten minutes:

> To Shomrim Bodyguard #1: "Does the name Nathan Davis mean anything to you? Michael Justman?"
> Answer: "Never heard of 'em."

> To 2 women: "Righteous Men being murdered?"
> Both: "Yes!"
> "Where? Who?"
> "Don't know but it's terrible!"
> "How do U know? Know victims? Told by friends?"
> "Just feel it."

After ten minutes I drift over toward Manning, who's now with a different threesome of women. I come in on the tail end of him telling a joke, apparently about an assimilated American Jew denying his religious identity.

>MANNING
>". . . I am not a Jew, my father is not a
>Jew, and my grandfather, *olev ha-sholom*,
>is not a Jew either."

The ladies laugh, but with an edge.

>ORTHODOX WOMAN #1
>(to Manning)
>How do you come to speak *"olev ha-sholom"*
>so perfectly? You are not a Jew?

>MANNING
>I'm Roman Catholic, ma'am. My wife was
>Jewish.

The women absorb this soberly. They don't literally glance to one another, but that's the sense of their reaction. I have joined the group fully now. I'm standing with the three ladies, facing Manning.

>ORTHODOX WOMAN #2
>You said "was." Did your wife cease to be
>a Jew?

Manning blanches. I myself know only that Manning's wife took her own life after the tragic death of her young son. Manning was put on leave immediately after, and later entered rehab. I know no further details, as I've said, and have deliberately not put myself in the way of acquiring any.

The three women clearly intuit the significance of Manning's use of the past tense. Their reaction is one of compassion.

The females are in their forties, all attractive, clearly wives and mothers. Despite living in an intentionally isolated community, they do not appear sheltered or cut off from the realities of the city or the world. The first woman asks Manning, gently but pointedly, if he has been listening carefully to the Rebbe's discourse.

> ORTHODOX WOMAN #1
> Did you understand what he said about
> HaSatan? The Evil One changes form. He
> can inhabit even our own hearts without
> us knowing it.

Manning regards her uncertainly.

> ORTHODOX WOMAN #2
> By taking your wife from her people, you
> took her from God.

Manning smiles uneasily.

> MANNING
> Well, perhaps a different interpretation
> of—

> ORTHODOX WOMAN #2
> No. From God.

Suddenly from across the auditorium comes a woman's scream.

Every face in the congregation spins toward the door at the top of the stairs, the chamber to which the Rebbe retired. One of the Rebbe's daughters stands in this space. She cries something in Yiddish, then collapses and plunges in a tangle of limbs.

The gathering erupts into pandemonium.

A bodyguard and two other men appear in this same upper doorway; they scuttle down the staircase to aid the Rebbe's daughter.

> ORTHODOX MAN
> (cries from stairway)
> The Rebbe! Someone has murdered the
> Rebbe!

Manning's right hand flies to the holster. Empty! Our weapons, we both now remember, have been secured by the Shomrim.

Manning takes off in a flat sprint toward the staircase. I tear behind him. The room has broken down into chaos. Mothers and fathers snatch up their children. The hall fills with cries of terror and grief.

As I plunge into the crowd, something makes me glance to the auditorium entry.

The woman stands there.

The woman from Georgetown.

The one who sent the "lamed vav" text via the burner phone.

She sees me.

For an instant the woman looks as if she will flee. Then she realizes I cannot stop for anything except to race after Manning.

Ahead of me, Manning swims against a tide of black hats and white beards. He's onto the speaker's platform now. He crosses to the landing and the staircase behind it, taking the steps two at a time. I can see several of the Rebbe's security team in the upper doorway, ashen and paralyzed.

Manning bowls past them into the upstairs chamber. I can hear him shouting to the people inside, "Who did it? Where is he?"

I've got my own shield high in my right hand. "Police officer!" I'm on the stairs now too.

An elderly Chasid swoons three steps above me. His black-mantled form swan-dives into my right shoulder. I tumble. I can hear Manning's voice from the stairs above me, calling something I can't make out. I peel the old man off me and pound, empty-handed, up the steps and through the door.

Ahead opens an old-fashioned, homey apartment. The Rebbe's body lies crumpled against one wall. His family and bodyguards stand and kneel over him in postures of shock and horror. Lamps, a table, and a heavy couch have been overturned.

"Where?" I'm shouting to the family, seeking Manning. "Where did the officer go?"

There!

The rear exit!

I tear across the open space and into a dark hinter chamber, apparently the access to a staircase leading down.

Manning stands at the far side of the space, facing to my right as I enter.

Directly across from him stands Jake Instancer.

For an instant I think, *The prof is going to help Manning go after the killer.*

Then I realize: Instancer *is* the killer.

Manning bull-rushes at the taller, younger man. He attacks like a wrestler, grappling with his adversary, seeking to throw him or pin him.

Instancer peels Manning away from him as effortlessly as if he were fending off a child. The professor seizes Manning by the collar. With his left arm only, Instancer lifts Manning a foot in the air. He flings him into the wall.

The breath goes out of Manning in one percussive whoop. He drops like a load of bricks.

An interval passes, no longer than half a second. In it Manning's eyes fix onto Instancer's. His glance says, *You were not at the library by accident. You set this whole scene up.*

Instancer does not speak, but the glint in his eye is unmistakable.

He turns toward me. Instancer meets my eye for a fraction of a second, then wheels and bolts down the stairs.

Manning lurches to his feet.

>   MANNING
>   (to me)
>   Go. Go!

Twenty seconds later I'm spilling, behind Manning, out the ground-level door and into the alley.

No one to the right.

No one to the left.

Rain has started—the leading front of an unseasonable tropical storm rising fast out of the Carolinas. Already drops the size of silver dollars are splatting onto the dark pavement and the hoods and roofs of parked cars.

I scramble behind Manning into the street. Security alarms are blaring. Shomrim men race from the auditorium.

Manning peers up the street and down. Lights are coming on in building after building. Heads appear in apartment windows. Cries in Yiddish resound. Already the space between the curbs is filling with grief-stricken Chasidim, men and women, pouring from buildings and brownstones.

Instancer is gone.

> MANNING

Fuck!

Manning's glance searches the shadows left and right. The mounting downpour makes it harder and harder to see. Suddenly, across on the opposite curb, Manning spots the woman.

She's alone, eyes wild.

She sees Manning.

> MANNING

You!

Manning shouts to the woman to freeze. She bolts. I take off straight at her. Manning sprints half a step behind me.

A twenty-year-old Hi-Top van sits double-parked at the curb. The woman leaps into the driver's seat. The engine starts. The van screeches away.

Manning and I still have no weapons.

> MANNING

Sonofabitch!

13

CHASE MODE

A N NYPD SELF-DRIVING VEHICLE is meant to operate auton-
omously. The car doesn't even have a steering wheel. In override
mode you accelerate, brake, and steer with a tiller that rises between the
driver's legs like the control stick on a fighter plane.

Manning plunges into the tiller seat and commands the unit ver-
bally to switch into manual. He unlocks the Remington twelve-gauge
from the ready rack between the seats. I snatch his backup sidearm, a
nine-millimeter P226, from its slot beneath the dash.

In the two seconds that the mystery woman appeared on the sidewalk, I got a good high-resolution photo of her. This pic I send now to the
car's automated pursuit system. I do this by hovering the phone over the
dash screen while pressing the SEND PHOTO icon. It's like holding a fugitive's sweaty shirt beneath the nose of a bloodhound. Instantly the photo,
including its FaceRec parameters, enters the pursuit database of every
street-corner surveillance camera, precinct house, and patrol vehicle in
the city.

Manning jams the tiller forward. The car lurches wildly into the
street. The reason there's no steering wheel on a self-driver is because

you aren't supposed to drive it. The whole point is that the technology is smarter than you.

Ahead half a block we can see the woman in her Hi-Top—an ancient Kia micro-camper with a pop-up top—swerving and careening through a sea of grief-seized Chasidim. Time is 2320. The Orthodox are pouring into the street in shirtsleeves, without umbrellas or rain gear. Many in their state of hysteria are hatless, covering their heads only with yarmulkes.

Manning hits the siren. Our unmarked unit has no exterior light bar, just white and red interior lamps forward, white and blue to the rear. The storm has broken. The volume of the downpour seems to double every thirty seconds. Through the beating wipers, we see nothing but beards and curls and black fedoras.

MANNING

Chase assist. Now.

Manning barks this to the dash sensors. All NYPD cruisers since '31, including the unmarked units issued to detectives, are grid-integrated, meaning their systems are linked electronically to the network of 277,000 aerial, interior, and street-corner surveillance pods that blanket the five boroughs so totally that, as the claim goes, a rat couldn't fart in a subway tunnel without someone at City Hall picking it up.

What that means for us now is that the photo I took sixty seconds ago is at this moment "in the pocket," meaning every surveillance cam in the city is seeking/tracking its object via FaceRec technology, which is so good, it can ID a fugitive from a profile or a three-quarter rear view, through a windshield, or even from a reflection in a mirror or a storefront window. (Why is the market so bullish for burner phones? Because people hate this Big Brother, Eye-in-the-Sky shit and will do anything to get around it.)

Our mystery woman's Hi-Top has hauled ass out of Fourteenth Avenue (the Rebbe's residence/auditorium is between Fiftieth Street and forty-ninth) and turned east on Forty-Ninth, rocketing toward Maimonides Medical Center. We're three blocks behind but we can see her big as life on three dash screens and two heads-up windshield displays.

MANNING

Where the hell is she going?

The woman blasts through the intersection at Forty-Eighth and Fort Hamilton Parkway. Her speed on the screen is fifty-four. In chase mode the system turns every light red in the path of a fleeing perp. Our girl either knows this or doesn't give a shit. Manning's tiller jacks us to sixty-six and accelerating.

The pursuit system has called in drones now. Our map display shows them as icons overhead, "pie plates" and "hummingbirds" that can follow a vehicle under the El, through a tunnel, even inside a multifloor parking garage. The system too has alerted the Six-Six and the Six-Eight. Precinct cars, under automated direction, are cutting off likely escape routes. DivSix is on the air now too. Area hospitals and paramedics are being alerted. All along the chase route, alarms are going off, red and yellow lights flashing to warn pedestrians to get the hell out of harm's way.

Our woman may be an off-the-gridder, but she knows not only how to handle a wheel but also how to outsmart a pursuit. The single vulnerability of an integrated chase system is a vehicle that runs straight at it. Entering Sunset Park, our fugitive hangs a hard U and cannonballs past us in the opposite direction.

Manning, I'm beginning to realize, learned to drive on vehicles with steering wheels. He's not worth shit on a tiller. Screaming out of Sunset Park, our AV sideswipes a garbage truck and nearly flips, bounding over a median into a double opposing lane.

```
                          ME
       What the fuck!
```

Our girl takes us through Greenwood Heights, out under the Gowanus Expressway, and into Industry City, hard by the docks and the bay.

We still can't see her.

She's too far ahead.

Through my earbud and on the console terminal we're receiving ID intel on the woman for the first time. No name. No FaceRec intersects. Neither Manning nor I possesses bandwidth at the moment to absorb any of this.

Where the hell is she going?

Forty blocks into the chase, the woman leaps a median, hangs a second one-eighty, followed by an immediate hard ninety, and highballs into a homeless encampment in an area known as "under the steel."

The camp is a maze of parked and squatting vehicles covering thirty blocks beneath an abandoned section of the old Belt Parkway. It's a chase nightmare. Every car, truck, and van radiates its own unique search signature, not to mention those of the human component of the habitat, whose combined facial contouring, body heat, sound, and physical motion meld to produce an overload of FaceRec, acoustic, thermal, and G&P input. Barrel fires and cooking pits are screwing up our search scans further. One of our drones has crashed into the collapsed overhead.

```
                       MANNING
       We're losing her!
```

The glowing speedo in front of Manning reads eighty-one. Our electric motor smells like a kitchen toaster. Suddenly . . .

There she is!

We're under the steel now too. I'm peering down an unlit lane that looks like Main Street of a Tunisian souk. Directly overhead, blocking all light both natural and man-made, looms the girder-and-concrete vault of the half-collapsed Belt Parkway. Beneath our tires spreads a slick of seawater, urine, cheap wine, and thirty years of gutter waste and petroleum by-products. Both flanks of this unlikely speedway are choked with shell tents, campers, RVs, mini-Winnies, converted panel vans and school buses, camper-shell pickups, gypsy wagons, rejiggered tanker shells, and every other mobile sleeping rig the ingenious mind of man can think of. Hibachi blazes and barbecue pits stud the slumscape.

Our female flees up this midnight Broadway. We're half a block behind when her left front tire blows. The Hi-Top nosedives to port, all four wheels spewing black smoke, bounces with unbelievable violence over a median, teeters, rights itself, and crashes head-on at fifty-plus into a ten-foot-wide, thirty-foot-high, graffiti-blackened concrete abutment.

Manning hauls the tiller into his belly. Our AV slews to a stop. Manning leaps out, twelve-gauge in hand, sprinting for the Hi-Top's driver's door. I dash toward the opposite flank.

On both sides of the crashed vehicle, precinct cruisers are skidding in. Uniformed officers, all with weapons drawn, race toward the nose-crumpled, smoking van.

MANNING

Hold fire! Hold fire!

Manning reaches the Hi-Top first, moving from the rear in a low crouch along the vehicle's flank. I'm approaching from the front, head-on to the windshield—left palm heel under the butt of the P226, right forefinger on the trigger, all safeties off, advancing one step at a time at ninety degrees to Manning so we don't wind up shooting each other, with my muzzle extended in front of me and my eyeline over the front sight.

I can smell the van's airbag—the nitrogen from the explosive charge and the talc from the sack itself.

Manning is shouting, "NYPD!" and ordering the woman to extend both hands, empty, out the driver's-side window. Her airbag's white lacerated shell drapes, limp and steaming, over the steering wheel and half of the dash. The woman herself sprawls facedown and motionless atop the deflated cocoon. I have two seconds to glimpse her through the windshield amid the reflection of the flashing red and yellow lights of the police and emergency vehicles surrounding the crash site; then Manning's left arm jerks the driver's door open hard. The woman pitches, head and shoulders foremost, out under the flashing lights.

Manning catches her before her skull hits the pavement. Is she dead? Manning cradles the woman with one hand behind her neck. Immediately two uniformed officers reinforce him and take the bulk of the female's weight into their arms. Manning checks her swiftly for weapons. One of the officers aims a tac light into the woman's eyes. She groans and tries to turn away.

Manning waves the other officers to stay back. His immediate priority, after securing the fugitive, is to clear the vehicle of any possible accomplice or booby trap that might turn us all into smoking body parts. From my position in the glare of the van's headlights I can achieve only the shallowest view-angle on the woman. Her face is bruised and blackened; both eyes are contused and shut. Her left arm is twisted at an unnatural angle. With one hand Manning snuffs the smoldering fabric of her collar, apparently set alight by the airbag detonation. He hands the woman into the care of the two officers and motions to me to follow him. I skim in his wake along the van's flank toward the right sliding door that leads into the living compartment.

Manning takes a position aft of the door. I'm covering him from a half crouch, directly flanking the van. Two uniformed officers from the Six-Eight back him from the rear.

One, two . . .

Manning yanks the door open. He plunges in. I pile in behind him. No one inside.

The patrol officers scramble up, flashlights in fists. Manning commandeers one. He's fully aboard now. So am I. Manning calls through the open driver's door to the two officers who hold the woman.

MANNING

Lock her up! Get a bus and get her to the
hospital.

A bus is an ambulance.

Manning shouts to the other officers to call in for the crime lab. He wants the Hi-Top combed for prints ASAP.

Manning himself pushes farther into the vehicle. The interior is as compact as a submarine—stowage space forward, sleeping berth above the cab. The right flank holds a fold-down table with two banquette seats and a galley kitchen with fridge, sink, and cooktop.

A homemade corkboard covers the left wall across from the table. The vertical surface takes up a quarter of the length of the vehicle, as tall as a standing man. Every square inch is plastered with typed and handwritten notes, photos, documents, maps, and index cards.

MANNING

What the fuck is this?

He takes a step back and aims the 750-lumen SureFire tac light at the corkboard. I shine mine too.

In the gleam of both our lamps, Manning glimpses what appear to be scriptural passages in Hebrew, Greek, Aramaic, whatever, side by side with photos of at least two dozen men arrayed in some order that seems to be deliberate and definitive. Numbers of the men's pix are X'd out. Esoteric-looking mathematical formulas cover a quarter of the Obsession Wall (which is what it apparently is), along with phone numbers and addresses, satellite-photo maps, occult signs, and arcane markings.

Dead center on the wall, with broad black Sharpie arrows pointing to it from all directions, is a poster-sized photo of our murderer and self-described associate professor of Judaic studies—Jake Instancer.

14

INTENSIVE CARE

ANY INDIVIDUAL ADMITTED to a medical facility while in the custody of the NYPD becomes by law the responsibility of the city of New York, specifically the Office of the District Attorney for the borough in which he or she was apprehended. The person is no longer under his or her own insurance. The city picks up the tab. There's an elaborate procedure for checking a suspect into a hospital, which I've never done but fortunately the paramedics have down cold and so do the admitting clerks. Nor can you take an individual in custody to just any hospital. The facility must be approved; it must operate under a contract with the city. That means Maimonides Medical Center in this case, thank goodness, which is a beautiful modern hospital with clean floors and nurses who speak English.

Manning has been required to return to the murder scene of the Rebbe. His orders to me as he packs me aboard the ambulance evacuating our runaway female are delivered with an intensity I've never seen from him before.

```
                    MANNING
       Stay glued to this woman, Dewey. Do not
       leave her side for any reason. Forget
       Gleason's bullshit about Russia, this
       female is the key to the case.
```

Manning holds the ambulance to deliver one final directive to me.

```
                    MANNING
       If anybody shows up at the hospital for
       her—I mean anybody . . . ID them and hold
       them till I get there. Feed them any line
       of bullshit you need to, but don't let
       them get away.
```

Why has Manning been ordered back to the crime scene? He is not only the initial officer on site, and thus technically responsible for securing the scene (which he has failed to do by absenting himself in a vehicle pursuit), but he is also a witness and indeed a participant in the flight of the suspected killer. Manning has grappled physically with this individual. He has received a disabling blow from the perpetrator, the consequence of which was to permit the perp to escape. Beyond this, Manning has accompanied the suspected murderer to the scene as his invited guest. In other words, whether he likes it or not, whether he has asked for it or not, Manning has become the law enforcement epicenter of this catastrophe.

How big is the story of the Rebbe's murder? By the time my ambulance reaches Maimonides, which is no more than twenty minutes after the actual killing, the tale is headlining on Buzzfeed, Politico, the Atlantic, Reddit, JPost, Breitbart, Upworthy, and Viral Nova. WCBS, WNBC,

WABC, WPIX, plus Fox 5, CNN, MSNBC, Amazon, and Al Jazeera have all made it "breaking news" with a banner, a chyron, and its own music sting. Social media is on fire. Both New York senators are being flown in by helicopter, or will be within the hour, to the site of sorrow. A tweet from the mayor vows he'll be on hand in twenty minutes. By dawn every Jewish, Protestant, Catholic, and Muslim leader in the tri-state area will have either spoken or appeared on TV or via Facebook or Twitter expressing shock, outrage, and grief.

At Maimonides I remain joined to our mystery woman at the hip throughout the admissions process and the initial physical examinations, including X-rays, concussion protocols, EKG, and wheeling her to the ladies' loo. A female patrol officer from the Six-Six joins me. By the manual, she should be the one to stand sentry over our mystery woman but, heeding Manning's orders, I refuse to be dislodged.

Two hours on, still no positive identification has been made. Despite numerous excellent prints having been acquired from the Hi-Top, CSU has so far made no matches to databases in the U.S. or Europe. FaceRec continues to yield zip. Even the woman's personal effects come up goose eggs. No ID, no phone. She has a wallet but it's as scrubbed as her identity on the web and in the administrative world—no credit cards, no family snapshots, not even cash, just street scrip, traceable to nowhere and nothing.

I have gleaned only two insights in my initial three hours as our female's guardian. The first comes in the ambulance.

PARAMEDIC #1
Hey, Detective . . . want something for
your report?

The medic turns the unconscious woman's left wrist into the light. Suicide scars.

PARAMEDIC #2
Pro-style. Not across the veins but
parallel.

The second medic calls my attention to the scar tissue. It has faded
to differing hues.

PARAMEDIC #2
Multiple attempts. On both wrists. And
take a squint at this.

Along the length of both forearms: burn scars.

ME
From which you conclude what?

PARAMEDIC #2
Self-mutilation?
        (shrugs)
This babe's had a rough life.

The woman remains unconscious throughout the ambulance trip
and for twenty-four minutes by my watch after entry to the ER. I have
handcuffed her per protocol. When the medics settle her on a gurney,
I secure her by one wrist to the rail. Down the hall we troop toward an
examination room. Suddenly our woman snaps alert. It takes her several seconds to realize where she is. Then, with a cry like an animal, she
claws herself upright, yanks the IV tube from her arm, and catapults off
the trolley.

The cuff on her left wrist jerks her back. The gurney totters. I tackle
her from one side; a six-foot orderly undercuts her from the other. Two

nurses right the rolling rig and expertly flip her back onto it. Apparently they have done this before.

I don't know what juice they inject our woman with, but her eyeballs roll back into their sockets like pinballs. She drops dead-weight onto the trolley. A second IV, this time delivering a stronger punch, is affixed.

Another hour passes in paperwork (for me and the patrol officer from the Six-Six) and medical evaluations for the woman. A team from DivSix arrives—Kiriakin and two Second Graders, both of whom have hit on me in the past and now hate my guts. They dismiss the patrol officer and turn to shoo me.

> SECOND GRADER #1
>
> The girl's ours now, Dewey. Take a hike.

> ME
>
> I'm here till Manning relieves me.

Kiriakin gets on the horn to Gleason, who's on-site at the Rebbe's now and can't or won't respond. Gleason's tech sergeant, though, reminds me on his own that the SWAT raid on the Russian Mafia is slated for 2230 tomorrow, with prep commencing four hours from now at Emergency Service Unit, Brooklyn South.

> KIRIAKIN
>
> Go home and get some sleep.

> ME
>
> I'm comfortable here.

Finally, near 0400, our woman is admitted to a private room on the ninth floor of the Gellman Building. I flop into the chair beside the bed.

> SECOND GRADER #2
>
> You staying here?

> ME
>
> You see me leaving?

The trio grunt in aggravation. Kiriakin and one detective vacate for coffee and donuts; the other takes up a post in the hall outside the room.

What a fucking night.

The SWAT raid is for real, though. I must be in the briefing room without fail three hours from now. Can I catch a few Z's? Should I? I'm too tired to even worry about Manning.

I close my eyes for three minutes and begin dreaming immediately about our woman running away. I jerk awake in a sweat. But she's there in the bed, cuffed to the rail, with an IV drip-dripping into her left arm.

I realize, with a shiver, that I'm concerned for her.

Yeah, it happens. Somehow over the past seven hours, this unknown female has become "mine."

My job is to protect her.

I'm not gonna let Kiriakin and his porker henchmen peek under her gown or make shitty cracks about her while she's out cold.

Who the hell is this woman anyway?

I get up and take a photo of her.

I stand at the foot of the bed and snap off a shot full-length, then cross to her side and crank off two more of her face.

I never realized the damage an airbag can do. It saved her life, yeah. But its explosive deployment has cracked two ribs and nearly broken her collarbone. Both eyes have been blacked. The left side of her face is purple from jaw to eyeline.

I lean over and fix her hair, or at least tug it out of her eyes.

She's, what . . . thirty?

Good skin.

Good teeth.

Somebody paid for orthodontia.

I'm just snapping another pic when the woman stirs and opens her eyes.

She says my name.

WTF?

Her skull sinks back into the pillow. Her lids droop shut.

> ME
> What's your name? How do you know mine?

No response. I try for thirty seconds, lifting her head, speaking softly. Again she manages to surface.

> WOMAN
> Help me.

Kiriakin will be back in minutes. I try to get the woman to speak more but the sedative is too strong. She manages to babble a half phrase or two . . .

She wants me to contact someone.

I tell her I can't.

> ME
> I'm a cop, honey. Not your girlfriend.

But I put a pencil in her hand and hold a pad beneath it. The woman struggles to write.

AMOS BEN-DAVID

Her handwriting is squiggles.

                    ME
     Amos Ben-David? The anthropologist? From
     Israel?

The woman manages a nod. I move closer.

                    ME
     Why were you at the Rebbe's tonight? Did
     you know what was going to happen?

She tries to speak. I'm bending over her, straining to hear.

                  WOMAN
        . . . followed him . . .

                    ME
     Followed who? Instancer?

                  WOMAN
     Manning.

                    ME
     You followed Manning? Why would you—

The woman's eyes roll shut. I seize her hand.

                    ME
     Stay with me! Don't crash! Why were you at

the Georgetown murder scene? Why did you
shout-out about the "LV" sign?

I squeeze the woman's hand harder. No response. Harder. I'm bending close, with my ear inches above her lips . . .

KIRIAKIN
What is this? Lesbo ladies' night?

Kiriakin and his two stooges tromp in and take over. They proceed to give me a yard of shit—about me sticking here, about me being Manning's flunky, about refusing to defer sufficiently to their male sense of entitlement. Manning's in trouble with Gleason, they tell me. He'll be off the case by morning and so will I.

I make no peep about Amos Ben-David. But my skull is spinning. How does a woman with no name and no home know one of the most celebrated scientists in the world?

Kiriakin pulls rank and kicks me out.

In the corridor I change my mind about helping our girl.

I find a corner and pull up one of the pix I took of her. I attach the shot to a text and, after a quick search under AMOS BEN-DAVID, send it to him via Facebook Messenger, Instagram DM, and to his mailbox at the Ecology Department of Bar-Ilan University in Tel Aviv.

This woman, identity unknown, is asking for you.
Maimonides Hospital, NYC.

I leave my return address in the clear.

Then I shoot the following text to Uribe at CSU, cc'ing Manning:

No print match on mystery girl in US, Euro databases?
Try Israel. A hunch.

Kiriakin emerges into the corridor.

>   KIRIAKIN
> You still here, sweetheart?

He orders me to get my ass to ESU South Brooklyn for the SWAT briefing. I hold up a moment, adopting a respectful tone.

>   ME
> Sir, you're Russian, right?

>   KIRIAKIN
> Two generations ago.

>   ME
> What's your take on this case? I mean the
> boss's fixation on—

>   KIRIAKIN
> The boss don't have no "fixations," Dewey.

>   ME
> You know what I mean, sir. Is this
> Russian thing bullshit or what?

Kiriakin is basically a good guy, despite his substandard taste in team members. He straightens and fixes me with a sober glower.

                    KIRIAKIN
     I'll tell you what _is_ bullshit—your hero
     Manning chasing leads he's been told to
     fuck off from.

Dawn's first storm-shrouded glimmer peeks through the grating at
the end of the hall.

                    KIRIAKIN
     Wanna keep your job, Dewey? Ask
     yourself who signs your professional
     evaluations . . . then do exactly what
     the fuck he tells you to.

BOOK FOUR

THE SERVICE

15

EMERGENCY SERVICE UNIT

Hᴇʀᴇ's ᴡʜᴀᴛ ʏᴏᴜ ɴᴇᴠᴇʀ ᴛʜɪɴᴋ ᴏꜰ as a woman when you embark upon a career in law enforcement:

The clothes.

Fashion. Style. What the hell are you gonna wear? My first day assigned to Manning, I clomped in in heels I had selected deliberately as the blockiest, clunkiest I could possibly be seen in public in.

> MANNING
>
> What is this? *Vogue* magazine?

Manning takes one peek and orders me to redefine my concept of appropriate footwear.

> MANNING
>
> You're a cop, Dewey. You want heels that
> can stomp a Puerto Rican to death.

I'm shocked.

                    ME
              (pissed off)
        How 'bout a Filipino?

                  MANNING
        Flips? A waste of shoe leather.

This is day one on the job for me, this action going down by the Nespresso machine with detectives and tech personnel sniggering from all corners. I can see that Manning is playing intentionally on the stereotype of the chauvinist Irish cop. Still it hurts.

He sends me after work to a haberdashery called Rubidoux's on 110th and Amsterdam. The place is row after row of shapeless female business suits—navy, black, gray, pinstripe. Even the sizes are fauxmale: S, M, L, and XL. The salesman (there are no women) asks simply, "How many?"

What exactly are the fashion guidelines for gal detectives on duty?

No earrings (they might snag on something, or get yanked by a perp). No jewelry. No nail polish (except clear). No nail art.

No necklines lower than your throat. No push-up bras. No cleavage.

No rings other than a wedding band.

No skirts. Slacks only.

Weapon worn in holster on hip or at small of back, never carried in bag.

Hair short or up, or pulled back into a bun. (French twist okay if it's "high and tight.")

No ponytails.

No smoking.

No drinking.

No gum chewing.

No hands in pockets.

In public, you stand—always.

Except when interviewing, sit only in a vehicle or at your desk.

> MANNING
>
> I know you think this is bullshit, Dewey.
> But a detective is like a priest in
> the eyes of the community. You have to
> simultaneously command respect and be
> accessible to confidences. Particularly
> you as a woman, because other females
> will look to you to understand their
> point of view. They'll open up to you,
> when they never would to a man.

Here is what an idiot I am: I invite Manning, a week later, down to my loft as a getting-to-know-you courtesy.

He accepts, God knows why.

The first place Manning cruises is my closet, which is (my fault) half exposed beside the open space that holds my bed.

> MANNING
>
> The Lo! This is yours?

"The Lo" is short for Polo. Ralph Lauren Polo. These jackets, sweaters, and gooses (goose-down jackets) were the supreme hip-hop fashion statement of the '90s and well into the new century—all boosted from Bloomies and other upscale outlets by street crews from Brooklyn who called themselves with pride "Lo Lifes."

> ME
>
> They belonged to my father.

Manning scans the hanging items, fixing at last on a shelf that holds a monogrammed cigarette case: MGV.

>   MANNING
>   Marcus Garvey Village. Your old man's
>   black?

>   ME
>   He died.

>   MANNING
>   Where?

I don't answer.

>   MANNING
>   I'm sorry.

Manning takes me out to dinner that night, the only time I've ever sat across from him and consumed a meal off actual plates and dishes. Manning, I can see, is moved by the sight of the threads in my closet— and the vanished era they evoke.

>   MANNING
>   Did you know your father?

My expression answers.

>   MANNING
>   I probably did. I was in Brownsville
>   then. A beat cop.

He asks if I ever wear the Lo.

                    ME
Around the loft sometimes.

                  MANNING
Never on the street?

                    ME
No.

Manning asks what the clothes mean to me. I have a serious answer, but I'm reluctant to verbalize it.

                  MANNING
Go ahead. You can talk straight with me.

I tell Manning that I understand and even respect the brilliance of fighting poverty and powerlessness with style. With fashion.

                    ME
Those crews in their day were the flyest
thing on the planet.

                  MANNING
But.

                    ME
In the end it didn't work. They died. They
wound up in Clinton.

Manning regards me thoughtfully.

                    MANNING
    So you applied to the academy.

The check comes. Manning grabs it.

                    MANNING
    You know I'm jerking your chain when I
    talk like that about flips and Ricans?

Outside, he walks me to my stop.

                    MANNING
    Don't sell the Lo. Ever.

I'm recalling that evening now, two and a half hours after being relieved by Kiriakin at Maimonides Medical Center, as a Brooklyn South armory sergeant sets into my fists a Mossberg 500 ZMB "Zombie Killer" shotgun and dubiously ogles my five-foot-four, 125-pound frame.

The SWAT raid on the Russian Mafia kicks off in fourteen hours. Am I really ready for this?

It's Saturday morning, 0830. The storm has slammed into the city, building from Cat 4 to Cat 5 to possible Superstorm. Per Gleason's instructions, all DivSix personnel assigned to the warrant service have assembled at Emergency Service Unit South Brooklyn, then proceeded in order of seniority to Weapons and Equipment Draw, where our two teams of four and one team of two (Manning and me) have been issued IBAs, individual body armor—not the Kevlite sleeveless vests that tac officers and bike cops wear but military-issue flak jackets, eleven-pounders, designed to protect against shrapnel, ball bearings, and everything up to and including a Quds Force IED.

The raid on the headquarters of the Russian Mafia is slated for 2230 this evening. The teams will be briefed here at ESU, then rebriefed at the assembly point near Coney Island, where they will link up with the operators who will lead our teams in the actual assault. From there the combined force will proceed in convoy to the target—a complex on Ocean Avenue in Brighton Beach constituted of two homes, an office, and a social club.

I have not had a minute to speak apart with Manning since he dispatched me to Maimonides last night. I have texted him, however, cc'ing Uribe, three times. Once to report the suicide scars on our still-unidentified female's wrists and to describe her terrified attempt to bolt from the hospital gurney (without interpretation on my part as to motive), once to inform Manning of her statement that she was at the Rebbe's last night because she had "followed" Manning, and last to document her Mayday request that I contact on her behalf Amos Ben-David in Israel. I add a note re: Ben-David's global stature and my own surprise, not to say astonishment, that our woman not only knows this individual but apparently considers him a contact-in-emergency friend.

ME

(by text)
Meanwhile how are you?

MANNING

(texts back)
Read it in the paper tomorrow.

My phone says 0845. I have been issued a helmet, a headset, and, as I said, a Zombie Killer shotgun. In the ladies' loo I scope myself in the mirror. I look fucking ridiculous.

At the academy we had only two days on "High-Risk Warrant Service," and even those sessions were abbreviated by Hurricane Alexandria (a hurricane in January, unheard-of as little as ten years ago), which put Wards Island, the site of our training in close-quarters combat, under a foot and a half of seawater. We were supposed to be given a half day on the range for "fam fire" (familiarization) on both twelve-gauge shotguns and M4 assault rifles. Neither happened. I've never held or thrown a flash-bang grenade. I wouldn't know a hooligan tool if I tripped over one.

Even in the supposedly elite workup at DivSix we've had no warning order, no ops order, and no operational briefing. We've had one short video brief in the Bunker with aerial drone footage of the buildings the operational teams will assault, but only one barely decipherable floor plan diagram, and no photos or physical descriptions of the individuals we're supposed to apprehend. Not to mention we have never worked with, or even met, the ESU operators we'll be conducting the service with. I for one have no idea how our teams will be integrated or if each division will be operating on its own.

The NYPD has no tactical entity designated as SWAT. Our version is called ESU, Emergency Service Unit. ESU operators are door-kickers. Their job is to "respond to high-risk tactical operations involving barricaded subjects, hostage situations, high-risk warrant service, tactical crowd control and dignitary/VIP protective operations."

In police parlance, a raid is never called by that term. It's a "service," i.e., a warrant service. To raid a location is to "carry out a service."

There are ten Emergency Service Squads distributed across the five boroughs. Squads are called "trucks." The truck we'll be working with is ESS-6, South Brooklyn. This truck consists of twelve operators working as a "stack," i.e., the front-to-back lineup that bursts through a door (though we have been assigned only six, a half-stack, because DivSix is considered "apprehension-capable"). We'll have a canine squad from ESU and an Apprehension Tactical Team as well.

Am I up for this?

Are our teams?

I'm striding two steps behind Gleason and Manning down a corridor of the Six-Eight Precinct station house, the headquarters for ESS-6 at the border between Sunset Park and Bay Ridge. Manning has just finished a ninety-second hallway pitch to our boss to include Jake Instancer on the bust list for tonight. Gleason, ears scarlet, dismisses this.

> GLEASON
>
> You know how much heartburn these black-
> hatted sonsofbitches are giving me? The
> mayor's all over my ass, along with two
> senators, four congressmen, the AJC, the
> Anti-Defamation League, and every Jewish
> organization in the city except JDate.
> I've got the White House on my callback
> sheet for Christ's sake. Why? Because
> your mug shows up in a hundred viral
> videos shot outside the Borough Park
> murder scene and when the press asks what
> you were doing there, twenty Chasidim on
> the street tell 'em you were going toe-
> to-toe with the devil—Beelzebub himself—
> and that because you lost the fistfight,
> Mr. Scratch is about to bring on the
> Apocalypse. What are you doing to me,
> Jimmy?

Silver falls in step beside our skipper.

> MANNING
>
> I was in Borough Park on my own time,
> Frank. And I'll tell you something else—

> GLEASON
>
> Don't tell me nothing! I don't wanna hear
> about the end of the world and I don't
> want a recap of the plot of *Rosemary's
> Baby*.

Manning again presses Gleason and Silver to include Jake Instancer on the warrant service list.

> MANNING
>
> Frank, I was in the room where the Rebbe
> bought it. The scene is a dead ringer for
> the murders here and in D.C.

> GLEASON
>
> With the LV sign on the forehead?

> MANNING
>
> We don't know.

Manning acknowledges what Gleason already knows from last night—that the Rebbe's family would not let any civil authority, police or medical, near the sage's remains.

> GLEASON
>
> We don't know—and we <u>won't</u>, will we?
> Because Orthodox Jews bury their dead the
> day after they croak.

As he strides, Manning dons the dark blue flak jacket with NYPD ESU across the shoulders and a Velcro patch with his blood type on the front.

I'm doing the same. Gleason is already suited up, as is Silver. All three carry shotguns or assault weapons.

I know, not yet from Manning but from a pair of tac officers of the Six-Eight I wolfed donuts and coffee with this a.m., that Manning has been on the hook all night, filing reports on the Rebbe's murder, three for DivSix, two each for the FBI and the NSA, as well as being deposed by two ADAs from the Manhattan District Attorney's Office and a prosecutor from the U.S. Attorney's, Southern District of New York. Lapel camera video of his encounter with Instancer at the Dorot Library and more from the Rebbe's *farbrengen* has been filed as evidence, not yet with the LV murders but under a separate case number. Likenesses of Instancer have been distributed to every police department in the metropolitan area and to all cable and network outlets as well as social media. Two DivSix teams, reinforced by twenty precinct officers, are at this moment canvassing the neighborhoods of Borough Park/Crown Heights and Columbia/Morningside Heights seeking any evidence or confirmation of truth regarding Instancer's claim to employment as an associate professor or his attestation that he is or was a member of, or associated with, the Chasidic community.

Meanwhile, I have received no response from Amos Ben-David in Israel (if in fact he even got my message), for which I am secretly and selfishly relieved. I was way out of line to send that text. The act was at best unprofessional; at worst it could be a career-ender. Maybe Ben-David susses this and is thus responding with silence. If so, I am grateful.

Gleason, Manning, and Silver turn a corner. ESU operators, in assault gear and packing shields, rams, and ballistic door breachers, emerge from a locker area to the side and stride ahead of us down the hall. The feeling is like a military operation.

The teams have finally been given photos and physical descriptions of the three individuals—Viktor A. Korchmar, Isais T. Mazdr, and Alemany "Yoo-hoo" Petracek—whom they are assigned to apprehend. All three suspects are present now on the premises to be assaulted, or so our teams have been informed at the briefing at Brooklyn South. This intelligence comes from "eyes-on" surveillance of the site, as the storm is too wild for drones to fly, and from one sniper overwatch team, in position now on the roof of the Russian Orthodox church across the street from the social club.

Our assault teams pass an open roll-up door on the left, through which we glimpse outside in a service yard a pair of armored Chevy Tahoes, with their engines idling and wipers beating, and several other military-type vehicles, including an ESU K-9 unit getting ready to roll. Medics and fire department personnel hurry along the hallway, heading apparently for the same place we are.

A half dozen paces before the briefing room door, Gleason tugs Manning to the side. I can just overhear as I pass.

                    GLEASON
    I made a place for you in DivSix, Jimmy,
    when you were fucking radioactive. This
    ain't just your ass on the line. Don't
    embarrass me.

Our group and the ESU operators enter a briefing room. Gleason and Manning follow, among other team members, including the dog handlers and communications personnel. The space is crammed and the mood is keyed-up and intense. More than two dozen officers—fortyish detectives from DivSix but mostly young muscular ESU operators—arm themselves and assemble before a briefing panel.

The ESU commander and Gleason take their places before a wall displaying oversized street maps and building diagrams of an area of city streets in Brighton Beach, Brooklyn, just a few blocks from Coney Island.

GLEASON

```
All right, everybody. Listen up.
```

What exactly, our boss asks the room, constitutes the legal basis for tonight's warrant service?

Gleason lays it out on wall-mounted briefing boards. My notes:

1. Russian victim #2, Alexsandr Golokoff of Filvovsky Park, Moscow, was murdered at his residence on the night of April 3– 4, 2034, sometime between the hours of 2300 and 0200.
2. Air passenger manifests [United, Aeroflot] confirm Alemany Petracek arrival in Moscow @24 hours prior to Golokoff murder—and departure from Moscow Sheremetyevo @8 hours post.
3. Traffic video provided by Moscow police, authenticated by Russian MVD (Ministry of Internal Affairs) confirms presence of rental vehicle (UAZ Bukhanka van, Alamo Rent A Car), receipt to Petracek, in victim's neighborhood at hour of murder.
4. U.S. victim #1, Nathan Davis, DOD 4/9/34, killed at Century Association, Manhattan, 2030 hours.
5. "Yoo-hoo" Petracek MD [metadata] phone log indicates calls from Petracek cell 4/1/34 and 4/4/34 durations 12:14 and 21:34 to Davis's private number [6 days and 9 days prior to murder]. No intercept tapes.
6. Security video 4/1/34 [9 days before Davis murder] @Davis building shows Petracek enter, sign security log, proceed to Davis residence floor. No interior video.

Much of this evidence, Gleason admits, is circumstantial. What has convinced him (not to mention the judge who okayed the no-knock warrant) that it justifies an ESU service, however, is the confirmation by

DivSix Team #1, Silver's crew, of linkages between Russian victim #2, Alexsandr Golokoff, and U.S. victims #1, Nathan Davis, and #2, Michael Justman—and connections between all three and the Russian security police, the FSB, which has been known to engage the services of American assassins, specifically those associated with Bratva, the "Russian Mafia," to carry out domestic and overseas espionage and murder.

The link between the three victims?

Climate change.

Silver's team reports that Michael Justman, in the months before and continuing up to the date he was murdered, had been the lead U.S. negotiator with the Russian Foreign Ministry on a proposed multinational, multitrillion-dollar carbon sequestration program. The project involved taking out of cultivation tens of millions of acres in the United States, Canada, Mexico, and eleven Central and South American countries, along with matching acreage in Russia, Chechnya, Ukraine, Georgia, Armenia, Azerbaijan, Kazakhstan, Uzbekistan, Turkmenistan, Tajikistan, and Kyrgyzstan, and restoring these spaces to native grasses and/or reforestation. The aim of the program, for which negotiations remain ongoing, is to retard and possibly begin to reverse the course of global climate change.

The program, according to Silver's team's report, was and is opposed vehemently both by fossil fuel interests (very powerful in Russia and Central Asia as well as in the States) and agribusiness conglomerates, whose financial interests, and even survival, are perceived by the parties themselves as being set at jeopardy by the proposed agreement. All three murder victims—Golokoff, Davis, and Justman, and indeed the fourth, Alexei Tcheckousky—share histories of clashing with the Kremlin, Rosneft, Gazprom, Lukoil, and other Russian petro-giants and in fact of being threatened, harassed, and intimidated by them. The two Russians indeed had been imprisoned for their activism.

Gleason's conclusion: the Rooskies, specifically these of the Brighton Beach Brotherhood, are the trigger-pullers, bigger than shit.

GLEASON

Here in my hand are the warrants for
these motherfuckers' arrests. You and I
are about to serve them.

The last items of intel that Manning and I receive before boarding the ESU vehicles come via text from Uribe.

Amos Ben-David, Uribe says, has within the hour flown in from London, where he was the featured speaker at a conference on global climate catastrophe. He has traveled by Uber directly from JFK to Maimonides Medical Center, where he was met by his longtime friend and colleague Ms. Ellie Landau, the celebrated attorney and Felix Frankfurter Professor of Law at Harvard Law School, author of the mega-bestseller *Landau for the Defense*, and omnipresent talking head on CNN, Fox, MSNBC, and all the networks.

Uribe reports that Ms. Landau arrived at Maimonides in possession of a judge's order, mandating the release from custody of Rabbi Rachel Davidson. (Yes, that is our mystery woman's name and profession.)

Ms. Landau's office is in the process now, Uribe continues, of filing a $10 million lawsuit against the city of New York and the NYPD, citing Manning by name for his role in the unlawful detention of her client, Rabbi Davidson, and naming Uribe as well for his part in illegally impounding Ms. Davidson's vehicle.

Final beat:

Positive identification of Ms. Davidson, Uribe reports, was achieved by processing her fingerprint file through the database of the IDF, the Israel Defense Forces. Rabbi Davidson, it turns out, was a *segen mishne*, a second lieutenant, in the reserve forces of the Israeli army before she was discharged dishonorably, twenty-one months ago, for "offenses against the Jewish religion."

16

THE SERVICE

THE FIFTEEN-SQUARE-BLOCK AREA south of Sheepshead Bay at the Belt Parkway, bounded by Ocean Parkway to the west, Manhattan Beach/Corbin Place on the east, and the Atlantic Ocean to the south, is known as "Little Russia" (occasionally "Little Odessa.")

Our party assembles now—three teams from DivSix (the original complement had been four but one has been called away on another assignment) along with fourteen operators of South Brooklyn ESU—under vehicle cover in a vacant lot behind a bakery and a Jewish deli south of Neptune Avenue and west of Brighton First Street.

Time is 2145, nine forty-five in the evening, of Saturday, April 22, 2034.

The gale, which had been classed as a Category 4 hurricane until 1330 this afternoon, has been upgraded first to Cat 5 and then to a Superstorm, named Dani, the fourteenth since Sandy in 2012. Brighton Beach Boulevard is under eight inches of water already, with runoff sluicing in rivers from the elevated subway and storm surge back-flooding furiously out of the street drains.

The Emergency Service Units have been in meetings and prep assemblies since 0800 this morning. Three times the warrant service has been called off. Three times it's been reinstated. Manning's latest migraine (I could see his eyes clouding during the early brief at Brooklyn South) seems to have passed; he has gotten a couple hours' snooze on the couch in the ESU skipper's office. I haven't had a wink and neither has anyone else.

Manning has time for one final fracas with Gleason before vanishing into the captain's office.

> MANNING
> Frank, you're telling me this street
> woman means nothing. Then how come the
> most famous attorney on the planet is
> suddenly standing up for her?

Gleason dismisses this. Who cares who's defending her?

> MANNING
> Come on, Francis! How many homicide
> cases have you and I brought to court?
> Has either of us ever . . . _ever_ had a
> defendant represented by Ellie Landau?
> This means something!

Gleason blows it off. "We'll talk about it tomorrow."

As for me, I confess the whole Righteous Man scenario has completely fled my brainpan. I'm too overwhelmed by what's happening right now.

The final ESU brief has wrapped. Manning has reappeared. Our teams have assembled.

We're out in the storm, behind the deli.

I've been issued a helmet, as I said, from beneath whose brim and behind whose visor I can't see jack shit. My headset is malfunctioning. The deluge drowns sound utterly. Here in the vacant lot, guys are shouting at max volume into each other's ears. There's no other way to make yourself heard. Gleason, issuing last-minute instructions, has to move man-to-man and bawl straight into our faces.

> GLEASON
>
> Forget staying dry. We're gonna be drenched two seconds after we dismount the vehicles. Don't fight it. At least the rain is warm.

Gleason orders his officers not to discard any gear, no matter how sodden or cumbersome it may become.

> GLEASON
>
> Every officer must display NYPD ESU at all times. It can save your life and it can save an innocent civilian's.

Remember, he says, we're after three men. (Though Gleason has, grudgingly and at the last minute, secured a magistrate's okay to append "Jake Instancer" to the bust list.)

> GLEASON
>
> This is not a war. Don't start pulling triggers unless someone pulls on you. Secure these three assholes and let's get the fuck outta here.

Manning pulls up at my shoulder now, returning from a confab with Silver and the ESU team leaders. The last warning Gleason issues is don't do anything that's gonna get you on the six o'clock news.

> GLEASON
> Follow procedure. Perform like
> professionals. Remember: every idiot on
> the street has an iPhone and they all
> want to shoot something that goes viral.

That's it.

From the assembly area the teams advance by vehicle, in this case two assault trucks carrying the ESU operators, two armored Tahoes for DivSix's teams, a comms truck to control intra-team and ops control traffic, a K-9 Toyota Land Cruiser, and four squad cars from the Six-Oh Precinct for traffic and crowd control if necessary.

I'm the only woman among the teams. I'm packing, as I said, a twelve-gauge Mossberg. I have never fired a shotgun in my life. I'm terrified I'll blow my own foot or somebody else's head off. Manning has been issued a Colt M4 Commando assault rifle with a selector switch that thumb-flips from semi to burst to auto.

"Use your nine-millimeter," he tells me (meaning my regular service weapon) as we dismount from our Tahoe onto Brighton Beach Avenue and commence the approach march to our assigned entry point—an eight-foot cyclone fence we are to overmount. "If you pull the trigger on that cannon, it'll knock you flat on your ass."

The target is a privately owned complex off Brighton Third Street between Ocean View Avenue and Brighton Beach Avenue. The compound includes a corner cigar and candy store, a social club adjoining; a preschool with four classrooms (in temporary buildings) with an adjacent playground featuring swings, sandboxes, jungle gyms, and an "ocean wave"; an office in the school proper; and a residence complex, like a small motel. Surrounding the compound on the nonstreet sides is a seven-foot perimeter wall topped by razor wire. Primary entry is off Brighton Third, via a two-vehicle-wide steel gate chain-locked on the inside. The ESU guys, prepping, reassure each other by saying, "No problem. It's just like Afghanistan."

I'm trotting behind Manning. Rain descends in torrents. My trousers have been bloused into my boots and sealed with duct tape (so they won't catch or snag on anything). I've got lampblack under my eyes. I'm drenched in sweat. Meanwhile, we're on an actual street, Brighton Fourth, one long block north of the elevated train line. Incredibly, people are out in the storm. We pass two kids, no older than twelve, in T-shirts and wading boots. "Who are you guys—the army?" says one. Manning chases them off.

We turn a corner into an alley. It's just me and Manning now. We're wearing wireless headsets with mikes. In my right ear I can hear the chatter from the assault teams moving into position out front, from the sniper team on the rooftop of the Orthodox church across the avenue, as well as the comms truck, our DivSix teams moving into blocking positions, and the guys from the Six-Oh sealing off the neighborhood.

Manning leads the way over the fence. He's a nimble bastard for fifty or whatever the hell age he is. We drop on the far side. We're in an alley behind the preschool. It's dark. No lights. The ESU operators have NVGs, night vision goggles. The rest of us are stuck with our own orbs. Manning dashes past a jungle gym and around several sandboxes sluicing stormwater to a door at the rear of the preschool.

He points to a spot.

Our position.

I take it. Manning himself scoots off to scope the alley. According to our brief, there is only one door, a rear egress of the school, which we will cover together. But when Manning returns from his look-see, he signs that he has found a second exit around the corner.

He will cover it.

He indicates the first door.

My door.

> MANNING
>
> You okay, Dewey?

> ME
>
> I'm cool.

> MANNING
>
> Don't fuck around.

> ME
>
> I'm cool.

Manning takes one step, then draws up. The sense is palpable that one or both of us could buy the farm sometime in the next few minutes.

> MANNING
>
> Whatever happens, stand your ground.

He raps my shoulder, then bolts to his station around the corner.

I'm alone.

Am I scared?

Fuck, yes.

I have decided to stick with my Zombie Killer, despite its blunderbuss-like drawbacks, mainly because I don't dare set it down. If I should some-how become separated from an issued weapon . . . I don't even wanna think about it.

I plant my soles and brace myself.

The ESU action unspools through my headset. Both ears fill with staccato military-style chatter. Three stacks of four men each will assault the compound. Two will go over walls (in fact they're in the act right now) while the third, using one of the ESU trucks as a ram, will break through the chained front gate. They'll do this in reverse, using the vehicle's rein-forced rear bumper as the battering instrument. This third stack, the one that would normally be in the truck, will already be dismounted; they'll rush through the gate as soon as the breach has been accomplished, then assault the front entry of the residence complex on foot.

Our post, Manning's and mine, is immediately behind the pre-school. The complex is actually four sub-buildings—double-wide trail-ers linked together like a train. A play yard separates the preschool from the residence complex and social club that the ESU teams are assaulting. In other words, Manning and I are, I'm telling myself, almost certainly safely out of the line of action. There's no reason to believe that a fugitive would flee across the play yard and into the preschool, let alone out the rear egress.

We're chill.

We're safe.

I'm telling myself this and running down my wish list.

I wish I had night-vision gear.

I wish I could hear through my headset.

I wish I had trained, at least a little, on shotguns.

I wish I wasn't alone.

I wish our ESU guys would get this fucking thing over with.

I'm starting to think about Gleason.

Maybe he's right. Maybe this Russian mob *is* the force behind the LV killings.

What am I saying? Of course Gleason is right. Why would a known assassin, Yoo-hoo Petracek, be in a victim's hallway, i.e., Nathan Davis's, in his apartment, with a freaking key, for Christ's sake, if not to case, to prep, to recon?

Of course Yoo-hoo killed Davis.

Did I seriously believe any other scenario?

The devil?

To bring about the Apocalypse?

I feel my brow flushing. It's 105° but it feels like 120. I'm streaming sweat, just from embarrassment. Note to self: when this raid is over, make sure Manning knows I'm onboard 100 percent with Gleason's FSB/Bratva scenario.

Suddenly: a dull boom.

> TEAM LEADER #1'S VOICE
> (through headset)
> POLICE! NYPD!

> ASSISTANT LEADER'S VOICE
> (through headset)
> Breach front entry! Breach front entry!

I tug one earphone clear so I can hear in real life. Was that a breaching charge? Did our guys use *explosives* to blow the front gate? My headset fills with multiple garbled exchanges, all in jargon that I'm only vaguely familiar with.

All three teams are in.

They're advancing room-to-room.

What's going on?

I wish I had a video feed.

I wish I had a drone feed.

Then: an explosion.

WTF?

Rain is dumping from the heavens in ungodly volumes, yet suddenly the two farthest buildings of the preschool erupt as if a bomb has hit them. I'm a hundred feet away, with two structures between me and ground zero. Still the heat and concussion strike like a physical blow.

Gunshots.

Shouting voices.

My headset explodes into chaos.

> MANNING'S VOICE
> (through headset)
> Dewey, you okay?

> ME
> What's happening?

> MANNING'S VOICE
> Sit tight.

> ME
> Where are you?

> MANNING'S VOICE
> Sit tight.

The initial fireball and blast have blown skyward and passed, succeeded now by shooting jets of flame twenty, thirty feet high. My alley lights up like Broadway. I can see Building #3 catch fire. My building, #4, remains for the moment untouched.

I hear more gunshots.

Close.

Not in my headset.

> TEAM LEADER'S VOICE
> (through headset)
> He's running!

Despite myself, I edge closer to my door.

> ME
> (into headset)
> Manning! What's going on?

> MANNING'S VOICE
> (through headset)
> Hold your position.

My Mossberg 500 Zombie Killer holds eight rounds of double-aught buckshot. It's a howitzer. I'm about three feet from the door, deafened by the gale and the downpour, when, without the door handle turning, the full solid mass of the portal explodes in my face and a 220-pound man charges at me at full speed.

I pull the trigger.

Nothing happens.

My finger is *outside* the trigger guard.

The fleeing man hits me like a linebacker.

I am bowled rearward, ass over teakettle. *Now* the shotgun goes off. Its kick hammers me straight into the ground. Both my feet are over my head. The weapon goes flying. I feel a heavy boot step on the center of my chest and push off.

The man sprints away down the alley.

ME

(into headset)

Manning!

Two seconds later another male comes hurtling out the door, and half a second after that, a third. All three run right over me and highball away. I'm sprawled on my back in the flaming, gale-drenched alley with my helmet twisted sideways around my skull and both hands achingly, impotently empty.

At this moment temporary Building #4 blows apart. You know in movies how you see the fireball in the background while in the foreground bodies go flying? That's exactly what happens in real life except you also go instantly deaf, blind, and stupid.

The force of the blast flattens my lungs as if I'd been slammed in the solar plexus by a sledgehammer. The other thing is the fireball doesn't just ignite any adjacent structures. It incinerates them.

Somehow Manning is beside me. I snatch the Zombie Killer off the deck. The alley has become a tunnel of flame. Manning jerks me to my feet with one hand. To my amazement, I can actually think. I'm not scared of the fire or of any further explosions. My single thought is, *Hang on to the shotgun.* If I have to file a property report stating that I have through carelessness or negligence lost a weapon issued to me by the city, I will never find work in law enforcement again.

Three ESU operators appear in the perpendicular alley. They're running. They shout something I can't make out.

                    MANNING
            (to me)
        Go!

Ten seconds later he and I are out of the alley, pounding past pan-caked, blazing Building #3, and sprinting in forty pounds of armor out the entry gate and onto Brighton Beach Avenue. Fugitives #2 and #3 have peeled off right and left and are being chased by various DivSix and ESU teams.

It's me and Manning, joined by two ESU operators, pounding in the wake of Fugitive #1.

Could it be Instancer?

Could he somehow be part of this?

We can see Fugitive #1, ahead, fleeing onto Surf Avenue. Floodwater is above his ankles, as it is above ours. It's not run run run, it's splash splash splash. Fugitive #1 turns off Surf, bolts down a gale-howling alley, then another, and out onto the strand itself.

To the right, shrieking in the storm, I glimpse the derelict structure of the Super Cyclone roller coaster. This is Coney Island, or what's left of it. The strand at Brighton Beach, which used to be hundreds of yards wide, accommodating bathers by the thousands, has been underwater since the '20s.

A twelve-foot seawall was erected in '27 intending to shield the row of apartment buildings fronting on Surf Avenue, but this has been over-whelmed twice, by Hurricane Alice in '29 and Superstorm Dominique in '31. The structures are shells now, occupied by squatters and migrants. The Rockaways have vanished from the map. Bay and Sound stink of sewage and contamination.

Our fugitive sprints onto the seawall. The ESU guys are half a block ahead of Manning and me. How hard is it to run in this gear and this gale and this heat? My eyeballs are flashing so lividly I can see the veins of my own corneas. My heart is about to erupt out of my chest. The shotgun in my fists feels like a ninety-pound barbell.

Manning slings his armor vest. I do too. We'll both catch hell tomorrow, but right now who gives a shit?

Fugitive #1 is Yoo-hoo. I see him plainly now, his bald dome reflecting as he dashes beneath a streetlamp. One of the ESU men trips and sprawls, hydroplaning on his chest like a boogie boarder. The other is starting to wobble with exhaustion.

Suddenly Manning turns on the jets.

I can't believe what I'm seeing. The dude is a handshake away from retirement. Suddenly he turns into a rocket ship.

Manning pulls ahead of me by ten feet, twenty, thirty. We're on the seawall now. This formation is nothing grander than a jumble of gigantic boulders, slick as snot in the gale and the downpour.

Ahead, Yoo-hoo is clambering hand-over-hand.

Waves higher than a man's head are crashing against this barricade of stone. The breakers booming up between the rocks have the force of an explosion. One hits me. Over I go. I'm thrashing for my life in a downsucking maelstrom. I catch the lip of a boulder and barely keep from getting washed out to sea.

Where is Manning?

He has caught up to Yoo-hoo. The first ESU operator races up behind him. ESU #1 commences whaling on Yoo-hoo's shins with his D-cell Maglite. Down they both go, between the rocks. Blasting surf obscures everything. Suddenly Yoo-hoo emerges. I'm on the rocks now too. I feel like I'm in an end-of-the-world movie.

Yoo-hoo starts running toward me.

Fuck.

He's twenty feet away.

Suddenly a form tackles him from one side. It's Manning. I can barely see with the sea spray, the deluge, and the dark, but it looks to me like he's got Yoo-hoo in a wrestling hold. I slip-and-slide closer. The ESU man recovers; he's closing too. I hear a dog barking behind me.

Yoo-hoo goes down, flailing wildly.

Manning has him pinned.

The ESU guy flex-cuffs Yoo-hoo.

Manning, exhausted, releases the assassin.

A German shepherd, soaked black, bounds up onto the boulder, dragging behind him by his lead his K-9 handler, who's even more drenched, and bleeding from various scrapes and cuts sustained on the rocks of the seawall.

I dash up, shouting to Manning, "Are you okay? Are you okay?" My mentor sprawls upright, wedged between two giant boulders, with a vortex of storm surge swirling around him. I shine my light into his face. I can see from his eyes he's got another migraine.

Eight hours later, 0745 the next morning, I'm sitting at my workstation at DivSix, still on zero Z's but after a hot shower at Brooklyn South and an hour at home to change (Manning himself has crashed like the dead on the couch in his office, with a shot of Imitrex in his bloodstream and a cold towel over his eyes), sneaking a peek on my terminal at hacked video (by me) of the interrogation of Alemany "You-hoo" Petracek.

The video is NYPD ceiling-cam footage from an interrogation room at the Six-Oh Precinct in Brooklyn. (Time code on the video shows it is six hours old, in other words recorded about ninety minutes after the actual apprehension on the seawall.)

In the video Yoo-hoo sits manacled by one wrist to a slide-bar on the table before him and by both ankles to a stanchion embedded in the floor. For some reason he has waived his right to have an attorney present. On-screen, Gleason, Silver, and two ESU sergeants visit upon Yoo-hoo wrath of Old Testament proportions, to which the assassin stands up with extraordinary composure and aplomb.

I'm watching with earbuds in and privacy screen engaged. If anyone in the office knew I was accessing this material (or anyone from the mayor's office down, for that matter), I would be in deep, deep doo-doo.

I cue the tape and let it roll.

For the first hundred and eighty seconds, Gleason on-screen confronts Yoo-hoo with airline and rental car records proving that he was in Moscow at the exact hour when Russian victim #2, Alexsandr Golokoff, was murdered.

YOO-HOO

I was there on vacation.

GLEASON

For fourteen hours?

Gleason tells Yoo-hoo he knows he's working for the FSB. He knows he's collaborating with freelance U.S. assets. Gleason demands that Yoo-hoo spill everything he's got on "Jake Instancer," or whatever this individual's real name is.

YOO-HOO

Who?

GLEASON

Jake fucking Instancer! We know he's a
contract killer! We know he's working with
you!

YOO-HOO

Never heard of him.

Three hundred and forty seconds of video follow, during which Gleason confronts Yoo-hoo with surveillance camera footage of Yoo-hoo in the hallway of the apartment building of New York Victim #1, Nathan Davis, nine days before Davis was murdered.

This interval is succeeded by Silver displaying before Yoo-hoo Verizon Wireless records showing calls from Yoo-hoo's cell to Davis's home on two separate occasions, nine days and six days prior to the murder.

                         YOO-HOO
    So what?

                         GLEASON
    You went to Davis's apartment. Why?

                         YOO-HOO
    To see him.

                         GLEASON
    Cut the bullshit.

                         YOO-HOO
    To visit him, if you don't fucking mind.

                         GLEASON
    You "visited" him?

                         YOO-HOO
    Is that against the law?

                         GLEASON
    And you called him.

                    YOO-HOO

    So what?

At this point, a shadow falls across my screen.

Manning stands behind me.

He says nothing, only watches in silence as the video continues.

For the next forty seconds it's Yoo-hoo who takes the offensive. "You assholes burned down a preschool! What if children had been present? What am I supposed to tell the kids tomorrow? That the cops broke in trying to kill their uncle Yoo-hoo?"

                    GLEASON

    Why did you phone Davis, you slimy piece
    of shit?

                    YOO-HOO

    He phoned me.

                    GLEASON

    My ass.

                    YOO-HOO

    He was scared. He wanted my help.

                    GLEASON

    Cut the shit.

                    YOO-HOO

    He thought someone was following him.
    Stalking him.

> GLEASON

So he called you?

> YOO-HOO

What are you, deaf?

> GLEASON

He phoned you. Why the fuck would he
phone <u>you</u>?

> YOO-HOO

I'm his cousin.

> GLEASON

What?

> YOO-HOO

I'm his fucking cousin.

Gleason glances to Silver.

> YOO-HOO

We grew up two blocks from each other. I
talk to him every day.

Even on the black-and-white video you can see all color drain from
Gleason's cheeks.

> YOO-HOO

You guys didn't know that? Holy shit.
You're even dumber than I thought.

GLEASON

You're his cousin?

YOO-HOO

Look it up.

GLEASON

You're Nathan Davis's cousin?

I don't have to glance to Manning to know what he's thinking.
Never overlook the obvious.

A day later, when this story hits network and cable, it will be augmented online by yearbook stills of Yoo-hoo and Davis at New Utrecht High School, Class of '03, side by side on the varsity basketball team—the "Utes." These photos will be accompanied by vacation video of Yoo-hoo, Davis, and their wives at the Ocean Club in Bermuda and several other high-end getaways.

The kicker, which I catch forty-eight hours later on CNN, is home video of a tuxedo-clad Yoo-hoo, eighteen months ago, beaming beside Nathan Davis's thirteen-year-old son, Marshall, at the boy's bar mitzvah at Temple Emanu-El on East Sixty-Fifth Street in Manhattan.

YOO-HOO
(to Gleason and Silver, on-camera in
interrogation room)
Wow. You geniuses have fucked yourself in
the ass big-time.

At this moment, a message box opens on my terminal screen. Uribe's face appears. He looks flushed and frantic.

> URIBE

Jimmy, it's me. Grab your shit!

Behind Uribe I glimpse parked vehicles, two mechanics in overalls, a garage service lift. Manning asks, "Where are you?"

> URIBE

At the Flushing impound lot, breaking down the girl rabbi's vehicle. Since when does a congregation leader pack one of these?

On-screen Uribe holds up a folding-stock Uzi submachine gun and a fistful of high-capacity magazines. Ms. Davidson's Hi-Top van is visible prominently behind Uribe, suspended on a lift rack with Uribe's Crime Scene team excavating its innards.

> URIBE

That's only half of what we found, Jimmy. Get over here ASAP. This babe is in these murders up to her eyeballs.

BOOK FIVE

A TURNING
TOWARD EVIL

17

IMPOUND LOT

Rᴀᴄʜᴇʟ Dᴀᴠɪᴅꜱᴏɴ'ꜱ ᴠᴀɴ, which was impounded in Brooklyn, has been hauled to the Queens tow pound on College Point Boulevard in Flushing, a catchall for vehicles impounded during the arrests of their owners, or vehicles used in crimes and/or seized as evidence.

Uribe is waiting on subterranean Level #3 as the elevator doors open and Manning steps out. Uribe meets Manning's glance. He rolls his eyes toward the spotlighted space in which sits the impounded Hi-Top.

Next to the vehicle stand Rachel and a striking-looking man of about forty whom I recognize at once, from his TED talks, as Dr. Amos Ben-David, the Israeli anthropologist and climate activist.

                        URIBE
                    (to Manning)
        They dropped outta the blue twenty
        minutes ago. The girl wants her ride back
        and everything in it.

                    MANNING
What did you tell her?

                    URIBE
I told her forget it. I got a warrant.

                    MANNING
Do you?

                    URIBE
Fuck, no. But the weapon and mags I
showed you . . . they're the least of it.
Wait till you see what else we found.

Time is 0845. In the nine hours since the conclusion of the Brighton Beach warrant service, two fresh factors have been incorporated into the LV murder files.

First, exhaustive canvassing of Borough Park/Crown Heights and Columbia University/Morningside Heights has turned up nothing on Jake Instancer. The department of Judaic studies has no record of him either as a student or a faculty member. He is unknown at every apartment and dormitory complex within ten blocks of the campus. Nor has his likeness drawn recognition from the proprietors of any local market, deli, bodega, newsstand, or dry cleaner. He has never ordered a pizza at Ray's or a caramel macchiato at Starbucks, dated a coed, propositioned a hooker, created a Facebook profile, or jogged on the grass in Riverside Park.

Ditto for Borough Park and the Chasidic community.

Instancer is a ghost.

Everything he told Manning is a lie.

Second, four more murders matching Instancer's MO have been turned up in searches of overseas databases—all committed within the past thirteen days. One in Brazil, another in China. The third is a Tarahumara Indian, killed in Colombia. Homicide #4 is from Germany.

Known total now, counting the Rebbe: nine.

Manning falls in step beside Uribe. His glance takes in the impound floor, Uribe's Crime Scene team, the Hi-Top van, as well as Rachel and Ben-David waiting beside the vehicle with expressions of impatience and indignation. I catch Manning's eye and start to alert him to who Ben-David is and what stature he carries in the wider world.

                    MANNING
          I know.

One of Manning's prime assets as an investigator is he can sling bullshit with anyone, at any level of society. He crosses in stride to Ms. Davidson, whose eyes remain blacked and bloodshot forty-eight hours after her get-together with a highway abutment. The left side of her face shines, livid and swollen; her hair is a rat's nest. Her right arm is in a sling. Inside her Converse low-tops I spy non-skid socklets from the hospital.

Manning greets Ms. Davidson and introduces himself and me to Dr. Ben-David.

Have our guests been offered coffee? Can Manning get them some? Bottled water? A soft drink?

Manning inquires after Ms. Davidson's physical well-being. Was her treatment at Maimonides satisfactory? Did the hospital run a concussion protocol on her? Has she been X-rayed for possible rib injuries? How about fluids? Is she hydrated? Has she gotten any sleep? Is she in pain?

I'm studying Ben-David.

The man, I confess, is a bit of a hero to me. I know his CV by heart. He's American-born (Long Island somewhere), undergrad at Yale, doctorate in Earth and Planetary Science from Johns Hopkins. He "made aliyah" to Israel at twenty-eight and immediately enlisted in the IDF as a private. Within eighteen months he was a captain. He's a major now, commanding a reserve paratroop battalion. In person he's shorter than I thought he'd be, but with forearms like a stevedore's and a presence in its own way as imposing as Manning's.

Ben-David informs Manning, "as a matter of courtesy," that he has engaged legal representation for Rabbi Davidson.

He names Ellie Landau.

Manning thanks Ben-David for so informing him and replies that he is aware of Ms. Landau's retention. He expresses admiration for Ms. Landau's professional standing and commends Ben-David on his discerning choice of representation.

Ben-David thanks me for sending the Mayday text from the hospital. "Forgive me if I have not responded," he says. "Things have been a bit hectic."

He adds, to Manning, that he has phoned Ms. Landau's office some ten or fifteen minutes ago and has been informed that Ms. Landau is on her way here to the impound lot as we speak.

Uribe joins the group, bringing coffee in Styrofoam cups with sugar, sweetener, powdered creamer, stirrers, and a half box of Yum Yum donuts.

                    BEN-DAVID
                 (indicating Uribe)
        Detective Manning, your associate informs
        us he has a search warrant, but so far he
        has failed to produce it.

Manning apologizes at once. Warrants these days, he says, are issued digitally. They're on your phone. Uribe, he explains, is a bit of a klutz; apparently he misfiled the document and can't figure out how to retrieve it.

We'll straighten the situation out, Manning promises.

"Meanwhile," he says, "as I'm sure you're aware or have been informed by these officers, possession of an automatic weapon and/or high-capacity magazines is a Class A felony under the Anti-Terrorism Act of 2031, in which instance probable cause is waived and the requirement of a search warrant becomes moot."

Manning indicates Uribe, whose team stands to his rear, beside the van, with the seized Uzi and its magazines displayed on an adjacent shop counter.

Manning begs Ms. Davidson and Dr. Ben-David's forgiveness if his colleague's tone or comportment have been brusque or "in any way untoward."

Did Ms. Davidson and Dr. Ben-David know, Manning asks, that Uribe is an MD? Indeed he is a licensed physician, medical examiner with the OCME, as well as a specialist in crime scene investigation. Dr. Uribe meant no disrespect, Manning assures Rachel and Ben-David, if "in the exigency of the moment" he has, perhaps, expressed himself in "the urban idiom."

Manning informs Ms. Davidson and Dr. Ben-David "as a courtesy, as well as a mandate of the statutory code" that he and his associates, i.e., Uribe and me, are required by law to wear on their persons at all times lapel cameras and digital recording devices. He indicates his own, pinned to his suit jacket—a device no bigger than a tie tack.

"This is for your protection as well as ours as law enforcement professionals," Manning says, "to ensure that all procedures are scrupulously adhered to. But you need to be aware, for your own sake, that everything any of us says or does is being recorded and may under certain circumstances be introduced as evidence in a criminal proceeding."

Ben-David thanks Manning. He asks if Manning wishes to be called "Detective" or "Lieutenant."

> MANNING
> Call me Jim.
>   (to Rachel)
> Ma'am, do you wish to be addressed as
> "Rabbi"?

Ms. Davidson glances from Manning to me. How much she recalls of our private exchange in her hospital room two nights ago, I have no idea. My own feelings toward her remain, despite my better judgment, protective.

> RACHEL
> "Ms. Davidson" will be fine.

> MANNING
> Ms. Davidson, Dr. Uribe informs me that
> his team has discovered within this
> vehicle . . . your vehicle, as your
> presence here and your demand to reclaim
> it attest . . .

Manning turns his body so that his lapel camera picks up the van.

> MANNING
> . . . certain "items of interest"
> to Homicide Division Six and to the

> Manhattan District Attorney's Office.
> Do you have any objection to me and
> Detective Dewey continuing the search
> that Dr. Uribe initiated?

> RACHEL
> I do.

> BEN-DAVID
> Detective, is this necessary?

> MANNING
> I'm afraid it is.

Ten minutes later Manning is standing beside the evidence table, jaw-to-jaw with Rachel and Ben-David.

All civil niceties have been deep-sixed.

Rachel's "Obsession Wall" has been taken from the van and brought forward under the lights. At its epicenter is the poster-sized photo of Jake Instancer.

The X'd out photographs of men, which Manning and I glimpsed thirty-six hours ago in the haste and dislocation after Ms. Davidson's vehicle crash, are seen now to be pix of the "LV" victims—Davis and Justman, the two in Russia, and the four others that Manning and DivSix had till only a few moments earlier been unaware of.

But the kicker, plucked by Uribe from the margins of the Obsession Wall, is a list of thirty-six names. The document is headed:

TZADIKIM NISTARIM

meaning in Hebrew, as Uribe informs us:

THE HIDDEN RIGHTEOUS MEN

Uribe hands the list to Manning. He states for Rachel and Ben-David's benefit as well as Manning's that his team has run the roster through DivSix's international crime database. On the list, Uribe says, is every "LV" victim so far, including the four newest ones.

> MANNING
> (to Uribe)
> Lemme guess. Famous men, all known
> for their moral rectitude and upright
> character.

Manning turns to Rachel.

> MANNING
> Ms. Davidson, are you the author of this
> list?

> BEN-DAVID
> Rabbi Davidson is saying nothing without
> the advice of counsel.

Ben-David steps to Rachel's side, confronting Manning. Manning holds the list up before them.

> MANNING
> (to Rachel)
> You compiled this document. This is your
> name on the title page.

Manning points to the blow-up photo of Instancer.

                    MANNING
        Who is this man? What is your connection
        to him?

Ben-David again protests. If indeed Manning's words are being
recorded, he says, they are going to look like bullying and intimidation
when played back in a judicial hearing or a court of law.
    Manning ignores this.

                    MANNING
                (to Rachel)
        Someone is murdering the Righteous Men,
        aren't they? Who? You? You sent me that
        "lamed vav" text—and the follow-up saying
        that all the victims are Jews. Why?

                    RACHEL
                (to Ben-David)
        Where's Ellie? You said she was on her
        way—

                    MANNING
        We tracked down your burner phone, Ms.
        Davidson. And you're talking to me.
        Answer my question!

> BEN-DAVID
> (to Manning)
> No one's talking to you without an
> attorney!

> MANNING
> (to Rachel)
> Your list is a hit list. You compiled it
> for the purpose of murder. Nine so far, to
> be exact.

> BEN-DAVID
> Stop this, Detective! Can't you see this
> young woman is in no state to answer you?

> MANNING
> (to Rachel)
> You're working with Instancer. He's
> murdering people off the list you
> compiled.

Rachel tries to snatch the document back from Manning. He jerks it away from her.

> MANNING
> Why were you at the Georgetown murder
> scene? You came all the way from New
> York. How did you know to be there?

Rachel's face shines purple and swollen beneath the lamps. I see tears welling in her blacked eyes.

MANNING

How did you know about the "LV" sign? Why
did you shout it out at Georgetown? Why
did you shout it at me?

RACHEL

Because you're the big-shot Detective.
You're DivSix. You're the All-Star.

Ben-David steps forward, thrusting himself physically between
Rachel and Manning.

BEN-DAVID

Leave her alone! Can't you see what you're
doing to her?

MANNING
(to Rachel)
Why were you at the Rebbe's two nights
ago? And don't hand me the bullshit you
gave Dewey about "following" me.

RACHEL

I did follow you.

MANNING

Why did you run when I ordered you to
stop?

RACHEL

To get you to chase me.

A vein stands out on Manning's temple.

> MANNING
>
> I can arrest you for murder right now, Ms.
> Davidson, based on nothing more than this
> list. And I can put you away for ten years
> for possession of that submachine gun.

At intervals in this exchange, I've been scanning the names on Rachel's list. Two leap out at me. I catch Manning's elbow. He won't look. He's too engaged in the moment.

> BEN-DAVID
>
> (to Manning)
> The list is Rabbi Davidson's Ph.D. thesis.
> She compiled this document three years
> ago, using the principles of gematria—

> MANNING
>
> Of what?

> BEN-DAVID
>
> Hebrew language numerology. This is a
> legitimate scholarly paper, Detective,
> compiled for academic purposes only. Rabbi
> Davidson has suffered enough because of
> it already.

For the first time Manning's eyes show real anger. He tugs Ben-David's arm, pulls it away from Rachel.

                    MANNING
             (to Rachel)
You were at the Rebbe's because you knew
Instancer was going to murder him. You're
working with him. Who is he? Who is
Instancer?

                    RACHEL
You know who he is.

                    MANNING
Tell me.

                    RACHEL
You know exactly who he is.

I break in on Manning a second time. He still won't look down at the names on the list.

                    RACHEL
Answer me this, Mr. Detective. Why were
you at the Rebbe's? Instancer brought you,
didn't he? How did he find you? Huh? Huh,
Mr. Smart Guy?

Rachel thrusts herself into Manning's face. Despite himself Manning backs off half a step.

                    RACHEL
Yeah, I followed you. I found out where
you live, at that crummy athletic club.

```
I followed you to the Jewish library.
I saw Instancer approach you. You fell
for his act like a ton of bricks. Tell
me. What line of bullshit did he feed
you?
```

This accusation chills Manning. Rachel sees it.

```
               RACHEL
He was waiting for you, you dumb fuck! He
picked you! You're being played, just like
the rest of us!
```

Ben-David tries to contain Rachel. She twists free.

```
               RACHEL
          (to Manning)
How did I know about the "LV" sign? I've
been tracking these murders in Europe
for months. Why did I run from you
outside the Rebbe's? Because I had to
make you see. I had to make you part of
this.
```

Rachel's posture becomes even more aggressive.

```
               RACHEL
And you are now, aren't you?
          (with satisfaction)
You've seen him. You've touched him.
```

At this instant the elevator doors open. Ellie Landau emerges.

I grab Manning's sleeve again and force him to read the two names I indicate on Rachel's list.

AMOS BEN-DAVID
ELLIE LANDAU

Manning's expression never alters.

He watches Ms. Landau step from the elevator. Two male associates in business suits accompany her. One wears fashionable spectacles and carries a leather briefcase; the other sports a butch cut and wears an earpiece. Ms. Landau crosses to the table in three strides.

                    BEN-DAVID
        Ellie!

Ben-David seizes the attorney's hand with relief, steering her to Rachel's side.

Ellie Landau inserts herself physically between Rachel and Manning. With a glance she takes in Rachel's distraught countenance, Manning's truculent posture, and the evidence table with its impounded weaponry and documents.

She notes as well the list—Rachel's list—in Manning's hands.

Clearly he has read it.

Clearly he is aware of the names upon it.

I'm facing my lapel cam directly toward Ms. Landau. I tap the volume control on the voice recorder. I want to be sure I get everything.

Ellie Landau looks exactly like her photos in the press and on TV—jet-black hair styled in a severe but feminine cut, with a streak of vivid white ascending from the forelock. What the images in the media can't show, however, is her charisma. Ellie Landau is a star and she knows it.

Ms. Landau says something to Rachel and Ben-David that none of us outside their circle can hear. She turns and, shielding Rachel and Ben-David both with her posture, faces Manning.

                    ELLIE LANDAU
        Detective Manning, I presume.

                    MANNING
        "Ellie Landau for the defense."

Ms. Landau smiles but does not extend her hand.

                    ELLIE LANDAU
        That document in your hand, Detective. Is
        it the list of Righteous Men from Rabbi
        Davidson's Ph.D. dissertation?

                    MANNING
        Righteous Men. And Righteous Women.

                    ELLIE LANDAU
        The Almighty has apparently grown more
        inclusive over the millennia.

Now it's Manning who smiles. Ellie Landau holds out her hand. Manning shakes it.

Manning's eyes never leave Ellie Landau's.

ELLIE LANDAU

You've seen my name on that list,
Detective. You've seen Dr. Ben-David's.
You're convinced the document is a hit
list. You're thinking, "Why would Ellie
Landau defend a woman who put her in the
crosshairs of a psychopath?"

Manning's expression says, *You're reading my mind.*

ELLIE LANDAU

That document is a hit list. And my
client did compile it. But she had no
idea, as she was doing so, that the list
would be used for that purpose . . . and
no idea of the motive or identity of the
killer.

MANNING

And what would that motive be, Ms.
Landau?

ELLIE LANDAU

You tell me, Detective. Or maybe you
should tell your boss at Division Six
Homicide.

Manning bristles.

MANNING

Who is Instancer? You know, don't you?

ELLIE LANDAU

I only know what can be proven in a court
of law.

MANNING

Don't fuck with me, counselor. I'll put
your client away.

ELLIE LANDAU

Will you, Detective? I don't think you've
got the juice.

Manning's shoulders rise the way they do when he's battling fury.

ELLIE LANDAU

Your boss thinks this line of
investigation is hogwash. What word did
he use? "Bullshit," wasn't it? That's
what my spies tell me. "Righteous
Men?" "Supernatural Killer?" "End of
the World?" Lieutenant Gleason thinks
you've gone off the deep end, Manning.
He thinks you've lost your shit. You're
embarrassing him and the whole division.
Worse, you're threatening his career, his
future . . .

MANNING

You're a brawler, Ellie. I'm impressed.

                    ELLIE LANDAU
You won't book my client, Detective,
because if you do, it'll be the end of
your career, which from what I understand
is hanging by a very slender thread
already.

Manning's eyes never leave Ellie Landau's.

                    MANNING
            (to me)
Detective Dewey, place Rabbi Davidson
under arrest. Handcuff her, take her in,
and book her.

I reach for my cuffs and start forward.

                    ELLIE LANDAU
            (to Manning)
On what charge, Detective, are you
detaining my client?

                    MANNING
Accessory to murder.

Outside, in the ongoing downpour, I palm the crown of Rachel's
head and steer her under the roofline into the rear seat of Manning's
AV. Ellie Landau's Escalade brakes at the curb, taking aboard Ellie,
Ben-David, and her bodyguard. Her law associate scurries across to
Manning, confirming with him the floor and room at DivSix to which

Manning will be taking Rabbi Davidson for booking. "Follow us," Manning tells him.

He gives me my instructions across the Crown Vic's roof.

> MANNING
>
> Identify every "LV" murder in Europe,
> Russia, Asia, and South and Central
> America, and don't stop till you've found
> 'em all. Cross-check dates and cities for
> flights from the States, hotels, taxis,
> Ubers . . . search every record including
> FaceRec videos from street-corner
> surveillance cameras.
>
> (indicates Rachel in car)
>
> If this woman was anywhere near any of
> those murders, I wanna know about it in
> detail.

Ben-David has crossed back to our Crown Vic in the downpour. Rain plasters his hair to his skull; his eyeglasses are fogged solid. Manning steps aside, permitting Ben-David to reassure Rachel that he and Ellie will be at DivSix the moment she arrives and that Ellie is already on the phone arranging a speedy release.

I'm still mystified by the anthropologist's ardor to defend Rachel. When he bolts back to the Escalade, I turn to Manning.

> ME
>
> Why is this famous guy here? I don't get
> it. Why does he care so much about this
> crazy woman?

MANNING

Ben-David in Hebrew means "son of David."

ME

So?

MANNING

Davidson.

I'm an idiot.

ME

He's her fucking brother.

18

THAT WHICH GOD HAS HIDDEN

I'M WATCHING MANNING interrogate Rachel. It's eight hours later, four-thirty in the afternoon of April 23, 2034. Manning is the lone detective conducting the interview. I'm observing from my desk at DivSix via remote camera. Across the table from Manning sit Rachel, Ellie Landau, and Dr. Ben-David, whom for reasons unknown to me Manning has permitted to remain. The room is the same one in which Gleason and Silver interrogated Yoo-hoo Petracek early this morning.

In the hours since the impound lot, I have web-scoured the hell out of Rachel and Ben-David.

They are indeed brother and sister, of Massapequa, Long Island, New York, the children and grandchildren of Conservative rabbis. Both spoke Hebrew before they could speak English. Ben-David Hebraized his name when he made aliyah to Israel in 2018. He is currently, as I said, a paratroop battalion commander in the reserve forces of the Jewish state. His younger sister, before her expulsion, was also an IDF reservist—a second lieutenant in Intelligence—as are hundreds, even thousands, of other Jewish-American citizens. She fought in the sixth and seventh Hamas Wars, in the tunnels.

For the first twenty minutes of the interrogation Manning presses Rachel on the origin of her list. Ben-David defends his sister with barely contained fury.

                         BEN-DAVID
         The list is Rachel's Ph.D. thesis. You
         have proof of this already, Detective. I
         have given it to you. What more do you
         need?

                         MANNING
         Nine men have been murdered, Dr. Ben-
         David. Every name is on Ms. Davidson's
         list. Explain that to me.

Manning intensifies his pressure on Rachel. Ellie Landau objects over and over to Manning's hostile, berating tone. She blocks Manning again and again from compelling Rachel to answer.

The physical layout of DivSix is different from that of a precinct house.

The office is built around "the Floor," a central arena containing the workstations of the Second and Third Grade detectives. Flanking this on one side is the Bunker, the big meeting room. On the other are conference areas and interrogation rooms. It is in the third and largest of these that Rachel is being interviewed.

The process simply of getting her here has consumed, as I said, the better part of eight hours today, because of Superstorm Dani. Trains are out, streets are flooded, bridges and tunnels closed. It has been impossible for the judicial officers, at least those who normally service DivSix and who all live in the New Jersey or Connecticut suburbs, to make their way into town.

Bottom line: Manning and I have had to transport Ms. Davidson, and her brother and lawyer, in person and by vehicle to the New York

State Supreme Court Building at 60 Centre Street on Foley Square. It takes us two hours to get there and, when we arrive, Centre Street is inundated. The East River seawall has been breached at South Ferry and at Old Slip. Lower Manhattan is under a foot of water.

So we walk.

Wade.

Our group—Manning, Rachel, Ben-David, Ellie Landau, and me— has been together now for six unbroken hours since the impound lot. Individuals are starting to get to know one another.

"Tell me the truth," Manning says to Ellie Landau as we approach Centre Street in salt water above our ankles. Manning is carrying the attorney's Manolos and sheltering her beneath his umbrella. "Why are you defending this woman?"

                    ELLIE LANDAU
          Maybe I believe in her.

                    MANNING
          Come on.

                    ELLIE LANDAU
          Maybe I don't like the idea of you
          locking her up. Maybe I believe she has
          critical work to do, and that the stakes
          for the human race could not be higher.

Two hours earlier, before our initial departure from DivSix, I had handed Manning a quickie report, gleaned by me from overseas trial transcripts and airline passenger manifests.

Ellie Landau, it turns out, has assisted in the defense of both Russian "LV" victims when they were charged with crimes by the Kremlin.

She was in Russia on four separate occasions.

As a foreigner, Ms. Landau could not officially represent the accused. But she stood present to aid their domestic counsels. She was in Moscow at the time Russian Victim #2, Alexsandr Golokoff, was murdered.

I have found as well, on Instagram, a video from January 2031. The tape is of Ms. Landau praying at the Wailing Wall in Jerusalem. The caption identifies her as part of a delegation from the United States. The group was led by the Lubavitcher Rebbe.

                    MANNING

They know each other, don't they? All of
them.

                    ELLIE LANDAU

To whom do you refer, Detective?

                    MANNING

Stop breaking my balls.

                    ELLIE LANDAU

And how might I do that, Jim? By telling
you I believe in the devil? Clearly you do.

                    MANNING

I'm a Catholic, Ms. Landau. I believe in
everything.

The courthouse at Centre Street shuts down when the last auxiliary power generator crashes. It's 3:40 in the afternoon. We still haven't received a hearing. Over Ellie Landau's objections Manning compels the traveling troupe back to DivSix's offices and begins the interrogation.

MANNING

Where did you first meet Instancer?

RACHEL

On a dig. An archaeological dig in
Israel.

Rachel turns to the button camera mounted in the ceiling of the interrogation room.

RACHEL

The "Gehenna dig." Look it up, Dewey.
November to January 2031.
      (to Manning)
He said he was a graduate student from
Columbia, studying at Bar-Ilan University
for the semester.

MANNING

And you believed him?

RACHEL

You did.

Ellie Landau again objects to Manning's hectoring tone. She cites her client's fraught state, as well as her history of emotional instability. She threatens Manning with administrative action if he continues in this "truculent and confrontational" manner.

Manning takes a breath.

He resumes.

If Ms. Davidson is indeed a rabbi, why is she living like a street person?

If she is truly a Ph.D., why is she camping in a van "under the steel"?

Why does she carry no ID, no credit cards, no phone, no money?

How did she come to compile her list of Righteous Men? For what purpose? Whose idea was it?

Again Ellie Landau refuses to let Rachel answer.

> ELLIE LANDAU
> (to Manning)
> Are you familiar with the Hebrew term
> *herem*?

> MANNING
> I'm not familiar with any Hebrew terms.

> ELLIE LANDAU
> It means excommunication.

The most senior religious officials of Israel, Ellie Landau tells Manning, are the Ashkenazi chief rabbi and the Sephardic chief rabbi. Acting in concert, these elders, with their council of scholars and advisors, constitute the supreme authority of the Jewish faith.

Charges were brought against Rachel twenty-seven months ago, Ellie Landau says. Rachel was compelled to appear in Jerusalem before this synod.

> MANNING
> For what crime?

ELLIE LANDAU

Publishing her dissertation. For printing
this document that you're so certain is a
hit list.

MANNING

I don't get it.

ELLIE LANDAU

Among the Orthodox, for anyone but the
most venerated scholars to dig into the
hidden lore is considered an outrage.
For a woman, such an act is unthinkable.
What Rachel did, in the world of the
devout, was sacrilege of the highest
order.

MANNING
(to Rachel)

They excommunicated you?

Rachel acknowledges. This makes an impression on Manning.

BEN-DAVID

Rachel lost everything—her livelihood,
her standing in the community, her
family, her future. Our own father
disowned her. She was dishonorably
discharged from the army. Death threats
were made against her.

Rachel's hands tremble. Her eyes plead with her brother to stop.

                    BEN-DAVID
    My sister cracked up, Manning. She tried
    to kill herself—twice. She spent six
    weeks in a locked ward at Tel HaShomer
    Hospital in Israel. Is that enough for
    you? That's why she's "under the steel"
    now. That's why even I don't know how to
    help her.

My fingers are hammering the keys for:

ASHKENAZI CHIEF RABBI AND SEPHARDIC CHIEF RABBI

appending Rachel's name and every other search parameter I can think
of. To my non-surprise, no official record comes up. But I'm getting article after article in *Maariv*, *Haaretz*, and the *Jerusalem Post*.

The proceedings of the hearing are secret, of course, including the
identity of the accused.

But not that of her counsel.

As I'm running this search, I'm speaking into Manning's earbud and
watching him in the interrogation room via the overhead camera. With
the most imperceptible of nods he waves me off.

                    MANNING
    When you went before the elders in
    Jerusalem, Ms. Davidson, were you
    represented by counsel?

Rachel makes no answer. But she glances, despite herself, toward Ellie Landau.

> MANNING
> Two women against the patriarchy. I'd
> have bought tickets to that.

Manning's expression reveals a new respect.

> BEN-DAVID
> Rachel went through hell. Can you
> understand that, Manning? Can you see
> that she's hanging on by a thread?

> MANNING
> And the submachine gun? The Obsession
> Board?

> ELLIE LANDAU
> Does someone put together an Obsession
> Board because they're in cahoots with
> its subject? Rachel isn't working with
> Instancer. She's hunting him. She's trying
> to stop him. The gun isn't to help him.
> He never uses a weapon anyway. It's to
> protect herself, as much as anything can
> protect against him!

The interrogation goes on for another hour. For the first time, Ellie Landau lets Rachel open up.

Rachel declares, haltingly at first and then with greater vigor, that she has been tracking Instancer for the past twenty-one months. Twice she got within a day of him—once in Dusseldorf, once in São Paulo.

Instancer broke no laws. He committed no crimes. Rachel says she couldn't figure out, at first, what his intentions were or why he was in these specific places.

Then she realized: he was establishing the whereabouts and studying the daily routines of individuals on her Righteous Men list.

He was casing them.

Rachel went to the men and warned them.

She told them their lives were in danger.

She identified herself, explained everything, pleaded with the men to realize their peril.

The men dismissed her. They rejected her. They turned her in to the police.

> RACHEL
>
> The cops ran their checks on me. Every ounce of shit came up. I was detained four times and deported twice.

Rachel raises her eyes again to the ceiling cam.

> RACHEL
>
> Look it up, Dewey. Ankara, October '32. Marseille, April '33 . . .

She rattles off four more, in Africa, Asia, and South America. She turns to Manning.

RACHEL

By the way, Detective, there aren't nine
murders. There are twenty-seven. Eighteen
before your first Russian victim.

I run the arrests Rachel claims. They're all true. I relay this to
Manning. As I'm monitoring all this from my desk, asking myself
do I believe Rachel's story, I'm simultaneously skimming her Ph.D.
dissertation.

It's fascinating:

Gematrial and Eschatological Implications
of the Legend of the Tzadikim Nistarim

The piece is 387 double-spaced pages. Eschatology is the study of the
End Times. I never knew this. Gematria, as Dr. Ben-David had explained
earlier, is Hebrew numerology.

The *tzadikim nistarim* are by definition "hidden."

Their identities are known only to God.

How, then, Manning is asking Rachel in the interrogation room, did
a twenty-seven-year-old, only-recently-ordained female rabbi figure it
out, when generations of scholars had all failed?

According to Rachel's paper, there are twenty-six different gematrial
systems, developed over centuries by Talmudists and learned masters
in Judaic esoterica working in Hebrew, Greek, Latin, Aramaic, and
Assyro-Babylonian-Greek, by which a single word (or part of a word),
a passage of scripture, or an individual's name can be broken down to
reveal its occult meaning or, perhaps more important, a clue to some
broader ethical, religious, or political issue. Here is one such formula
from Rachel's paper:

$$F(x) = (10^{\ \text{floor}((x-1) \div 9)}) \times ((x-1) \text{ rem } 9 + 1)$$

I google this. It's for real. I'm reading Rachel's dissertation with one eye and keeping tabs on Manning's interrogation of her with the other.

> RACHEL
> (to Manning)
> I have tools that the ancient rabbis
> didn't.

It is possible, according to Ms. Davidson's dissertation, to employ contemporary computer modeling techniques to analyze via gematrial systems the names of all candidates for inclusion in the list of living *tzadikim* and to determine, within a reasonable margin of error, who the likely individuals might be.

Rachel came up with two lists.

The greater contained 1,787 names, non-Jews as well as Jews.

Then the core document.

Thirty-six names.

> MANNING
> How certain are you, Ms. Davidson, about
> these thirty-six?

> RACHEL
> We're trying to read the contents of the
> mind of God, Detective. It's not an exact
> science.

Manning studies Rachel hard. Does he believe her? Does he believe this whole outrageous scenario?

<pre>
                    MANNING
     In Jerusalem, Ms. Davidson . . . what
     exactly was the charge against you? What
     were you accused of?

                  ELLIE LANDAU
     You don't have to answer that, Rachel.
</pre>

Rachel meets Manning's eye.

<pre>
                    RACHEL
     I was charged with "revealing that which
     God has hidden."
</pre>

The interrogation continues into the evening. I'm working on three monitors simultaneously, confirming and consolidating for Manning's inspection (and for submission to the district attorney's office) Rachel's record of intellectual brilliance, psychological fragility, and general proclivity for fucking up her own life.

Sometime after dark I look up from my screens to see Gleason emerging from the Bunker, where he has been working since noon with two other teams of investigators.

Our chief summons Manning from the interrogation room, confers with him briefly in the corridor, then crosses to the Floor, where he orders two Third Graders to follow through on some procedural matter that I can't hear. I'm watching on my screen as Manning reenters the interrogation room. He does not sit. Ellie Landau rises. Ben-David stands as well.

From my workstation I see the group exit the interrogation room. Gleason is waiting at the exit station that leads to the elevators. I see Manning's shoulders ride up the way they do when he's furious. I rise and hurry over.

Gleason has released Rachel.

No charges will be filed.

Ms. Davidson is free to go.

Ellie Landau, Ben-David, and Rachel exit toward the elevators.

Manning's glower remains fixed on Gleason.

> GLEASON
> (to Manning)
> What are you looking at me for?

Gleason tells Manning that while he, Manning, has been defending the planet from the Apocalypse, real detectives have been on the job, doing real detective work.

> GLEASON
> The victims all knew each other, Manning.
> Including the newest one from China and
> the Tarahumara Indian.

> MANNING
> I've been telling you that for days.

> GLEASON
> They knew each other because they were
> all terrified. Not of the devil. Of the
> fossil fuel industry.

Gleason shows Manning phone and web intercepts proving that the nine victims identified so far communicated regularly with one another, and had been doing so for years, via conventional channels as well as secure courier and other encrypted media.

Every one of the "LV" victims, Gleason says, was a climate activist.

Their fear was of the cadre of killers and defamation specialists utilized by the FSB and the energy extraction industry worldwide, including U.S.-based entities, Big Agribusiness, and the petro-oligarchs of Central Asia and the former Soviet bloc, of whom the red-white-and-blue Solntsevskaya Bratva, the Russian Mafia based here in New York, was and is a principal man-killing instrument.

                    MANNING
Then who is Instancer?

                    GLEASON
An asset. A freelancer. A hired gun.

                    MANNING
With all respect, Frank . . . bullshit.

Manning asks Gleason if his decision to release Rachel Davidson has anything to do with Ellie Landau's ten-million-dollar lawsuit against the city. Gleason has not, by any chance, received a phone call from the mayor?

Could Gleason's decision, Manning says, possibly be linked to his own political ambitions? Or maybe the fact that half the judges in the city have either studied under Ellie Landau or are sucking up to her now for their own career aggrandizement?

                    GLEASON
My decision, Manning, if it's any of your
fucking business, has to do with this
division—with DivSix—and with keeping
your "investigation" from taking it, and
all of us, down the tubes.

Gleason tells Manning to go home.

> MANNING
>
> I don't wanna go home.

> GLEASON
>
> Go anyway. The line of investigation
> you're following ends tonight.

I steer Manning to the elevators. When he and I emerge at street level, Ben-David, Ellie Landau, and Rachel are still on-site, sheltering from the downpour under the south-facing awning.

It's a moment. In some crazy way, the relentless friction of this long day has produced a bond among the participants. Manning slides in between Ben-David and Ellie Landau. I find a space at Rachel's shoulder.

Ben-David is telling Ellie Landau that he will take Rachel home with him now, uptown to his place at Riverside and Ninety-Ninth. Manning reacts with concern.

> MANNING
>
> If you're going, let me and Dewey drive
> you.

"I'll take them," Ellie Landau says. Her car and driver will be here in a few moments. Ben-David thanks her but waves the offer off, citing the storm and the flooded streets.

> BEN-DAVID
>
> I'm still a New Yorker, Ellie. We'll catch
> the local at Seventy-Second and be home
> in three stops.

Rachel and Ben-David take off.

It's Manning and Ellie Landau now, with me, under the awning.

Manning shifts one step upwind of Ms. Landau, opening his umbrella to shield her from the gusting wet. His eyes betray frustration, exasperation. It looks like he's half ready to give up on the case.

Ellie Landau sees this. Manning's face is turned away from her, looking out into the storm.

> ELLIE LANDAU
> Will you take something from me, Manning,
> and not use it against my client?

Manning turns back.

> ELLIE LANDAU
> When I was in Moscow two weeks ago, I saw
> Instancer.

> MANNING
> What?

> ELLIE LANDAU
> I had no idea who he was. I didn't
> make the connection till two days ago,
> when the first police sketches began
> circulating.

Manning has come to full nuclear alert. His glance to me says, *Make sure you're recording every syllable.*

Ellie Landau tells Manning that she had flown to Moscow to assist in the defense of Alexsandr Golokoff, who was facing a hearing before a Kremlin tribunal. The Sabbath, she says, fell on the night before. Ellie was at shul in a private home. In attendance, she says, were a dozen or so, all Russians, friends of Mr. Golokoff.

> ELLIE LANDAU
> Instancer was among them. He sat alone.
> He spoke to no one, and no one seemed to
> know him. He was wearing a yarmulke and a
> prayer shawl. I was struck by him because
> of his appearance.

Manning presses Ellie to be more specific.

> ELLIE LANDAU
> He was electrifying. Charismatic. I
> couldn't tear my eyes off him.

Ellie Landau tells Manning that Golokoff—"your 'Russian victim number two'"—was supposed to meet her there, that night, at the private home.

> ELLIE LANDAU
> But he never showed. When I got back to
> my hotel I saw on TV that he had been
> murdered. I knew instantly that this
> young man was the killer. He showed up
> at shul, I felt certain, out of some
> diabolical intention to let me know. He
> knew who I was. He was mocking me.

Manning asks Ellie Landau what conclusion she draws from this encounter. If her supposition about Instancer being Golokoff's killer is true, what does she believe it means? He's a hired assassin? An FSB agent? A religious nut?

> ELLIE LANDAU
> I believe what you believe, Detective. We
> both know who he is.

Ellie Landau's car pulls in at the curb and stops. Time is 1930, seven-thirty in the evening. The driver springs out and scurries around to open the right rear door. Ms. Landau is about to step out from beneath the awning.

Her phone pings with an incoming text.

Ellie checks it.

It's a video.

Ms. Landau taps the PLAY arrow.

She reacts with dismay.

> MANNING
> What?

Ellie Landau stares at her phone in alarm.

Manning steps in to see.

> ELLIE LANDAU
> This is live! It's happening right
> now . . .

On Ellie Landau's screen a video streams.

It's Instancer.

On a subway platform somewhere.

He's wearing the same jeans, T-shirt, and hoodie he wore at the Rebbe's.

The video is a selfie.

He's filming himself.

In chalk, on a steel subway column, Instancer finishes scratching the last of twenty-seven vertical marks, in five groups of five, with horizontal slashes to mark the fifth in each, then two more verticals to complete the tally.

> INSTANCER
> (on video, speaking to camera)
> Twenty-seven down out of thirty-six.
> Twenty-eight coming up.

Instancer grins. The video goes dark.

> MANNING
> Where is he? Wind the video back!

Ellie Landau obeys.

Manning peers.

Above Instancer's chalk marks, in a sign-square on the column, is the street number of the subway stop:

72

19

SEVENTY-SECOND STREET STATION

OUR SELF-DRIVER slaloms to a stop at Broadway and Seventy-Second. Manning hits the sidewalk on a dead run. I'm two paces behind him.

We're sprinting in the downpour for the Seventy-Second Street subway stop of the IRT Broadway–Seventh Avenue line.

Time is 1955, five minutes to eight. Manning has ordered Ellie Landau to go home, stopping for nothing, and to keep her driver and security man with her. He has called for backup to DivSix and all contiguous precincts. I have tried every channel, phone, text, DM, and social media to reach and warn Ben-David and Rachel. She, we know, has no phone at all, and Ben-David . . . who knows? Maybe he's one of those Luddites who turns his off.

Entrance to the Seventy-Second Street station is via two above-ground control houses, on traffic islands in the middle of Broadway. Seventy-Second Street runs between the two. There are stairs down to the tracks, uptown and downtown, from both houses, and two elevators.

Manning points to the control house south of Seventy-Second.

> MANNING

> Take the downtown side.

We're half a block east, bolting into traffic from the corner of Seventy-Second and Broadway, running flat-out through the sluicing downpour. Manning's SIG Sauer is in his hand. He signs to me to unholster my weapon.

> MANNING

> Aim dead-center. Empty the full mag into
> him. Whatever you do, do NOT let him get
> past you.

I have never heard a shoot-to-kill order. Holy shit. I watch Manning burst through the heavy double doors of the control house and tear down the uptown stairwell.

That's the side Ben-David will be on. The dangerous side. The side where Instancer will be.

I plunge down the stairwell to the downtown side.

Seventy-Second Street is an express stop on one of the two major West Side lines. It has four tracks and two island platforms—one uptown and one downtown. Riders access these down flights of stairs from the mezzanine level. The uptown platform receives the local on one side, the express on the other. Same for the downtown platform. Between the two island platforms are two tracks—one for the uptown express, one for the downtown. Ben-David and Rachel, heading for Ninety-Sixth Street, should be on the uptown platform.

I'm thinking this as I vault the turnstile and skitter out onto the downtown platform, scanning north and south as fast as my neck can swivel. The platforms each hold two dozen people or more, spread out over 100, 150 feet. Despite the storm, trains are still running up here.

Who could Instancer be going after? Rachel? Ben-David? Both? I have no idea.

"Police officer!" I'm shouting, shield in one hand, weapon in the other.

Bystanders are gawking. I see no Ben-David, no Rachel, no Instancer on my side of the station. Where's Manning? I dash to the center of the platform, peering across the two tracks that separate my platform from the uptown platform on the far side. I'm thinking two things:

1. Don't shoot anybody not named Instancer.
2. Why would Instancer send that selfie to Ellie Landau? Did he know that Rachel and Ben-David were on their way to the Seventy-Second Street station? How? Did he know that Manning was with Ellie Landau? How? Was the message really for Manning?

Why?

Why would Instancer send it?

I hear a train coming.

There's Manning. I spot him, across the tracks on the uptown platform.

I see Ben-David but not Rachel.

Ben-David is uptown of Manning, about a hundred feet.

ME

There! There!

I'm pointing across the tracks and shouting to Manning. In the cavernous underground with the din of the approaching train, Manning can't hear.

I see Instancer.

He's approaching Ben-David from the downtown side.

ME

Manning! Manning!

I dash to a spot directly across from Instancer and Ben-David. I call Ben-David's name. I'm shouting, waving my hands and arms.

Ben-David can't hear me.

I've never jumped onto a subway track in my life.

WTF.

I leap. I land. People on the platform are pointing and shouting.

Now Manning sees me.

So does Ben-David.

ME

(shouting to Ben-David)

It's him! It's him! Get outta there!

I'm pointing at Instancer. But I'm too far away in too dim a light. Ben-David doesn't realize it's me. What is he thinking? Probably that some maniac has jumped onto the tracks.

At that instant, Rachel appears.

She sees me.

She sees Ben-David.

She sees Instancer.

Rachel's location is a hundred feet downtown of Ben-David. In other words, Instancer is between her and Ben-David.

Manning is on the same side but fifty feet behind Rachel.

Rachel bolts like a sprinter at Instancer.

Here comes the train.

Manning sees Rachel; he takes off, flat-out, after her.

The train is an uptown express, on the second track in front of me. It runs flush to the platform that holds Ben-David, Instancer, Rachel, and Manning.

I'm scrambling over the first set of tracks—the downtown express—dodging the third rail.

I see Instancer seize Ben-David.

He grabs him with one hand by the throat. Manning is racing toward the pair. He's seventy-five feet away, shouting something I can't hear. Rachel is twenty-five feet from Instancer and Ben-David, running and shrieking almost as loud as the train.

The subway booms into the station, metal-to-metal brakes screaming.

Instancer clutches Ben-David.

Rachel flings herself onto Instancer from behind.

She attacks like a wild animal, clawing for Instancer's eyes, seeking his throat to choke him, thrashing furiously, trying to knock him off balance.

Manning is forty feet back, running all-out, weapon drawn.

He's shouting to Rachel to get herself clear.

The train screeches toward the writhing trio of Ben-David, Instancer, and Rachel.

Instancer flings Rachel off him.

He re-seizes Ben-David by the throat.

Somehow Ben-David shakes free.

He flings himself onto the track, directly in the path of the train.

I'm screaming. Bystanders wail. The train is twenty feet from Ben-David.

He scrambles wildly, dives clear.

Manning skids up, shouting to Rachel to get out of the way.

She does.

Manning rises into a shooting stance, point-blank before Instancer.

I see muzzle flashes—three in rapid succession. Then the train, brakes screeching, passes between me and the platform, eclipsing all sight of Instancer and Manning.

Ben-David is on the downtown express track, right in front of me. The train, huge and dark and stinking of hot steel and smoking brake pads, power-slides past on the uptown express track in a broadside of sparks.

I grab Ben-David.

I haul him to his feet.

Astonishingly, two bystanders, both black kids in gangbanger garb, have leapt onto the tracks to help us.

"Police officer!" I bawl into their startled faces, flashing my shield. I shove Ben-David into the boys' arms. "Get him to the downtown platform. Be careful!"

I spin toward the uptown side. I see more muzzle flashes from the far flank of the train, then two forms, no doubt Manning and Instancer, dashing along the platform, one in pursuit of the other.

Alarms are going off all over the station. Red, yellow, and blue lights flash along both platforms and all four tracks. The train has finally stopped. I'm on the track. I stumble around the train's rear. Finally I can see.

Instancer faces Manning on the platform.

Fifteen feet between them.

Instancer is unarmed, in jeans and hoodie. If any of Manning's rounds have hit him, I detect no sign.

Manning fires again.

Bangbangbangbang.

Bystanders are shrieking and plunging for cover.

The double-stack magazine of Manning's P226 holds fifteen nine-millimeter hollow-points that at close range produce more hydrostatic shock on a human target than the mule-kick of an Army Colt .45 M1911.

The weapon's report is ear-shattering in a confined space like a subway platform.

Manning's initial fusillade shreds Instancer's T-shirt and hoodie as if they were tissue. The salvo slams into Instancer's chest.

The impact rocks Instancer, but does not penetrate.

He does not go down.

My own nine-millimeter is in my hands.

Manning fires again.

I do too.

Bullets tear into Instancer from two directions.

The din is deafening. The muzzle flashes from Manning's weapon leap out so far they actually touch Instancer.

Instancer's eyes never leave Manning's.

He staggers but remains upright.

No blood.

No rending of flesh.

The bullet strikes rock him backward. But he remains on his feet.

With a look first to Manning, then to me, Instancer springs from the platform, lightly and powerfully, onto the uptown express track to the rear of the stopped train.

He flees in the downtown direction into the dark.

Manning leaps after him, reloading.

Two pairs of uniformed officers (the backup teams Manning had called for) sprint now onto the platform from adjacent stairwells. They vault after Manning into the pursuit.

Something makes me turn and glance to the platform above me. Rachel stands at the brink, her hair spiky wild, the whites of her eyes livid and bloodshot.

                    RACHEL
     Go after him! What are you waiting for?

I take off. Instancer is already fifty yards down the track. Flashing alarm lights obscure him. I'm struggling to keep my footing on the wet, greasy railroad ties. I hear one of the uniforms shout that the fugitive has bolted through a door or hatch into a lateral shaftway.

I'm sixty feet behind Manning and forty back of the first patrol officers. I see Manning, then the officers, duck right and into the lateral doorway.

I follow.

The passageway leads to a steam tunnel. You drop through a circular hatch and down a ladder well.

What the fuck?

This second tunnel runs parallel to the subway line but one level below. A single narrow-gauge track runs down its midline, apparently for maintenance handcars. The tunnel is an intestine of insulated high-pressure steam pipes, mounted along walls glistening with oily, gunk-dripping stormwater. Red and yellow emergency lights flash. Alarms sound. Jetting steam obscures everything.

I hear a gunshot and race after it.

Fifty yards.

A hundred.

Suddenly the tunnel opens onto a vaulted, tile-walled cavern. Flood-water thunders like Niagara from a dozen breaches in the overhead. A catwalk crosses the atrium. Storm runoff sluices in unimaginable volumes across the void. Roiling, viscous fluid fills the belly of the vault, thirty feet below.

Instancer flees across the catwalk.

Manning chases him.

The patrol officers pursue along a second walkway, farther uptown.

Suddenly Instancer trips. He slips and plunges down a four-step descender, but catches himself, nimble as a cat, and hauls himself back up.

He races into another hatchway.

A continuation of the steam tunnel.

I crab-scoot across the catwalk, clinging to the rails in a death grip.

Into the second steam tunnel.

A hundred feet ahead, Manning overhauls Instancer.

The pair grapple.

I'm slogging as fast as I can, straining to see. Steam jets everywhere from the wall-mounted pipes.

I see Manning seize Instancer in some kind of wrestler's hold. For an instant it looks as if Manning gains the upper hand. Then Instancer punches with his elbow into one of the steam pipes.

The vessel punctures.

Scalding steam blasts into Manning and Instancer, obscuring them both.

I glimpse Manning among the steam as he reels, shielding his face.

He lets go of Instancer.

Instancer, lit scarlet by the flashing emergency lights, stands stock-still amid the searing steam.

He turns and bolts.

Another tunnel. A level farther down. I drop off a ladder into flood-water up to my waist. Rats the size of small dogs dot the surface. The water is frigid. I see Manning ahead. Another muzzle flash.

We must be a hundred feet below the street now.

Ladder wells.

I climb two.

Tracks!

I see Manning, a hundred yards ahead. We're in a subway tunnel. A working track. Back at the level we started from. My hair is soaked with grease, the toe-boxes of my clodhoppers slosh with what feels like half a gallon of industrial solvent. Snot and saliva drain in runnels down my chin.

Lights.

A subway station!

I'm thirty yards behind Manning now, on the track bed. Instancer is another seventy yards ahead of Manning.

I see Instancer enter the lighted area of the station and haul himself up onto the platform. He stops and looks back.

He pulls something from his shirt pocket.

Manning has drawn up on the track bed, weapon in hand.

Manning's chest heaves. He gasps for air.

Instancer holds a phone.

He punches numbers.

I stagger up to Manning.

Manning's phone rings.

People on the platform ahead are reacting to Instancer's sudden appearance. I can see faces peering down the tracks toward me and Manning.

Manning hits ACCEPT.

I hear Instancer tell Manning an address.

Instancer takes the phone, a burner no doubt, and smashes it screen-first into one of the steel columns on the platform.

He slings the busted mess onto the tracks and bolts up the stairs and out.

                              MANNING
                         (to me)
              Ellie Landau's address. What is it?

My phone finds it. Manning's look says it's the same one Instancer just gave him. Four blocks from here. Three seconds later he's calling for precinct backup and phoning ahead to Security at Ellie's building.

We're out on the sidewalk now, racing full-tilt.

Manning gets Ellie Landau on the line. He's half running, half staggering from exhaustion. Manning tells Ellie what has happened. He orders her to lock down every entry to her apartment, interior and exterior, and to keep her driver and security man in front of her, weapons drawn, ready for anything. I can half hear Ellie from the earhole of Manning's phone:

                    ELLIE LANDAU
        My building is super-secure. I pay enough
        for the service, believe me.

Manning and I reach Ellie's building. Manning highballs into the lobby, past doormen, security personnel, precinct officers.

No break-in reported.

No forced entry.

No intruders picked up on security cameras.

But when we hit Ellie Landau's penthouse floor, the door to her apartment is wide open. Ellie's driver sprawls facedown on the floor. A nine-millimeter automatic lies smoking beside him. Spent shell cases litter the entryway.

Inside the apartment, whose ceilings are double-high and whose east-facing windows give onto a heart-stopping panorama of Central Park and the East Side skyline beyond, lights are on. Nothing appears disturbed.

Till we reach the master bedroom.

In the doorway lies the crumpled form of the security man. His weapon, an old-school Smith & Wesson .38, lies a body length away from his outstretched right hand, its smoking barrel searing the nub ends of the carpet pile.

                    MANNING
        The bathroom.

Manning steps over the security man's body. The bathroom's mirrored double doors are shattered, as if someone had been flung bodily against them.

Manning enters, weapon in hand.

MANNING

Christ.

He draws up.

I stop at his shoulder.

Ellie Landau's nightgown-clad body lies, limp and broken, over the rim of a porcelain lion's-leg tub. Her left hand clutches the shower curtain, which she has, in her fall, pulled down on top of herself like a shroud.

A Glock 19, with its slide open and locked, indicating that its magazine has been fully discharged, lies on the marble floor beside her. Cartridge cases, still releasing wisps of spent cordite, are scattered atop a microfiber bath mat and under the tub. The inner surface of the bathroom door holds a tight group of nine shots, fired through the door from the inside.

Manning withdraws a handkerchief from his jacket pocket.

He kneels.

Setting the cloth over the fingertips of his right hand, he reaches and checks Ellie Landau's laryngeal airway.

His expression confirms, *Crushed.*

20

A RIGHTEOUS WOMAN

URIBE IN SCRUBS stands beside the stainless steel table, upon which Ellie Landau's corpse lies, naked (though covered from the collarbone down by a paper surgical sheet), faceup, skull shaved. An autopsy tech readies the bone saw, like the one the Metro D.C. medical examiner used to uncap the skull of Michael Justman.

URIBE
(to Manning)
You don't have to stay for this, Jimmy.

The Forensic Pathology Center of the Office of the Chief Medical Examiner is at 421 East Twenty-Sixth Street, adjacent to Bellevue Hospital and one block west of the FDR Drive. Autopsies are performed on the eighth floor, between the hours of nine and noon. That's the workday schedule for the MEs. It has been overridden in the emergency. Uribe will work at night.

Manning signs to Uribe that he will remain. Manning must confirm the existence or absence of an "LV" sign between the eyes of the decedent. He needs as well to determine for himself, and to acquire Uribe's sign-off to that effect, that cause of death is from a crushed tracheal airway.

Then there's something else.

Manning's terminal responsibility, at least in his mind, is to the family of Ellie Landau, for whom religious custom directs that the deceased's remains be interred within twenty-four hours or as soon thereafter as circumstances permit.

In the minutes after the murder, I search and acquire the contact information for the immediate family. Manning makes the calls. We're still at Ellie Landau's apartment. Uribe and CSU have arrived. Neighbors and emergency personnel fill the hallway. The press are downstairs in droves. When Ms. Landau's grown children arrive—her daughter Lauren, also an attorney, and son Cameron, an orthopedic surgeon—it will be Manning's job to get their permission for the medical examiner to perform an autopsy.

This is the shit they don't tell you about when you acquire your gold detective's shield. I see grief in Manning's eyes, the first time he's ever shown it.

At 2250, a few minutes before eleven, Lauren and Cameron arrive. Manning speaks with them privately. Ellie Landau's children insist on viewing their mother's body in its terminal posture. They are tough, these two. Manning gives them as long as they need, which is not long. When the siblings emerge I see them shake his hand. Manning's eyes, I can tell even from across the room, are clouding from an oncoming migraine.

Permission has been granted.

The forensic examination proceeds.

A memorial service for Ellie Landau will be held the following day.

The medical examiner's office transfers Ms. Landau's remains from OCME to Temple Beth Shalom at Park and Ninety-First, arriving at one-thirty in the morning. Manning rides with the body. I follow in our Crown Vic. Amazingly nearly a dozen family members, friends, and colleagues wait to receive the corpse and sit with it. Rachel and Ben-David are there, in the same clothes they wore in the subway. Both are grim and shaken. They speak privately with Lauren and Cameron.

The memorial service is scheduled for eleven this morning, Monday. The mourners will sit up with Ellie's remains through the night. The men in the room all wear yarmulkes. Prayer shawls cover their shoulders. They chant softly or recite prayers.

Throughout this interval I've been handling the press and supervising the precinct officers in securing the crime scene. I find a minute in transit to Beth Shalom to jump on the phone to Uribe and get the results of the autopsy. Yes, our ME confirms, the "LV" sign was present, exactly as on the corpses of Justman and Davis. COD, Uribe says, will go in his report as "trauma to tracheal airway."

As I'm entering these notes to my files and Manning's, a text comes in for me from Iceland—the Reykjavík metropolitan police. WTF? I check local time. It's six-thirty in the morning there. The message is from a homicide detective named Elisabet Gottmundsdottir. I've never heard of her, nor have I communicated with her via any medium.

To Det. Covina Duwai, Division Six, New York Police Dept.:
Monitoring your RIRC [Request for Interjurisdictional Remission of Confidentiality] re female person of interest in "LV" murders in Dusseldorf, Marseille and Riga. We have one here too, of 10 August 2033, eight months ago. This homicide has been linked to the others by forensic pathology only within the past 24 hours.

My state of exhaustion vanishes. In .01 seconds I am awake and wired.

Your request for FaceRec video file release has
been approved by our office. Attached please find a
sequential compilation. File total is 27. Most are from
traffic-flow and sidewalk surveillance cameras and are
unremarkable. Please note however the 22-second clip
from a convenience store security camera at 9 August
33 (the morning before the aforementioned murder)
that commences at 10:44:45. I think you may find it of
interest.

Elisabet Gottmundsdottir, Detective Inspector

I cue the video and tap the PLAY arrow. I'm head-down in a corner at
the front of the service room, with the young rabbi who will serve as the
officiant for the memorial service approaching me and looking, I swear to
God, like he's about to hit on me. I bury my nose deeper into my phone.

On the screen appears a woman who can be no one but Rachel. The
face is the same, posture, hair, everything. She is standing beside some
kind of self-serve coffee machine in intense, even passionate confron-
tation with a tall, broad-shouldered man appearing to be about thirty
years old whose back is to the camera. Suddenly Rachel slaps the man,
open-handed, across the face, so violently that the take-out cup in her
other hand goes flying, sending hot coffee everywhere.

The man does not turn or move.

Rachel bawls something furious at the man, then wheels and stalks
from the store. The clip ends when the man, still with his back turned,
moves in the opposite direction and vanishes from the viewing field of
the camera.

I bolt from the young rabbi before he can open his mouth to say hello.

I find Manning.

I roll the video.

He watches through his two-dollar Walgreens reading specs, peeking over their upper rims at Rachel herself, seated piously in a row of chairs at the rear of the room.

> ME
>
> When you questioned her at the impound
> lot, she said the last time she saw
> Instancer was in Israel in '32. This
> video is from August '33.

> MANNING
>
> But is that Instancer on the video? We
> can't see his face.

> ME
>
> C'mon!

I urge Manning to confront Rachel with this right now. Walk over and shove the video in her face. To my amazement, he resists.

> MANNING
>
> I thought you were her protector.

> ME
>
> Fuck that. She's lying to us!

I see from Manning's eyes that his head is splitting. It's all I can do to stifle my impulse to challenge Rachel myself. Whatever Manning is thinking, I know he is ten jumps ahead of me. I bite my tongue.

The young rabbi comes over and introduces himself. He's the age of Ellie Landau's children. In fact, he says, he knew them both growing up. Ellie Landau was, he tells Manning and me, like a second mother to him.

As the young rabbi speaks, he checks incoming news and texts on his phone. The story of Ellie Landau's murder is leading every channel. Hits on social media are approaching a million, even at two in the morning. The press, the young rabbi says, has made the connection between the killing of Ms. Landau and the murder of the Lubavitcher Rebbe. Reports are linking these to the attempt upon Ben-David's life tonight, and the violent demises of Davis and Justman and the two Russians. Rumors are circulating of other, similar homicides worldwide. The press knows somehow of the "LV" mark, though as yet they have no idea what to make of it. I start to excuse myself when the young rabbi begins to pump me, as well, for information. Manning catches my arm.

                    MANNING
        Where are you going?

                      ME
        To confront Rachel.

                    MANNING
        The fuck you are.

Ben-David joins our group. I'm getting that metallic taste on my tongue that tells me my blood sugar is approaching zero. I have to get Manning home. He needs sleep. So do I. But when I turn toward him to speak, I can tell by the way he cocks his shoulder that he will rebuff any well-intentioned intervention.

                    MANNING
              (to young rabbi)
        Is there a "hell" in the Jewish religion?

                    YOUNG RABBI
        It's called Gei-Hinnom.

                     MANNING
        Like Gehenna?

                    YOUNG RABBI
        Same thing.

                       ME
        Like the dig? The archaeological site
        where Rachel met Instancer.

I'm cursing myself for not following up on the name. I should
have put these together. I see on Manning's face that he's doing this
just now.

                    BEN-DAVID
        The site is quite famous, actually. It's
        almost a tourist attraction. I've worked
        on it myself.

Ben-David tells Manning that after he emigrated to Israel he volunteered for two summers. It was he, he says, who suggested to Rachel that
she apply to work on the dig herself.

                    YOUNG RABBI
                 (to Manning)
        For centuries the "portal to hell" was
        thought to be a specific cleft in the

earth north of Jerusalem. But about
twenty years ago the Gehenna site was
discovered. It's near Megiddo—Armageddon
of the Bible. The Gehenna site seems
more hellish than the old one. There's a
geothermal field directly beneath it.

Manning absorbs this.

> MANNING
> Is there a devil in the Jewish faith?

> YOUNG RABBI
> The Adversary. HaSatan.

> MANNING
> Could this devil just materialize? I mean
> walk out of hell and catch a cab into the
> city?

The young rabbi smiles.

> YOUNG RABBI
> According to the Talmud, an unholy entity
> must be "conducted" into the physical
> world by a mortal being. It needs
> someone to escort it. In the literature
> this "conductor" is often a female. A
> mother figure, a sister . . . frequently
> unwitting.

Manning is interrupted by a follow-up call from Uribe. It comes in over my phone; I take it for him. Our ME is heading home, he says, after this long, grim day. The final item of intel Uribe imparts is that he has, just five minutes earlier, received a message from the Queens impound lot, where Rachel's Hi-Top van was being held.

            URIBE

     Your girl's vehicle has been released per
     Gleason's order. Someone picked it up.
     Every item we had impounded as evidence
     has been replaced aboard. The van itself
     is back in Brownsville now, "under the
     steel."

I relay this to Manning. Ben-David moves off to the rear of the room, takes a seat beside his sister. The young rabbi is called away to other duties.

I'm standing beside Manning with the Icelandic video on my phone and Uribe's message about Rachel's van echoing in my ears.

My right hand, seemingly acting under its own direction, catches Manning's sleeve. From my mouth I hear the following:

            ME

     The Hi-Top. Let's toss it.

21

UNDER THE STEEL

A "DIRT-BOX" is a police cell interceptor. It's like a wiretap but for cell phones, illegal as hell without a warrant. I've got one in our car's equipment compartment, along with a password randomizer and other homemade and off-the-shelf hacking gear. With these, we can pick off any incoming calls and crack (I hope) any security protecting Rachel's drop phones or laptops.

We go.

It's fun.

Our Maglites have blue filters. Their beams can't be seen by an observer unless they shine straight into his eyes. With them Manning and I scour the innards of Rachel's home on wheels.

Her Uzi has been confiscated for mandatory destruction. It's not here. But I find handwritten journals and trip diaries. Rachel wasn't lying about traveling to Dusseldorf and São Paulo, not to mention two dozen other overseas cities.

Her journals are in Hebrew. I photograph the first three pages of four notebooks and dispatch them to DivSix's professional translation software. They come back fast—ninety seconds—but as mathematical gobbledygook, a pigpen code like the Freemasons used. I see the trick. Rachel is using the principles of gematria. I ask the software, "How long to crack?" Answer: "3–4 wks."

I order the computer to break the files down by the first five most frequently used words, figuring that one of them might be "Instancer," from which I might to able to extrapolate integers and get a start on decryption. But this too comes back as a jumble.

Meanwhile, DivSix's super-randomizer is attempting to hack the pass codes on Rachel's three laptops. The machine's AI brain can generate a billion terms a second, learning and narrowing its search as it goes. Rachel apparently has prepared for this. We're stumped. All I can find that's intelligible is letterhead correspondence between Rachel and some two dozen professors, scientists, and activists around the world— apparently Righteous Men she was trying to warn of danger.

At least this reinforces Rachel's claim of hunting Instancer, not helping him.

Rachel's primary laptop is protected by four passwords in chaos-code sequence. The randomizer cracks the first three. I enter "Gehenna," then "Megiddo," twenty more.

On "Tz@dikim99," the machine opens.

Again, every entry is in Hebrew.

ME

Fuck!

At least this time Rachel's stuff is not in cipher. I enter "Reykja-vik" in the search box. Up come hotel records, travel docs, surveil-lance logs.

MANNING

What the hell is this?

ME

Iceland. On five dollars a day.

At the Academy Annex in College Point we were taught the rudiments of hacking and blackout operations on the net. Rachel is light-years beyond this. She can code. She's a master of encryption and decryption. Did she learn this in Israel, in IDF Intelligence? She knows how to generate dummy identities and use them to hop on a flight to anywhere, pay for everything once she gets there, then sail the bill into the cyber shitcan. Passports are child's play for her. She has cranked out eleven e-versions that I can find without strenuous searching—five USA, two UK, one Danish, and three Israeli—all "liberated" from real people, with Rachel's retinal, facial, and digital signatures stripped in. She can breeze through customs anywhere on the planet and leave no record that can be traced back to her. Money? It grows on trees for Rachel. She can hack into bank accounts, crack ATM codes, create credit card identities for herself, or steal an account outright. She knows how to use trapdoors, spider holes, crossovers, double-backs, and all kinds of masking, cloaking, and identity-snatch techniques. She employs these, as best I can decipher, to perform "drive-bys," i.e., isolated EEs ("episodes of encroachment") into the confidential personal and professional information of an organization or individual, and the targeted entities never even know their data has been compromised.

ME

This is how she travels. How she pays for
everything.

Manning has pored through every drawer and compartment in the vehicle. He's beyond exhausted. He flops down beside me on the banquette, staring in frustration at Rachel's laptop screen.

MANNING

Find me something that puts her with
Instancer at one of these murders.

I'm trying.

Mail?

Nothing.

Files? Sanitized or firewalled.

I bang through folder after folder. I can't pull up texts, photos, videos. Even Rachel's trash is indecipherable.

Manning rubs his eyes. He looks like his head is about to split open.

ME

Okay. Enough.

I'm just clicking SHUT DOWN when the mail sound beeps and a mini-window opens in the upper right corner of the third of Rachel's screens.

Source: UNKNOWN.

Message:

THIS WHAT YOU'RE LOOKING FOR?

A link.

I click it.

Up comes a video.

A smartphone selfie with a time and date code from four years ago.

The video is of a man and a woman in a shower.

Soap on the lens.

Man and woman laughing.

The woman's in front, close to the lens, facing it. Giggling continues.

The woman wipes the lens.

It's Rachel.

A man's soapy hands cup her breasts from behind.

Rachel responds erotically.

The man nuzzles her neck.

It's Instancer.

MANNING

Sonofabitch.

Rachel, her hair wet and shampoo-y, turns back within Instancer's arms.

They kiss, deep and passionate.

Rachel's arms wrap around Instancer's neck.

ME

What the fuck?

A new message comes in. More links.

I click the first.

Rachel and Instancer humping on some beach.

The second: Rachel and Instancer in desert shorts and hats on an archaeological dig.

The rest: more of the same.

I'm backtracing frantically, though I know the sending source is another burner.

MANNING

Stop.

He signs to me to button up the vehicle.

We kill our Maglites.

We dismount.

MANNING

Gimme your phone.

Manning takes it, punches a number.

Someone answers.

Manning speaks for fifteen seconds, then closes the call and tosses me the phone.

MANNING

You hungry?

Twenty minutes later Manning is ordering espressos and plates of angel wings in a window booth at an all-night dive called Café Dacha under the El in Little Russia. Time is 0330.

Across from Manning sits Yoo-hoo Petracek.

One of Manning's mantras is:

Ask the question that's so obvious no one thinks to ask it.

MANNING

(to Yoo-hoo)

You were in Moscow the night Alexsandr Golokoff was murdered. But you didn't do it. Who did?

Scary and creepy as the Bratva assassin is, I must confess I have a soft spot for him. He has no bullshit. He is what he is, and it's all out front.

                    YOO-HOO
Gleason burned you?

                    MANNING
Not officially. Not yet.

                    YOO-HOO
But you're toast.

                    MANNING
Crisp on both sides.

Our espressos and pastries arrive. Café Dacha is the only place on Brighton Beach Avenue open despite the flooding. The counter and half the tables are occupied by fire and emergency crews. Yoo-hoo waits till the waiter, who appears to be the owner as well, chats for a moment and moves off.

                    YOO-HOO
I never knew the target's name. I had
the address and a photo and the security
code.

Yoo-hoo glances to a pair of patrol officers entering, then turns back to Manning.

                    YOO-HOO
Your buddy Gleason wasn't wrong.

Yoo-hoo confirms that he flew to Moscow to "perform a professional service." He proceeded to the victim's residence. He gained entrance. He was advancing upon the prey.

                    YOO-HOO
But somebody else got in before me.

Yoo-hoo describes a man of about thirty, tall, broad shoulders . . .
Manning displays a police sketch of Instancer.
Yoo-hoo nods.

                    YOO-HOO
He did the job before I could.

                    MANNING
You saw him?

                    YOO-HOO
He crushed the dude's throat. One hand.
No gloves. No booties. No hairnet. I was
as close to him as I am to that door over
there.

                    MANNING
He see you?

                    YOO-HOO
If he did, he didn't give a shit. He
walked out the front door like the place
belonged to him.

I'm recording and taking notes at the same time. I'm thinking, *Ask
the obvious question.*

ME

Anything else? Did you see anything else?

YOO-HOO

A car got him.

ME

A car? A self-driver?

YOO-HOO

A real car. It pulled up to the curb.

ME

Could you see the driver?

YOO-HOO

Not enough to recognize her.

MANNING

Her? It was a woman?

Manning turns to me. I pull up a pic of Rachel on my phone. I hold the phone out to Yoo-hoo.

YOO-HOO

Bingo.

22

INSIDE A MIGRAINE

MANNING DOESN'T SAY a word all the way back to Manhattan. He takes the passenger seat and turns the car over to me. His eyes are the color of coal. I'm afraid, not just for him but of him. His skull is splitting, I know. He takes one shot of Imitrex and has me detour to the only open Walgreens in the city (according to the POI on our dash), on Atlantic Avenue in Bed-Stuy, to pick up two more kits.

                    ME
    What do you want me to do about Rachel?

It occurs to me that Manning might take matters into his own hands. I know he feels suckered. I know he feels played.

But he offers no answer.

He just wants me to get him home.

In the two and a half hours since we left the scene of Ellie Landau's murder, the weather has made a screeching one-eighty. It has gone from Noah's Ark inundation to a blistering-dry desert sirocco. Gusts of fifty and more, according to WPIX-FM, howl down a Flatbush Avenue whose low spots look like the Mississippi River, with cars and buses marooned in midstream. Our AV zigs and zags along frontage roads and side streets, high-pointing around flooded intersections and downed power transformers. Flatbush Avenue is blocked at Tillary Street by a blown-over tractor-trailer. The Manhattan Bridge is the only span still functioning, though its EZ-Pass toll plaza is half a foot deep, dark, and empty.

Temp on the dash reads 106.7 with an up arrow.

Time is 0410 when our car breasts the streambed that Central Park West has become between Sixty-Eighth and Seventy-Second. The iron gate outside the Midtown Athletic Club is chained and padlocked. Manning's grunt says, *Take me around to the kitchen.* He's in too much pain to speak.

I drop Manning off (he refuses my hand to steady him) and watch him trudge, one shoe-splat at a time, up the unlit, flotsam-strewn alley to enter the club via his customary rear ingress. For the first time since I've known him, Manning looks old to me.

Rachel and Ben-David are waiting outside my loft. They look as hollow-eyed as Manning.

>   ME
>
>   What are you doing here? How'd you even
>   get my address?

They're scared.

I'm thinking, *Indicate nothing about where you've been tonight since Ellie Landau's murder and say zip about what you've learned.*

>   ME
>
>   I hope you like Asian food, 'cause that's
>   all I got.

I tell the car where to park (Howard Street, amazingly, is dry; there are actual spaces) and lead Rachel and Ben-David up the stairs and inside.

Ben-David asks about Manning. Clearly he and Rachel had hoped to find him with me and still on the job. I tell them Manning's down with a migraine.

Ben-David says he and Rachel have been trying for the past two hours to get a flight out to Israel. But JFK and LGA are shut down with the gale. No planes are taking off as far south as Charlotte and as far north as New Brunswick.

I ask why they left the memorial room at Beth Shalom.

> BEN-DAVID
>
> I couldn't take it anymore.

I tell him to sit. I'll whip up some eggs and coffee.

I'm trying to remember everything that's happened to Ben-David tonight. He's been attacked on a subway platform (the bruise marks are still visible on his throat), he has leapt onto the tracks in front of a train, experienced the murder of his friend Ellie—and the killer is still out there, probably searching for him right now to finish the job.

> ME
>
> How does it feel being a Righteous Man?

> BEN-DAVID
>
> It's the kind of attention I can do
> without.

I indicate the bathroom. Clean up, I tell him. Take a shower. I offer Rachel and Ben-David dry clothes. From the Lo. My father's stuff.

> ME
>
> Here. For what good it'll do.

Ben-David showers. He takes cargo pants and a tee. Rachel wants nothing. She towel-dries her hair and uses her fingers to work out the tangles. When I hand her a hot coffee, she meets my eye, something she's never done. "Thank you," she says.

> ME
>
> For what?

> RACHEL
>
> For that night in the hospital.

I scramble eggs with bean sprouts and snow peas. I have to close the windows against the gale. The interior is sweltering. We park ourselves on the floor, the three of us with our plates, in the dark away from the door and the windows.

> RACHEL
>
> Where's Manning now?

I describe his location. The feed from his GPS locator displays on my phone. His lapel camera records automatically.

As I'm saying this, the indicator light above Manning's icon goes dark.

> RACHEL
>
> What just happened? Why did that light go
> out?

The light, I tell her, is Manning.

                              ME
        He's gone into his shell.

The gale booms louder outside. My floor-to-ceiling windows rattle like thunder. The whole building shudders.

                          BEN-DAVID
        What's happening with Manning? Is he all
        right?

I describe Manning's room to Rachel and Ben-David. The narrow bunk. The single chair. The crucifix on the wall, the framed photo of his dead wife and son . . .

Manning, I tell them, has already self-administered a hundred milligrams of Imitrex. He may inject himself again. He's already taken five hundred milligrams of Cafergot, on top of his naprocene skin patch.

He'll be alone, I say.

He'll have shut off all phones.

He'll lock the door.

He'll turn out the lights and draw the blinds against any streetlamps or sounds. He'll lie on his back on the bed. He'll put a wet towel over his eyes.

Manning's skull, I tell Rachel and Ben-David, will feel like an iron spike has been driven through it. He'll try to think but he won't be able to. When the pain hits he'll be too stricken to speak.

Rachel asks how I know this.

                              ME
        I've watched him. Not in his room. He
        doesn't know I've even been there. But

I've watched him go through this, in the
office, on the road . . .

RACHEL

Are you in love with him?

I laugh.

ME

He's my boss.

RACHEL

Don't bullshit me.

I tell them more about Manning's state.

He'll be on his back in bed. Still fully clothed. Shoes on. He'll have forgotten to take them off and now he'll be in too much pain to make the effort.

His weapon in its holster will be hanging over the bedpost.

I know Manning disciplines himself to breathe.

I know he can feel the drugs when they kick in.

I know they never work soon enough, and they never take away the pain.

Here's what I *don't* know, and won't until the next frantic hour:

Manning is indeed on his bed, lights out, fully clothed, forcing himself to breathe, when . . .

He senses another presence in the room.

He feels fear.

Fear because he knows he's incapacitated.

Fear because he can't move.

With excruciating effort Manning elevates his head off the pillow. Even three inches takes all his strength. To tug the towel off his face is like hauling a sheet of lead. He forces his eyelids apart . . .

A man is sitting in the single chair across the room.

> INSTANCER
>
> I'm sorry, Detective. Did I wake you?

God only knows what's going through Manning's mind now. Recounting the experience later, he can't even guess at time duration. He remembers recognizing Instancer. He remembers the jeans, the T-shirt, the hoodie.

> INSTANCER
>
> I'm a little miffed at you, Manning. You
> tried to kill me tonight. Twice. Don't
> tell me that wasn't your intention.

Manning can feel the storm outside. His fourth-floor room looks out onto Sixty-Eighth Street. The gale howls off the park and bends, screaming, down the crosstown street.

Manning struggles to speak. He can't make his lips move.

> MANNING
> (barely audible)
> Who are you?

> INSTANCER
>
> Who am I? You're the shit-hot detective.
> You tell me.

Instancer rises. He picks up the chair he's been sitting in and crosses with it to Manning's bedside. He sits. Manning strains to keep his head up, but he can't. His eyes dart to his service weapon in its shoulder holster draped over the bedpost.

> INSTANCER
>
> Don't even think about it.

Instancer leans forward, directly over Manning.

> INSTANCER
>
> Oh, I see. You've got a headache. Does it hurt?

Instancer slips his left hand beneath Manning's neck. He elevates Manning's head several inches off the pillow.

> INSTANCER
>
> Where's the pain? Here?

With a crisp, two-finger punch of his right hand, Instancer hammers Manning between the eyes. Manning's body jackknifes in agony. He cries out.

> INSTANCER
>
> Oh, I'm sorry, did that hurt?

Instancer punches Manning again in the exact same spot. Again Manning cries out. He squirms wildly, trying to wriggle away. Instancer seizes him and pulls him back.

Instancer slaps Manning violently across the temple. Manning thrashes in his tormentor's grasp, seeking to grapple with him. Instancer eludes Manning's grasp with ease. Again he pulls Manning upright, again he hammers him, even harder, between the eyes.

INSTANCER
Who am I? The question is who are you?

The bud in my left ear is monitoring Manning. It's turned down to MIN.

But now I hear something.

I thumb the volume up and activate the video feed on my phone.

On my screen appears real-time video from Manning's lapel cam.

I see Instancer, pacing in the center of Manning's room.

RACHEL
What's happening? What are you looking at?

I show Rachel and Ben-David the screen. I'm on my feet, grabbing my holster and calling my Crown Vic.

ME
(to Rachel)
Stay here.

RACHEL
Are you crazy?

In ten seconds she and Ben-David and I are out the door and sprinting down the stairs to the curb, at which my self-driving car is pulling up right now.

In Manning's room Instancer continues pacing. Manning writhes, clutching his skull.

> INSTANCER
> You know, I didn't take to you at first,
> Manning. I thought you were kind of a
> dick.

It takes all of Manning's strength to make his lips form words.

> MANNING
> How did you know I would be at the Jewish
> library?

> INSTANCER
> Uncanny, wasn't it?

> MANNING
> Why me? Why am I part of this?

> INSTANCER
> Because I picked you. Because you're the
> man!

Instancer crosses back to Manning, seizes him, and hauls him upright.

> INSTANCER
> Wake up, Manning! Get your head back into
> the game!

Instancer wallops Manning across the temple with his open right hand. When Manning tries to defend himself, Instancer backhands him across the opposite temple.

MANNING
The game? What is the game?

Manning lunges at Instancer. His feet slip. He spills into the wall. The crucifix falls and shatters; the framed photo of Manning's wife and son crashes to the deck.

Instancer seizes Manning by the collar. He lifts him off the floor, one-handed. Instancer carries Manning to the window that faces out, four stories up, onto West Sixty-Eighth Street. Instancer smashes the frame and glass using Manning's head and back as a battering ram. Glass and splintered wood blast everywhere. The gale from the storm screams in, filling the room.

INSTANCER
How do you like this weather, Manning?
Apocalyptic, wouldn't you say?

Holding Manning suspended, Instancer thrusts him bodily through the shattered window and frame, out into the gale.

INSTANCER
How pissed off do you think the Almighty
is right now? At you. At all of humanity.
Look what you've done to this beautiful
world He gave you.

At this moment Rachel, Ben-David and I screech up outside in my self-driver.

> INSTANCER
> (to Manning)
> The only thing standing between the human
> race and annihilation is the existence of
> the Thirty-Six Righteous Men. And they're
> dropping fast, aren't they?

Instancer suspends Manning fully outside the building, four stories above the sidewalk. He holds him by one hand.

> INSTANCER
> What's the game, Manning? The game is
> global extinction. The game is the end
> of the world. You get it, Manning. You
> understand me. That's why I like you.
> That's why I want you with me at the end.

From the street, Rachel, Ben-David, and I can see Instancer, twisting Manning into the gale. Instancer harangues him, jaw-to-jaw. We can see Manning's arms flailing and the soles of his shoes dangling in thin air.

Rachel, Ben-David, and I bolt to the rear alley, hurtle through the kitchen entrance and into the stairwell. I'm taking the steps two at a time. Rachel and Ben-David follow, half a flight behind.

In the room, Instancer hauls Manning back from outside. Shards of window glass crunch beneath his soles.

                    INSTANCER
You're going to tell my story, Manning.
That's the detective's role, isn't it? To
get inside the villain's head. To "become"
the villain.

I kick the door at the latch plate with my right butch-heeled stom-per. The jamb splinters. I burst into the room with my nine-millimeter extended in both hands. Rachel and Ben-David push through behind me.

Instancer regards us without the slightest measure of surprise or alarm.

                    INSTANCER
          (to Manning)
"The evildoer doesn't want to be caught.
He wants to be <u>known</u>. He wants to be
<u>understood</u>. He wants his suffering to be
appreciated and his point of view to be
granted respect."

Instancer dumps Manning back into the room's single chair. Its legs splinter. Manning crashes to the floor.

I'm frozen. My finger is on the trigger but I can't make myself move.

Instancer reaches to Manning's jacket. From the lapel he tugs the lens and mini-mike of the recorder.

                    INSTANCER
Got it all for your report, Dewey?

He tosses me the device.

INSTANCER

See you next, you know where.

Instancer strides, absent all haste, between Rachel and Ben-David and me toward the door.

INSTANCER
(to Rachel, as he passes)
Hello, dear.

BOOK SIX

ARMAGEDDON

23

THIS IS HOW THE WORLD ENDS, PART ONE

O UR EL AL 797 bangs down onto the tarmac at Ben Gurion International in the most ungodly crosswind I have ever experienced. Before the aircraft's undercarriage has even touched down, the starboard wing starts ballooning under a gust that we'll learn later hits seventy-one knots (the maximum crosswind a plane of that size is permitted to land in is twenty-five), which means the tip of the opposite wing, with its fuel tanks and fuel lines, not to mention its two port-side engines, is plunging toward the tarmac.

Passengers are screaming. My window seat is right above the starboard wing. I can see the ailerons screw-driving up up up as all engines fire on full thrust. The plane slams down, bounces twice, and stabilizes. Passengers are hanging on to each other and every surface they can catch hold of. The engines scream into reverse; brakes come up howling. The pilots finally wrestle the jet to a halt so close to the end of the runway that the aircraft has no room to execute a reversion under its own power; it has to be towed back onto the tarmac not by one tug but by three. It takes more than an hour to reach the gate, with gale-force winds scouring the field and gust-blown grit abrading the jet's skin like a sandblaster.

Date is Friday, April 28, four days after Manning's migraine encounter with Instancer.

Rachel has bolted.

Day One. Telling no one, not even her brother. She got on a plane somehow and fled to Israel.

Manning is beyond furious, not just at her but at himself for not arresting her immediately after the migraine incident.

Has Manning slept in the past ninety-six hours? If he has, it's been in snatches only, despite me staying glued to him and forcing him to lie down and close his eyes at every interval where his participation is not absolutely essential.

In the minutes immediately following Instancer's exit from Manning's room at the athletic club, Manning has somehow managed to get to his feet and gain some measure of control over the pain behind his eyes. His room looks like the aftermath of a cyclone. Shattered glass and splintered wood litter the floor. The gale howls in through the void where the window used to be. Other athletic club residents, all male, clad in pajamas and shower shoes, are rubbernecking from the hallway, gawking at the mess and at Manning's beat-up face. I'm displaying my shield (and Manning's), assuring the company that everything's under control.

After twenty minutes, when patrol officers from the Two-Oh have arrived and shooed the natives back to their rooms or down to the coffee-and-bagel bar (time is 0550; the sun is just peeking up), our deeply unnerved party collects in the kitchen manager's office in the basement. I have never seen Manning in the state he's in now. Rachel ventures to ask if he's all right . . .

                    MANNING
    All right? No, I'm not all right.

Manning had been gathering himself in a chair beside the kitchen
manager's desk. Now he rises, turns toward Rachel.

                    MANNING
    Somebody just broke down a wall using my
    head as a battering ram. Somebody pounded
    my skull till the bone almost split.

Manning orders me to pull up the video from the convenience store
in Reykjavík. He snatches the phone and thrusts it before Rachel's eyes.
On the screen she sees herself slap Instancer across the face.

                    MANNING
    You told me you hadn't seen Instancer
    in three years. This video is from nine
    months ago.

                    RACHEL
    We've been through this. I couldn't
    tell you everything or you would never
    believe me.

Ben-David, glimpsing the video, reacts with shock. Rachel sees this.
She turns her back.

Manning catches her arm and hauls her around to face him. Ben-
David thrusts himself between his sister and Manning. He's cursing
Manning and pulling Manning's hand off Rachel's arm. In the adja-

cent kitchen, a pair of staff workers are wheeling the coffee cart into the lobby for the residents. They gape at the fracas in the office until I chase them.

>   MANNING
>   (to Rachel)
>   You were with Instancer from the start.
>   Tell me the truth. Tell me from the
>   beginning.

>   RACHEL
>   I've told you from the beginning!

>   MANNING
>   You said you met Instancer on an
>   archaeological dig. Was that a lie?

>   RACHEL
>   I've told you the truth about everything!

Manning hands me the phone and orders me to pull up the shower video. I do. Manning snatches the device back. He thrusts the video before Rachel's face.

>   MANNING
>   Tell me the truth about this.

Ben-David, glimpsing the screen, again reacts with surprise and dismay. Immediately he defends his sister. For the second time he plants himself physically between Manning and Rachel.

> BEN-DAVID
>
> This video proves nothing, Manning.
> Rachel has already admitted to a
> relationship. Stop terrorizing her!

Ben-David tells Manning again, as he had earlier this evening at Beth Shalom, that Rachel had volunteered for the Gehenna dig at his, Ben-David's, suggestion. Rachel had just been ordained after three arduous years of rabbinical studies. Ben-David thought the physical toil would be restorative for her. The experience would deepen her understanding of biblical lore and amplify her sense of the antiquity of the Jewish people.

> BEN-DAVID
>
> Yes, Rachel met Instancer at Gehenna. But
> she had no idea what he was. He fooled
> her. He fooled everyone. He appeared like
> a normal person.

Manning glowers. Ben-David describes the Gehenna excavation. An exploration shaft tunneled beneath the earth for nine levels, a hundred and twenty feet down. A geothermal field lay a quarter mile below that. Temperatures were so extreme at the deepest two levels, Ben-David says, that all access was sealed off. Thermal barricades were erected. Students and visitors were forbidden to descend past these warning markers.

> MANNING
> (to Rachel)
> But you went anyway.

Rachel sobs.

                    MANNING
You went down, didn't you?

                    BEN-DAVID
Stop bullying her!

                    MANNING
Something happened down there, didn't it?

Again Manning thrusts my phone with the shower video before Rachel's eyes.

                    MANNING
You went deeper than anyone else. Past
the barriers. You went all the way down,
didn't you? What happened? What happened
down there?

                    RACHEL
He appeared.

                    MANNING
Who?

                    RACHEL
Who the fuck do you think?

Manning seizes Rachel by both shoulders.

> RACHEL

He said he was a grad student working on
the dig.

> MANNING
> (scoffs)

And you believed him?

> RACHEL

I've told you all this! He looked like he
does now! He was cute. He was funny. He
flirted with me.

> MANNING

So you did what?

Rachel won't answer.

> MANNING

What, goddamn you? You did what?

> RACHEL

I couldn't help myself.

Rachel turns. She tries to bolt. Manning catches her and hauls her
back. He slaps Rachel across the face. Ben-David seizes Manning's arm,
tries to pull him away.

> RACHEL

He overwhelmed me! I couldn't—

MANNING

Couldn't what? Couldn't stop? Couldn't
resist him?

Now I jump in. I push past Manning to Rachel's side.

ME

That's enough, Manning!

BEN-DAVID

Stop this!

ME

Leave her alone!

Manning's open hand is raised to swat Rachel again. He restrains himself, barely.

MANNING

You "conducted" him in. You were the
human medium he used to enter the world.

RACHEL

How could I know? He looked like a
person! I couldn't stop! I couldn't help
myself!

Rachel's eyes meet Manning's in anguish. Manning faces me and Ben-David, who are lined up against him, protecting Rachel.
Rachel breaks down.

Manning steps back.

> MANNING
> (to Rachel)
> Whose idea was it to compile the list?
> The Righteous Man list.

Rachel's tears answer for her.

> MANNING
> You did it for him. You couldn't help
> yourself.

24

THE DOROT LIBRARY, REVISITED

MANNING

How do we kill him? There's gotta be some
way.

BEN-DAVID

He can't be killed. If he could be, your
bullets would've done it on the subway
platform.

We're at the Jewish Library. An hour past dawn. Rachel has vanished. Manning and I let her out of our sight for thirty seconds and she bolted. She's on an El Al jet to Israel right now, though we won't learn this for another ninety minutes when she texts her brother from somewhere over the North Atlantic. Manning is furious with himself, and none too happy with me.

He stands now before an oaken table (the same one where he first met Instancer) in the main reading room of the Dorot Library at Forty-

Second and Fifth. Before him sprawls a welter of esoteric texts and scripture in Hebrew, Aramaic, Greek, and Latin.

                    MANNING
              (to Ben-David)
          Tell me the ground rules. Instancer must
          have a weakness.

From the kitchen at the athletic club, Manning ordered me to phone Gleason, who in turn called heaven-knows-who. Somehow, at oh-dark-thirty in the middle of the worst weather calamity of the past dozen years, the main branch of the New York Public Library unlocked its doors and let our party in.

The research librarian of the Dorot division of the library has made his way in from his home in Park Slope to assist. He enters from the librarian's station now, lugging an additional armload of research material.

                    BEN-DAVID
          He's supernatural, Manning! The definition
          is he <u>has no weaknesses</u>.

                    MANNING
          Bullshit. If Instancer had unlimited
          powers, he wouldn't have needed Rachel to
          compile the list of Righteous Men and he
          wouldn't have had to stalk them before he
          struck. Besides, he <u>wants something</u>. And
          anyone who wants something is vulnerable.

The librarian's glance darts from face to face.

LIBRARIAN

What exactly are we trying to accomplish
here? What is the question we're trying
to answer?

MANNING
(to Ben-David)
And he's vain. That's why he leaves the
"LV" sign . . . why he's sucked every one
of us in to his drama. It's not enough for
him to wipe out the human race. He wants
to leave a record to show how clever he
was.

BEN-DAVID

Record for whom? If nobody's left to read
it.

MANNING

For God.

An hour passes. The great thing about New York is that even in the
aftermath of a superstorm, you can still get coffee and bagels delivered.
The side table of the reading room looks like a deli counter, supporting a
spread of sandwich wrappers, take-out cups and lids, cream cheese containers, sugar packets, and plastic utensils.

I'm helping the librarian tote in further armloads of bound arcana—
huge, heavy tomes that reek like a tomb. Everything is pre-Gutenberg, or
only a few years post. Illustrations are hand-rendered or etched or wood-
cut. Text is either inscribed letter by letter, or laid out in hand-set type.

Pages crinkle at the touch. We have to wear gloves, white cotton, to handle the covers, and must turn the leaves with surgical care. "If it means anything to you," the librarian tells Manning, "the volumes you're poring through are collectively worth seventeen-point-two million."

What powers do these Satanic entities possess? Our group pores over pix of Evil Ones stalking across fields of sulfur and brimstone. They descend from the aether on wings like dragons. They spit flame. Thunderbolts shoot from their sockets.

> BEN-DAVID
> We can't rely solely on myth and legend.
> How we fight must be based on what we
> know empirically, what we've seen with our
> own eyes . . .

Ben-David cites his own clash with Instancer on the subway platform.

> BEN-DAVID
> You grappled with him, Manning. So did I.
> He's real. He's physical. When he grabbed
> me, he even felt warm.

> ME
> Physical? Then how does he get into
> secure buildings leaving no sign?
> How does he kill ten people on four
> continents in the past fifteen days?

> BEN-DAVID
> I don't know.

```
               ME
How does he know Manning's mantras? How
does Instancer quote verbatim stuff he
couldn't possibly have heard?
```

```
            BEN-DAVID
I don't know.
```

Another ninety minutes pass. Rachel's text comes in from her plane to Israel. Outside the library, the windstorm continues to rage. I'm staring at medieval renderings of behorned demons (as well as a smattering of human-like creatures) emerging from smoldering clefts in the earth.

Not all, but most are escorted by females—innocent maidens, bewhiskered crones, maternal archetypes.

In the midst of this I'm on the phone at Manning's instruction to El Al, BEA, Lufthansa, and KLM trying to book Ben-David onto a flight to Tel Aviv. He's frantic to reach his sister and Manning is equally determined to find out where she's going and for what purpose.

```
            BEN-DAVID
Genesis 32:24 tells of Jacob wrestling
with an angel. But the Greek and Hebrew
translations say "man."
```

```
             MANNING
Meaning what?
```

Ben-David locates the passage in one of the Old Testaments. An illustration depicts two human-scale figures struggling on the earth beneath a horned moon in a setting beside a river.

                    BEN-DAVID
A man. See? Something or someone who
could be grappled with physically.

The librarian confirms this. Devil or rebel angel, he says, this entity
would be in material form.

                    LIBRARIAN
To enter the world, the teachings say, a
supernatural being must become physical.
It must take on the limitations of the
flesh, at least some of them.

                    BEN-DAVID
              (to Manning)
When you shot Instancer, the bullets
struck something solid. They didn't pass
through him as if he were a ghost. Their
impact rocked him. The bullets knocked
him back.

Manning paces in frustration.

                    MANNING
Where does the world end?

                    BEN-DAVID
What?

                    MANNING

Instancer said he wanted me with him at
"the end." What does the Bible say? Is
there a place—a specific location?

                    BEN-DAVID

Megiddo.

                    MANNING

Instancer said "you know where."

                    LIBRARIAN

The hill of Megiddo. Armageddon.

                    MANNING

The archaeological dig. Gehenna. Where
is it?

                    LIBRARIAN

It's there. It's the next hill.

                    BEN-DAVID

That does us no good.

                    MANNING

It tells us where Instancer will be.

                    BEN-DAVID

But not when. And not how to stop him.

                    MANNING

He'll be there. It's where he came from.
"The end" plays out at the beginning.

Manning crosses to a stack of books.

                    MANNING

If Instancer can be "conducted" into the
world, can he be conducted <u>out</u>?

He points to an etching in one of the texts. The illustration depicts a
demonic figure ascending from the inferno, led by a female child.

                    MANNING

The devil is escorted <u>into</u> this world,
right? Then there must be a way to escort
him out. That's the law. You said it,
Amos. Those are the ground rules.

                    BEN-DAVID

This is all myth and legend, Manning.
There's no such thing as "the law."

                    MANNING

There's always a law.

                    BEN-DAVID

Right.
        (sarcastic)
All you have to do is get Instancer to
the mouth of hell and kick him back down.

                    MANNING
    He can't return from there unconducted?
    That's the law.

                    BEN-DAVID
    I told you, there is no law!

We're all getting punchy. The greater library is closed with the flooding and the scorching windstorm. Power keeps going on and off. We're
out of coffee. The battery in my phone is fading . . .

This whole stunt feels like a fool's errand.

How can we kill the unkillable?

Are we crazy to put Ben-David on a plane to Israel? What if Instancer's already there? What if Rachel fled to be with him? Will she be an
accomplice to the murder of her own brother?

The librarian has begun clearing the books.

Manning slumps, silent, in a chair at the central table.

Ben-David keeps working. He's reviewing, out loud, all we have
gleaned this morning from the ancient texts or have theorized on our
own about supernatural beings and their potential vulnerabilities.

I can't tell if Manning is even listening.

Angels, Ben-David says, appear over and over in the Bible.

Angels can go bad.

They can rebel against God.

Is that Instancer?

Is he HaSatan?

Can anything stop him?

Manning remains slumped in his chair. He hasn't spoken in
minutes.

My eyes have crossed. I'm in and out of a REM state. Ben-David is explaining to Manning that in the Jewish religion God is One, meaning everything that is, is a part of the Almighty. Including the angels, including the devils.

Including Instancer.

All perform the will of the Almighty, whether they know it or not.

"How does that help us?" I say. "How do we kill this motherfucker?"

> BEN-DAVID
>
> He can't be killed. He can't be wounded.
> He fears nothing, not even God. He thinks
> he's smarter than God. Can he read our
> minds? Are we pawns for his amusement?
> Is he toying with us, playing us for
> fools?

> MANNING
>
> He can fall.

> BEN-DAVID
>
> What?

Manning says this so softly I barely hear it.

> MANNING
>   (to me)
> On the catwalk in the subway, remember?
> Instancer slipped. He fell.

> BEN-DAVID
>
> What are you talking about?

Manning sits up.

                    MANNING
He can fall. He's subject to gravity.

Manning shoots me a look that says, *Get this down. Don't forget it.*
He cranes all the way upright.

                    MANNING
We can't overpower him. We can't kill him.
But we can make him fall.

25

THIS IS HOW THE WORLD ENDS, PART TWO

WE'RE ON EL AL FLIGHT 26 to Tel Aviv, Manning and me. Forty-eight hours have passed. I'm checking my news feed every ten minutes.

Four more "LV" murders have been reported. Ben-David has decamped for the Holy Land two days ahead of us, alone, on the last El Al flight out of Kennedy. Rachel had bolted ten hours earlier.

Our exodus, Manning's and mine, plays out forty-eight hours after that.

It unspools like this:

Wednesday, April 26 (the day Ben-David flies to Israel), I'm in the office, at my desk, when I see Gleason's tech sergeant exit the chief's office and cross to Manning's. The spaces are only a hallway apart, both with glass walls. The tech stops in Manning's doorway, obviously delivering a message from the boss. Word around DivSix since the blow-up between Gleason and Manning two days ago is that Manning is about to be yanked from the "LV" investigation. Manning rises now and crosses from his own office to Gleason's. I'm watching from my workstation as he enters. Lieutenant Silver is in Gleason's office as well, along with Detective Kiriakin. Gleason's tech sergeant hurries in, trailing Manning.

Words are exchanged between Gleason and Manning.

Through the glass I see Manning pull out his badge and gun and slap them onto Gleason's desktop.

I get up and cross to Gleason's doorway. No one stops me, so I march in. Gleason, without looking at me (his eyes never leave Manning's), instructs his tech sergeant to put in motion the paperwork that will promote me to Detective Second Grade, raise my salary by $21,348, and install me in Manning's slot on the division table of organization.

Gleason is giving me Manning's job.

To my astonishment, I feel my right hand reaching to the holster at the small of my back while my left removes my shield from the belt clasp at the front right of my trousers. Without a word I set my badge and weapon next to Manning's on Gleason's desktop.

                    MANNING
        Dewey, are you out of your mind?

Manning turns to me and tells me I'm an idiot.

                      ME
        You're going to Israel. I'm going with you.

Manning's look to me says, *What makes you think I even want you along?*

                    MANNING
        What do you imagine you are, Dewey—my
        "partner"? I've been babysitting you since
        Day One. I don't need you and I don't want

```
you. You're an albatross. Every move I
make, I have to look over my shoulder to
make sure you're not tripping over your
own butch-heeled shoes. You're a burden!
You're a liability!
```

Once, when my father was still alive, he took me into his arms and told me he loved me. This from Manning feels at least as good.

ME

```
I'll get us adjacent seats.
```

I said Ben-David's flight was El Al's last out of Kennedy. This is true. Manning and I make our departure out of Halifax.

Why Halifax? Because JFK's runways have been rendered unusable indefinitely due to seawater incursion and "float" beneath their surfaces. (The other NY-NJ-CT fields ceased all operations seven years ago except those employing regional jets.)

We drive to Logan in Boston, then Portland, Maine, hoping that our inbound flight has been cleared to set down. Except wind shear from the third storm in seven days is so extreme at ground level and so unpredictable that air traffic control won't give the El Al extended-cabin 797 clearance to land at either of these fields. The aircraft is rerouted to Halifax, Nova Scotia. Manning and I overnight twice en route, at the Airport Radisson in Portland, then at a Holiday Inn Express in New Brunswick.

Throughout this pilgrimage Manning maintains what spotty contact he can with Ben-David (atmospheric conditions are so unstable that cell and satellite service is basically zilch) to make sure he's safe, to update him on our delay situation, to press him on his promise to meet us at Ben Gurion when we land, and to urge him to latch on to Rachel and to not let her out of his sight.

The plan, agreed upon in New York on that final morning at the Dorot Library, is to lure Instancer to the sulfurous portal from which he first emerged and then, somehow, send him back down there for keeps.

What I can't figure out is why Manning is so insistent on holding tight to Rachel. Forget her, I tell him. Let her go! If she *is* working with Instancer, as half our evidence and instincts say she is, she'll do everything in her power to sabotage us. She'll play innocent, like she has from the start. Then in the fatal moment she'll betray us.

                    ME
     Don't tell me you trust her now?

                    MANNING
     I don't even trust you, Dewey.

Meanwhile, I'm poring over maps of the Holy Land. Before, I had only the sketchiest notion of the geography of Israel and her Arab neighbors. Forty-eight hours of delays and forced layovers, however, have given me ample opportunity to bone up.

I had no idea that Israel was so small, the size of New Jersey. You can drive cross-country in an hour and ten minutes.

I'm memorizing place names and topography. I know now where Tel Aviv is (on the coastal plain, along the Mediterranean) and where Jerusalem sits (about sixty miles east, and high—twenty-five hundred feet—on the crest of the drop-off into Jordan and the highway across the desert to Amman).

I find Megiddo. It's in the north, near the Sea of Galilee. The Gehenna dig is there, so close the two names butt against each other on the map.

In the waiting area at Halifax Stanfield International, a fellow passenger—a nun in a habit—watches me paging through maps and guidebooks. She asks what my purpose is in traveling to the Holy Land.

                                    ME

        We're going to confront the devil at
        Armageddon and stop him from destroying
        the world.

"Well," she says without a trace of irony, "good luck with that."

I'm beginning as well to grasp the link between climate and geography.

Africa and the Middle East are the canaries in the global weather coal mine. What happens there today happens in Kansas tomorrow. Khamsins, simooms, siroccos. I had never heard of any of these five years ago. They're the hot, dry winds that formerly tormented the region only in season, rising out of the Sahara and the Arabian Peninsula. Now they're year-round and twenty degrees Celsius hotter than they've ever been. Commercial air traffic to the Middle East (and even military flights) is down to a fifth of what it had been only a few years ago.

The place is too hot to fly.

I'm filing reports, working on my timeline, and logging onto every Hebrew and Arabic political site I can find.

Ben-David's return to Israel is front-page news. Not only is he the leading climate activist in the Jewish state and in fact the world, and thus the go-to talking head for the mounting eco-catastrophes, but also his involvement in the "LV murders" (called in Israel the Tzadikim Nistarim Killings) makes him above-the-fold fare and clickbait on every site on the web and social media. Among the Haredim, the ultra-Orthodox, this story is the only news.

I pull up a video on Israel Channel KAN 11. It's Ben-David from two days ago, disembarking at Ben Gurion International. Report-

ers mob him, frantic to hear what he has to say about the imminent global climate calamity and to learn why he has returned now
to Israel. "Are these extreme weather events the result of 'natural'
phenomena?" a female journalist asks Ben-David. "Or is God's hand
behind them all?"

> BEN-DAVID
> Trust me, all such distinctions are
> irrelevant at this point.

The correspondents press Ben-David, demanding to know if the
apocalyptic floods and firestorms are "real" or "biblical."

> BEN-DAVID
> The concepts of "God" or "the devil" are
> not necessary to grasp the catastrophe
> that's looming. That, the human race has
> produced all by itself.

The news cuts to insert-video of a massive drilling project amid
melting glaciers.

> BEN-DAVID
> The Greenland ice cap, as we all know,
> has been functionally eradicated since
> 2031. What's there now? A twenty-two-
> billion-dollar petroleum extraction effort
> financed by ExxonMobil.

The segment switches back to Ben-David.

BEN-DAVID

Baghdad hit 141° Fahrenheit yesterday.
In Central Asia, temperatures are being
recorded that have not been reached since
the Cretaceous Period two and a half
million years ago. We're talking about an
extinction-level reordering. Sub-Saharan
Africa has virtually emptied out. Twenty-
seven million dead in famine and war.
Ninety million migrants on the move. The
world knows all this. It's on the news
every night. Four hundred thousand are
camped at Megiddo, here in Israel, right
now, waiting to witness the End of Days.
Believe me, we don't need "God" or "Satan"
to see that the curtain is coming down.

Our plane finally appears at dawn of the third day. After a six-hour delay due to atmospheric instability, Manning and I take off at last, but are compelled by a "weather anomaly" to set down barely three hours later at Narsarsuaq Airport in Greenland.

There we witness, on a scale even more dispiriting than Ben-David's description, the harbor-, housing-, and road-construction operations of the ExxonMobil drilling enterprise preparatory to tapping the petroleum deposits beneath the vanished ice. Tens of thousands of roughnecks are pouring in to work this new field. Temperature in April is 93° Fahrenheit, twenty degrees above records from a decade earlier. Up this close to the Arctic Circle you can see the carbon accumulation in the upper atmosphere. It looks like a dirty windshield.

The jet stream as well looks and feels different at this latitude. It's gray-brown. You can see it. West-to-east tailwinds that used to add 50–150 knots to a liner's airspeed now jack it up by 350. Planes don't even try to buck headwinds. Permitted altitude maxes out at twenty-four thousand feet. Rides are rough, and the abuse passengers take from eco-demonstrators for contributing to upper-atmosphere destabilization is worse. Protests are permanent outside every airport. Passengers are assaulted with stones and bottles, even bags of excrement.

FLYING IS EARTH DYING
PLEASE . . . CRASH

Narsarsuaq Airport had been until eighteen months ago, we are told, nothing more than a pit stop for private jets and an emergency landing field for commercial liners, with no passenger facilities beyond restrooms and a snack bar. Now it's the third-largest airfield in the world. Bulldozers and earthmovers are everywhere. Diesel stink saturates the air. While we lay over, I grab my laptop and camp directly under the Wi-Fi hub.

Finally we get through on WhatsApp to Ben-David.

```
                    MANNING
        Where are you, Amos? Are you safe?


                    BEN-DAVID
        I've got a battalion of paratroopers
        around me. Does that ease your mind?
```

To Manning's concern about Rachel, Ben-David replies, "She's here. She's fine. There's nothing to worry about."

Finally with a web connection, I continue my search for Instancer. I spend the full delay running passenger queries for every Mideast-bound commercial, private, charter, and fractional flight out of East Coast fields including New Brunswick, Nova Scotia, Prince Edward Island, and Newfoundland.

> MANNING
>
> You're wasting your time, Dewey. Instancer
> probably passed us half an hour ago.
> Without an airplane.

Airborne again, I settle in and scan channels for the latest. The top two stories on Israel KAN 11 are migrant wars on the Egyptian border— armed clashes at the Gaza towns of Rafah and Khan Younis—and water riots in Jerusalem.

Coach on El Al is not bad. Because it's international and overwater, the seats have legroom. You get a pillow and a blanket. When you order a drink, it comes in a real glass.

My seatmate (the best I could get for Manning is across the aisle) is a female ER physician from Medicine Hat, Alberta. She's part of a travel contingent of twenty-four, seated in a block between rows fourteen and seventeen. Their society is called the Sovereign Light Brethren. The party is bound for Jerusalem, she tells me in a voice fizzing with good cheer, anticipating Christ's return and the initiation of the Rapture.

> SEATMATE
>
> Did you hear? Our plane is the last into
> Tel Aviv. No more after us. Ben Gurion
> Airport has become unusable. Ground-level
> winds are too strong.

According to my new friend, more than two hundred thousand pilgrims are gathered already in camps in the Kidron Valley and on the western slopes of the Mount of Olives, overlooking the Old City of Jerusalem. Hundreds have perished from heat, thirst, and sickness, she says. Still the believers keep coming, driven by the mounting environmental catastrophes and the belief that the hand of the Almighty is behind them. My seatmate shows me pix of the tent city where her group will be quartered. The place looks like Andersonville. But the lady's eyes shine.

Conditions are worse at Megiddo, she tells me, where nearly half a million have congregated in heat that hits 120° every day. I've already researched this in detail. Video of the site shows a tent-and-RV camp that sprawls for miles in all directions.

                    SEATMATE
          They've been there, some of them, for four
          and half years.

I cue up for her a YouTube clip from one of Ben-David's TED talks:

                    BEN-DAVID
          The world doesn't end like a Hollywood
          movie. We've been conditioned to imagine
          an isolated singularity, one cataclysmic
          calamity like the asteroid cloud that
          killed off the dinosaurs. The slow-motion
          extinction we're witnessing now is far
          closer to how the process is actually
          unfolding. A million deaths at a time, five
          million, ten million. In the last fourteen
          days twenty million have perished. In
          eighteen months, a hundred and ninety
          million. This is how the world ends. It's
          not "going to happen." It is happening.

26

PARATROOPERS

FORTY-FIVE MINUTES LATER, our 797 is on the ground and Manning is clashing with a new antagonist.

A few minutes before landing, the aircraft's first officer had hiked back from the cockpit to deliver a message, received on the plane's secure radio and passed now to Manning as a handwritten note.

> *Manning,*
> *Upon deplaning, you will be met by Lt. Dana Peled.*
> *She is the operations officer of the reserve paratroop battalion*
> *that I command. Lt. Peled will expedite your passage through Secu-*
> *rity and Customs and will transport you to my location.*
>
> *B-D.*

```
                  MANNING
        What is this bullshit?
```

Manning thanks the first officer but he's furious. He hands me the note. I can feel the heat radiating from his shoulders.

Indeed Lieutenant Peled is waiting for us at the mouth of the jet-way, accompanied by a male soldier, a sergeant. She's a tall, attractive brunette with long hair pulled tight into a bun beneath her paratrooper's red beret. She welcomes us (the male sergeant, named Giora, has brought bottled water and trail mix) and apologizes for Major Ben-David's absence.

Lieutenant Peled's orders are to take us to Ben-David without delay. She has three Humvees waiting outside. Expect a trip, she says, of about two and a half hours. When I address her as "Lieutenant," she says, "Please call me Dana [pronounced DAH-na]." Her garb is red boots, khaki trousers, and shirt. Over her shoulder, on a sling, she carries a folding-stock Uzi.

> MANNING
>
> I don't mean to be rude, Dana. But where
> the fuck is Ben-David? He was supposed to
> meet us here.

> DANA
>
> My apologies, sir. Major Ben-David is with
> our battalion at a place called Ein Gedi
> on the Dead Sea.

Manning strides beside Dana into the terminal.

> MANNING
>
> What has Ben-David told you? Do you have
> any idea why my partner and I have come
> from the States?

DANA

Sir, Major Ben-David is assembling tech
gear for the Emergency Eco-Conference in
Cyprus in six days. He's under orders too.

MANNING

In other words, you know nothing?

DANA

About what, sir?

Despite his anger, Manning's expression softens toward the lieutenant. She's protecting her superior. She's a good officer.

MANNING

Who's with Ben-David now? Is his sister
there? Are there soldiers around him? Is
he secure?

Dana confirms that Rabbi Rachel Davidson has arrived at the battalion's location. She is sharing quarters with her brother, Major Ben-David.

DANA

I assure you, sir, he's as safe as the Pope.

Manning's anger relents. Dana's defensive posture abates as well.
Dana explains that their battalion is a reserve formation, activated only
ten days ago for the climate crisis and the migrant emergencies.

Apparently every Jewish male in Israel under the age of forty serves in one reserve unit or another. The entire country is an army and has been since its founding in 1948.

Dana indicates the direction to Baggage Claim. She makes it a point to stride in step with Manning.

> DANA
>
> Sir, if you'll forgive me for asking . . .
> what happened to your face?

Manning's jaw and forehead are still blue-black and puffy from his encounter with Instancer.

> MANNING
>
> Someone pushed it through a wall.

> DANA
>
> The reason I ask is Major Ben-David's face
> looks the same.

> MANNING
>
> Same someone.

Manning and I collect our bags. The party troops out toward the Hummers. The airport's plate-glass windows have been boarded up with heavy plywood—not against terrorists, Dana informs us, but because the glass keeps getting blown in by the wind. The terminal itself is an indoor dust bowl. My tongue is coated already with acrid grit. "What is that taste?" I ask Giora, the male sergeant.

"Air," he says.

"There's some good news," says Dana as we stride past the security line. She declares that Israeli-Palestinian relations have progressed over the past two years from "cordial" (her word) to "fraternal" and now even "communal."

                    DANA
        The end of the world will do that for
        you.

We step outside into an atmosphere only a few degrees shy of combustion. I actually stop. I can't believe how hot it is.

Dana, who seems to take the furnace blast in stride, is telling Manning that she realizes he and I are jet-lagged. She advises us strongly to remain awake till our normal bedtimes. We'll adjust faster that way. Priority one from this moment, Dana says, is hydration. She will be monitoring us and enforcing compliance.

                    DANA
        Carry a minimum of two quarts at all
        times. If you must choose between a
        weapon and water, take water.

Our Humvees wait at the curb under the guard of four other paratroopers. The vehicles are dun-colored, desert-camouflaged. All three are armored and topped by turrets mounting .50-caliber machine guns.

A male sergeant standing by one of the Humvees holds up the vehicle's radio handset and calls something to Dana in Hebrew.

Ben-David is on the line for Manning.

Manning takes the phone.

Ben-David apologizes for being unable to meet Manning at the airport in person. He promises to make up for it. He tells Manning he has ordered Dana to stop en route at an IDF armory.

> BEN-DAVID
> It's a candy store. Take anything you
> want.

Exiting passengers flow past our little convoy, heading for taxis, Ubers, and shuttles. I can't stop my eyes from searching every face and shadow.

Manning catches me.

> MANNING
> He's here. I feel him.

27

ZOMBIE KILLERS

O N THE WAY TO EIN GEDI, we stop as promised at an IDF armory at a satellite base in a suburb called Ramat Gan. The site is a converted high school. Israeli-made Merkava battle tanks are parked in rows under camo covers on what used to be the soccer field. The tanks are not for war, Dana says, but to control migrant clashes and civilian water riots.

The armory itself, the locked and guarded weapons repository, is down two flights in a bombproof bunker.

We prowl, watched over by military police, through locked-down rows of assault rifles, heavy and light machine guns, even vehicle-mountable anti-tank and antiaircraft systems.

Manning inquires of Dana what Ben-David has told her of our weapons requirements.

DANA

He said to equip you for fighting in
tunnels.

The armory commander appears. He's a stocky fellow, about thirty, with a shaved skull topped by a knit *kippah*, a skullcap, that he somehow manages to keep in place even when he bends over. He greets Manning with a handshake and me with a curt bow.

ARMORY COMMANDER
You were not here. You saw nothing.

The commander leads Manning and me behind a security partition and down an additional flight of stairs. We pass through another secure door and cross another floor stacked with weaponry.

The commander stops before a brown steel case about the size of a steamer trunk. He opens it with an electronic code. The Hebrew name for the IDF is Zahal. It's an acronym, the commander says, that simply means "Israel Defense Forces." The case is stencil-marked in Hebrew and English.

ZAHAL
XT1—SF/AV–AP

The final letters, the commander says, mean "Shoulder-Fired/Anti-Vehicle–Anti-Personnel."

Three weapons nest in the case. The commander removes one. It looks like a stubby, fat RPG.

ARMORY COMMANDER
Follow me, please.

The commander leads us down another flight of stairs to an underground firing range. The weapon, he tells Manning, is called in Hebrew *machabi*, "Maccabee," but is referred to more commonly as a "tunnel-buster." Fans blow air. Temperature becomes cool.

> ARMORY COMMANDER
> These weapons were developed during the
> fifth and sixth Hamas Wars. The warhead
> is concussive only. It explodes in a
> manner similar to a shaped charge, that
> is, in one direction only, but the blast
> is concentrated not into a tiny area but
> dispersed across a wide and high front.

The commander holds the weapon out before Manning.

> ARMORY COMMANDER
> Would you like to try it?

A range attendant outfits Manning with a helmet, protective glasses, and noise-canceling earmuffs. All of us are issued the same. We are escorted into a sound-insulated, fireproof bunker. The range is visible through a slit of six-inch protective glass.

The range simulates an infiltration tunnel. Pop-up silhouettes of enemy fighters rise at various distances. In the center of the tunnel at about seventy-five feet squats a Studebaker Lark, the real thing, an old clunker sedan from the sixties.

The range security officer demonstrates how to seat the weapon properly atop the right shoulder. He guides Manning into the proper firing stance. The armory commander indicates two safeties, which Manning unlocks with care, and the trigger, enclosed within a pistol-type grip.

<pre>
        RANGE SECURITY OFFICER
There's no sight. You don't need one. A
blind man could fire this thing.
</pre>

He tells Manning not to be concerned about recoil. The rocket-propelled projectile whooshes from the tube under its own power. The weapon's kick is less than that of a twelve-gauge shotgun.

I'm in the bunker, watching through the armorglass. The commander and range officer step inside this shelter as well. I glance to Dana. She's grinning, securing her ear protection tight to her head.

The range officer signs, *Ready.*

Security lights on the firing line turn from red to green.

Manning fires.

The projectile leaps from the tube like a round from a bazooka, spewing a fiery plume rearward. The warhead detonates like a sonic boom. The whole underground structure shudders. I feel the air sucked from my lungs. I nearly keel over.

Overhead lamps blaze in the tunnel. Powerful recessed fans suck the grit and debris clear. The commander and range officer step out from the bunker and cross to Manning on the firing line. Manning has tugged his ear protectors off. His face is black everywhere except where the goggles shielded his eyes.

Little by little, the tunnel becomes clear of dust.

<pre>
             MANNING
   Where's the car?
</pre>

In the place where the Studebaker had been, we see only a smoking engine block, on its side, and the steel chassis frame, peeled completely of paint.

ARMORY COMMANDER

Exactly.

Manning takes three.

On the way out we pass a rack of Mossberg 500 ZMB shotguns, like the one that bowled me over during the warrant service at Brooklyn South.

MANNING

(to commander)

And one of these for my partner.

Ninety minutes down the road our convoy is halted by a skirmish in a migrant camp outside a town called Arad. It takes Israeli Special Forces units—Sayeret Matkal—working with their Palestinian counterparts almost two hours to restore order and clear the highway. Returning to board our Humvees, I see two of our young paratroopers giggling at something on a phone.

I look.

It's the shower video, the one with Instancer cupping Rachel's bare breasts in his soapy hands.

DANA

(to paratroopers)

Put that shit away!

The soldiers obey reluctantly. When I turn to Dana, she averts her gaze. Either Ben-David has told her more about our enterprise than she has indicated or she and the troops she commands have figured it out on their own.

28

EIN GEDI

O UR PARTY REACHES Kibbutz Ein Gedi at the peak of the late afternoon heat. Ben-David is waiting in the sun at the end of the entry drive. I'm startled at the depth of feeling produced by this reunion. Manning shakes Ben-David's hand with real emotion. Ben-David has to pretend to wipe sweat from his eyes.

                    MANNING
          Where's Rachel?

                    BEN-DAVID
          She's safe. Don't worry. We've heard
          nothing from you-know-who.

Ben-David shows Manning the latest from KAN 11:
Four new "LV" murders in the past twelve hours—two in Israel, one in Egypt, one in Turkey.
Thirty-two.
Thirty-three.

Thirty-four.

Thirty-five.

> BEN-DAVID
>
> What number does that make me?

Ben-David leads us inside to the dining hall. He's in uniform—boots and desert hat, rumpled khaki trousers and even more wrinkled utility shirt. The digital thermometer on the wall reads 45.5 Celsius (114° Fahrenheit) even with a breeze and a line of industrial fans cranking.

Dana returns from the office to tell us there's been another "schedule alteration." Two civilian tractor-trailers were supposed to pick up Ben-David's equipment—prototypes of solar power generation gear—and take it to the port of Haifa, from which it will be transported by sea to Cyprus for the climate conference six days hence. But an emergency has called the vehicles away. We'll have to deliver the stuff ourselves, using army trucks and repacking everything.

> DANA
>
> I'm sorry. We're all drafted for loading
> duty and it's going to take all night.

We start working at sunset. Rachel has joined us, coming from the kibbutz dormitory where she has been sleeping. The Dead Sea shore for six contiguous miles north of Ein Gedi has been converted, we are told, into a half-military, half-civilian Eco-Research Park. The salt-heavy waters, which conduct electrical current nearly as efficiently as copper wire, have been employed for three decades in experiments by government agencies and civilian start-ups seeking tech breakthroughs to combat climate change. A consortium associated with the Technion, the Israel Institute of Technology at Haifa, runs this facility. Ben-David has been the intellectual guru and emotional catalyst behind many of these projects.

The building we're in looks like the Apple campus in Silicon Valley. Everything is Cube Modern and automated, powered by sun and wind. The bay is air-conditioned, thank God. The loading is done by forklifts manned by facility crews. Our job, under Ben-David's supervision, is to sort and rewrap the hundreds of pieces of equipment, which had been bundled for transport on forty-foot-long trailers and now must be broken down to fit on three-ton army trucks.

The gear, Ben-David tells us, is a revolutionary type of aeration apparatus for a system that climate engineers call SROG, Seawater Re-Oxygenation and Generation.

SROG technology mimics the process of photosynthesis in plants. It uses sunlight and salt water to produce electricity, which is then stored in an equally innovative medium constituted of 99.99 percent silica, i.e., sand.

This system alone, if deployed worldwide, says Ben-David, could retard if not reverse the most dangerous aspects of atmospheric carbon accretion.

Our party labors till midnight, when plans change again.

A fierce khamsin has come up with the fall of darkness. By ten the storm has become electric. Swarms of *migdalim* mini-tornadoes ("towers" in Hebrew) roar across the surface of the Dead Sea. Lightning strikes by dozens boom over the biblical landscape.

Electrical power has failed. A/C crashes. Temp soars to 105°, then 110°. No one can sleep. Across the loading area I spot Manning in some kind of clash with Rachel, with Ben-David in the middle and Dana and several other troopers looking on.

Do I care? I'm exhausted and dehydrated. My body clock is fifteen hours out of whack, and to top it all off I'm getting my period. Cramps knot my guts. I can't remember why I'm here or what I imagined we had hoped to accomplish.

I cross toward the fracas in time to hear Rachel confronting Ben-David and pointing indignantly at Manning.

>   RACHEL
> Why is he even here? Why did you let him
> come?

Rachel is telling Ben-David he must go to Haifa, to the port from which he and this equipment will sail for Cyprus. "Don't listen to him!" she's saying, indicating Manning.

>   RACHEL
> The climate conference is everything!
> You're the world's last hope, Amos! You
> can't risk your life. You must get to
> Cyprus!

Manning, with admirable self-restraint at triple digits Fahrenheit, makes the case that Cyprus can wait. The conference is six days away. We must go to Gehenna *now*, Manning says, with or without the trucks and equipment.

>   MANNING
> This was the plan, Amos. You agreed to it
> in New York.

>   RACHEL
> Don't listen to him! You're <u>bait</u> to him,
> that's all. He wants you at Gehenna to
> draw Instancer. He doesn't care if you
> die!

Manning tells Ben-David he'll die if he goes anywhere *except* Gehenna.

> MANNING
>
> Instancer will kill you on the road,
> Amos. He'll kill you in Haifa, he'll kill
> you at the Cyprus conference, he doesn't
> care. When you're gone, the full slate of
> Righteous Men will have been eliminated.
> The only place we have a chance against
> Instancer is at the dig—at Gehenna.

> RACHEL
>
> Don't believe him, Amos! You're Number
> Thirty-Six to him, nothing more.

The paratroopers look on. How much of this can they make sense of? Do they have any idea who Instancer is, or what the stakes are in this debate?

Ben-David glances to his sister, then to Manning. He turns at last to Dana and the troops.

> BEN-DAVID
>
> Carry on as you were instructed,
> Lieutenant. The convoy will move out, as
> soon as the storm abates, for Haifa.

29

SHIT HAPPENS IN THE HOLY LAND

Ein Gedi to Haifa is 140 miles. It takes us twenty-seven hours just to get to Jerusalem, a third of the way.

The electrical storm refuses to subside. Ben-David orders the start anyway. We pull out at 1030 precisely on April 28, 2034.

I have never seen atmospheric conditions as hostile as these, or a landscape as bleak and devoid of life. Surface temperature of the macadam on Highway 90 is 55° Celsius (130° Fahrenheit). The asphalt has literally melted. We drive over dust and sand mixed with petroleum-derived goo.

Our convoy is Manning and Ben-David in army truck #1 with a soldier-driver, Eli. They are led by Humvee #1 with Dana as convoy commander, the sergeant from the airport, Giora, and a third trooper to man the .50-caliber in the turret. Truck #2 is, like the first, an IDF "six-by" with a male soldier-driver, Hemi, short for Menachem. I ride beside Rachel in the tall, open, unbearably broiling cab. Behind us, the tarp-covered cargo bed is stacked roof-high with tech gear and distillation apparatus, part of the equipment that Ben-David is bringing with him to the Cyprus eco-conference. A second and third Humvee trail ours, providing rear security.

Manning has lost the argument of Gehenna versus Haifa.

He insists, however, upon riding at Ben-David's side. He takes the Zombie Killer and packs one of the tunnel-busters behind the truck cab's seat. His instructions to me, acceded to by Ben-David, are to rivet myself to Rachel. I am to ride with her, hydrate with her, march to the ladies' loo with her. She is not to be permitted to stray from my sight or supervision under any circumstances. Nor will Manning let her be issued a weapon. Further, at his insistence, I have outfitted Rachel with an NYPD-issue lapel cam and audio recorder exactly like the ones Manning and I wear.

> ME
>
> (to Rachel)
>
> From now on, every word you speak, every
> sound within your hearing, and everything
> this camera sees will be recorded. You
> don't have to do a thing. It's automatic.
> Goes straight to the cloud, meaning the
> permanent database of the NYPD.

The convoy vehicles themselves are equipped with sophisticated Israeli-made comm gear, including interior and exterior cameras linking all vehicles to the column commander, i.e., Ben-David, and to one another. Every trooper wears a mike and headset. Every console/instrument panel mounts separate tablet-type screens for each truck and Humvee. All are tied in by laser and GPS locators, so that each vehicle knows where all others are at all times. Rachel's police recorders are for Manning and me only, so that we miss nothing of what she does or says.

The convoy proceeds north out of Ein Gedi on highway 90. The Dead Sea is on our right. We stop briefly at the research facility at Mitspe Shalem. There Ben-David picks up more eco-equipment for Cyprus.

The loading proceeds in heat so intense even the birds and lizards have taken cover. Dana and her security party are nearing a breaking point, not so much from the heat or the labor, but from the tension produced by the foreknowledge of what they might have to confront, i.e., Instancer—and the fact that this eventuality has apparently not been addressed by their commander.

Here under the eaves Dana stands and confronts Ben-David.

She does so with respect but with passion.

> DANA
>
> Amos, our orders are to escort you and this equipment to Haifa and to see you safely aboard ship for Cyprus. This of course we shall do. However . . .

Giora, Hemi, and the other troopers listen intently. Dana gestures to Manning, to Rachel, and to me.

> DANA
>
> None of us in the security party is blind or deaf. We have read the news and heard the rumors. We know who these people are and why they are here—

> BEN-DAVID
>
> And your question is?

                    DANA
We are soldiers, Amos. We are not afraid
to fight.

Ben-David's glance scans the faces of the other paratroopers. Clearly
they stand with their lieutenant.

                  BEN-DAVID
Our destination, Dana, remains Haifa.
Should that change, I promise you will be
the first to know.

The crews finish loading the equipment—titanium tanks for the
SROG system. Titanium apparently is more impermeable even than
stainless steel in corrosive environments. Our convoy is three trucks
now instead of two, escorted by the same three Humvees.

What is it like to drive in a khamsin? Through our truck's windshield (I remain with Rachel in six-by #2), which is caked with dust so
thick that high noon feels like midnight, the ribbon of desert road, half
liquid and whipped relentlessly by a foot-high stream of sandstorm grit,
is virtually invisible. Stones the size of golf balls bound across the road
surface and pound into our tires and mudguards.

In the cab, speech is impossible. Our "deuce-and-a-half" weighs six
tons empty, nine loaded. We are buffeted like a microbus. Our driver,
Hemi, wrestles the wheel gamely. How he can see the road, I have no idea.

The convoy is derailed again at Almog, south of Jericho. Migrant
riots have produced a mass evacuation. Highway 90 north is closed.

We turn west toward Jerusalem. Ben-David's plan is to take Highway 1 to 6, the Rabin Highway, and head north on this route to Haifa.
But the westbound lanes are backed up for miles with inhabitants flee-

ing toward the coast. Our convoy struggles past Wadi Qelt and Khan al-Ahmar.

This is the West Bank. The territories. Checkpoints manned by security men of the Palestinian Authority and others by soldiers of the IDF halt our convoy over and over. We reach the outskirts of East Jerusalem at sundown in a standstill crush. It takes four hours to cross from Highway 417 at Jahalin to the Old City, a distance of less than five miles.

Through all this, Manning stays glued to Ben-David. When he's not physically at his side, his eye remains on him. I do the same for Rachel. But while Manning's job is to protect Ben-David from Instancer, mine is to keep watch on Rachel to shield Manning. How on edge are we? A column of vehicles is defenseless in densely packed traffic, and our convoy's situation is worse because of the anarchy and civil disorder within the city.

Demonstrators, Israelis as well as Palestinians and migrants, apparently have run amok protesting a reduced ration of drinking water. Our convoy enters the city from the southeast, from Bethlehem via the Jericho road. Firemen are knocking down blazes in wrecked and looted storefronts; they use chemical foam instead of water. Police in riot gear have cordoned off half the city. Our vehicles snake through the bedlam, thanks only to Dana, in the lead Humvee, flashing her ID and talking smack at each checkpoint.

Our party overnights in the trucks in a neighborhood called Abu Tor outside the Old City. Time is 0130, April 30. Drivers catch what sleep they can sprawled across the bench seats in their cabs; everyone else tosses in pools of sweat atop the stretch-wrapped cargo. All night the windstorm continues unabated.

Reveille arrives at 0430. Our party wash with hand wipes, brush our teeth using thimble-splashes from water bottles.

The trucks roll out at 0510. Traffic is already dense with motor vehicles, many of which have apparently been in the streets all night trying to flee the city, and also with pedestrians pulling carts and wagons hauling families and their possessions. We have to shut down to keep from boiling over.

Six hours pass. Time is 1130 before we escape the warren of local streets and at last crawl onto Highway 1 West. The sun is high now. The dust storm has eased. For a mile or more, we make speed. But at Abu Ghosh, still inside the city limits, our column runs into an even more massive traffic jam. Police and emergency vehicles creep forward along the shoulders amid a chaos of honking horns, stalled and overheated cars, and ragged refugees in the hundreds, many carrying children or wheeling old folks and belongings, all tramping toward the coast on foot.

Our driver, Hemi, goes forward to investigate the holdup. I start to step out myself but the metal of the exterior door handle is so scorching from the sun that I jerk my hand back, cursing. "Stay in the cab," calls Hemi. "Don't be a hero."

Manning stands on the roadside in the searing sun, packing the Zombie Killer, keeping watch over our convoy commander. Ben-David himself is on the military radio to Dana and Giora, seeking alternative routes. I check my phone for external temp: 121° F.

Hemi comes slogging back, his shirt soaked in sweat. He mounts to the cab. He's wearing gloves on both hands. "Another water riot," he says. Apparently mobs have attacked a convoy of tankers a few miles ahead.

We turn back for Highway 60. We will bypass Ramallah, a Palestinian city in the West Bank, and take mountain roads along the border with Jordan. "Might get a little breezy up there," says Hemi.

Our convoy covers five miles or so, climbing all the way, with traffic thinning dramatically behind us.

The Ramallah road is as jammed as Highway 1. Dana, breaking the trail, signals for the convoy to veer right onto a bypass route. The vehicles follow in order, in second gear and then in first, onto an unpaved, single-track road that hugs on its left a parched basalt ridge and teeters on its right above the sharp, sere drop-off to the Jordanian desert.

Ten miles down the bypass one of the trucks behind us overheats. The convoy stops. As soon as the engines are shut off, the other two six-bys boil over. An hour is spent transferring coolant from one of the sea-water evaporators in the cargo bays to the radiators of the trucks.

Time is now 1330. Heat is beyond my capacity to describe. I'm hunkering with Rachel in the shade under Ben-David's deuce-and-a-half. We have left the bypass road and turned onto a bypass-of-the-bypass. Unpaved, unmarked. I can't find it on any map or on my phone. The Jordan Valley desert—the Ghor—sprawls below us on the right. Temperature down there must be 150. Across the entire expanse, which is barren as a floor of linoleum, heat lightning crackles—scores of strikes every minute across a vista of what seems like at least thirty miles.

West, the grade descends through rugged hill country to the coastal plain and the Mediterranean. The result along the summit is an east-to-west gale like a furnace blast. Wind-driven sand and gravel howl up from the desert floor with the force of an industrial abrader. Did I mention it was hot? Dana, with her head wrapped in a checkered kefiyyeh, ducks into the shade under the truck.

When she sees Rachel she stiffens.

DANA

You still here?

RACHEL

Fuck you.

DANA

Tell us something. You have to tell us
something.

                    RACHEL
        About what?

                    DANA
        Him.

Dana wears a pistol on one hip. She carries her Uzi on a sling over
her shoulder.

                    DANA
        What are we up against? Do we have
        a chance? Will our tunnel-busters do
        anything?

                    RACHEL
        What am I, a weapons expert?

                    DANA
        You're why we're here. You're the cause of
        all this.

Manning appears, kneeling on the windward side. He has to hang
on to the flank of the truck, wearing gloves now, to keep from getting
blown over.

He tells us the trucks are ready.

We're moving out.

An hour later, in a gale that has only increased in fury, our convoy
grinds to another halt, this time on a knife-edge crest beneath a lime-
stone crag.

"Goats!" comes the squawking voice and image—Dana's—from the

Humvee #1 tablet screen on our truck's console. Through the chalky windshield I can make out a flock of hundreds, driven by Bedouin herders, shambling in the gale along the road crest.

Giora and Ben-David are waving from ahead. The convoy lumbers off the road into a bulldozed cutout on the slope beneath the crag.

Shelter.

Temperature drops immediately to about 110. Crazy as it sounds, this feels cool.

Giora, Hemi, and the soldiers pile out and scramble to top off their radiators, check their loads, and tighten down all lashings. Dana dismounts from the lead Humvee and comes back to us.

                    DANA
              (to all)
     Hydrate! I mean it. Get some water in you!

Rachel clomps past me with an odd expression. She stalks toward the front of the column. When I call to her, she doesn't answer. I chase her.

Some kind of commotion has broken out ahead. I see Ben-David's chest and shoulders above the milling goats. Two Bedouins in robes are speaking to him in an agitated state. Manning crosses toward them.

The flock blocks the road completely. The herders carry shepherd's staffs. Their garb is hooded robes and sandals. Little boys carry leather slings like David in the Old Testament.

The Bedouin patriarch speaks to Ben-David in Arabic. Rachel has pushed forward. She stands at Ben-David's shoulder. I shove through, beside her and Dana.

               DANA
        (indicates Bedouin elder)
   He says a man met him on the road and
   gave him a message for us.

Apparently the patriarch wants money. Ben-David digs in his pockets. He hands the man several bills. The elder accepts them. He produces the note.

Ben-David indicates Manning. The Bedouin hands Manning the note. He points to the summit of the crag looming overhead.

A man stands there, a hundred feet above us, silhouetted against the burning sky.

Rachel peers.

Dana reaches for binoculars.

Manning and Ben-David squint, shielding their eyes against the glare and the churning dust.

The man is Instancer.

Every hair on my body stands up.

Instancer holds motionless. The gale booms around him, whipping his khaki shirt and military-style trousers. His hair blows sideways in the wind. He stands beside some kind of desert-rigged truck. He's alone.

I turn instinctively to Rachel.

Her expression betrays nothing.

Dana peers at Instancer through binoculars. I see her adjust the focus knob, pulling the eyepieces deep and hard against her sockets.

I rap Dana's shoulder, for a look.

               DANA
   Get your own.

I'm peering as hard as I can at Instancer. He makes no movement. Just looks down at us. Too far away to make out his expression.

Manning opens the note, scans it, and passes it to Ben-David. Rachel pushes to Ben-David's side. He hands the paper to her.

Whatever the message says, it sobers these three completely. I see Manning meet Ben-David's eye.

Ben-David glances toward Rachel, then back to Manning.

> BEN-DAVID
> (to Dana)
> Lieutenant, arm your men.

Instancer holds his position directly above us.

His note is passed to me.

It's an iPhone photo.

I squint in the sun-glare.

The pic is a close-up of the hood of a desert truck, apparently the same vehicle Instancer is standing beside now.

In the dust on the hood a finger has scrawled:

C U IN HELL

Manning has crossed to Ben-David. He is speaking to him with quiet but urgent intensity. I can't hear what they're saying; they're too far away. Whatever action Manning is urging, Ben-David is rejecting it.

The herders, with fresh energy, drive their flock clear of the road.

I see Manning indicate Rachel. He's speaking with greater vehemence to Ben-David. Ben-David continues to rebuff him.

Instancer watches from the crest of the crag.

Suddenly Manning turns his back on Ben-David. He strides toward

Rachel, who stands beside me on the shoulder of the road. Manning seizes her by the elbow, hauls her roughly toward the front of the column, toward Dana's lead Humvee.

Dana herself continues staring through binoculars at Instancer.

Ben-David pursues Manning. He orders him to release Rachel. I'm crossing with long strides after both of them.

The lead Humvee's driver and gunner stare as Manning approaches, dragging Rachel.

> MANNING
>
> You two, dismount! I'm taking the vehicle.

The soldiers look to Ben-David, who is scampering as fast as he can to catch up.

> MANNING
> (to soldiers)
>
> Get out, I said!

Ben-David overtakes Manning. He orders him to take his hands off Rachel.

The soldiers are staring. Ben-David tears the flap open on his holster. Manning hears the military Glock 19 come out. He hears it cock.

> BEN-DAVID
>
> Stop, goddamn you! Where do you think
> you're going?

Manning turns back.

> MANNING
>
> Where are we going? The same place
> Instancer's going. The only place we
> can go.

Manning again shoves Rachel toward the Humvee's door.

> MANNING
> (to Ben-David)
> Keep behind us in your truck. I want to
> see your headlights in my rearview every
> second.

Instancer watches from the peak. Every eye has turned toward him. He mounts to the cab of his truck. We see the vehicle clearly now—a Chevrolet Chinook 5500 HD, the biggest, most powerful stock pickup on the planet. The engine starts. The oversize all-terrain tires churn into the dust.

Dana has at last joined our group. Manning orders her and the soldiers to break out the tunnel-busters. He hands me the Zombie Killer.

> MANNING
> (to all, re: Ben-David)
> Protect him!

I'm scanning the faces of the troopers. Manning has taken over the convoy completely. He has usurped Ben-David as commander and overpowered the others by the sheer force of his personality. That, and the desperate urgency that has overtaken all of us with the apparition of the Adversary.

                    MANNING
               (to Rachel)
          Get in. Take the wheel.

                    RACHEL
          Go to hell.

                    MANNING
          I intend to. And you're going with me.

Instancer's truck reverses out of its overlook position, shifts into a forward gear, and accelerates from sight down the far slope.

Manning watches for a long moment, then turns back to Rachel.

                    MANNING
          You conducted Instancer into this world
          and, by God, you're gonna conduct him out.

BOOK SEVEN

END OF DAYS

30

MEGIDDO

W E'RE FOLLOWING Manning and Rachel.

Three hours have passed. The convoy has found its way down, at last, off the crest line. The trucks lumber west through a storm front growing more violent by the minute.

From Beit She'an, Highway 71 runs northwest twenty miles to Afula, a sizable agricultural town, then Route 65 turns southwest, ten miles to Megiddo. It's kibbutz country, farmland parched to ash.

I have been fretting that we would somehow fail to find Gehenna. The absurdity of this now becomes apparent. From ten miles east of Afula, both sides of the highway, and indeed the driving lanes of the road itself, are packed solid with refugees and displaced persons streaming toward that exact location.

                              ME
        Who are these people?

                        BEN-DAVID
        End-of-the-Worlders.

Pilgrims in the tens of thousands shuffle westward. Heat tornadoes shimmer in the distance; cloud formations press menacingly upon the Earth. Khamsin-driven grunge compels each trekker to seek protection beneath hoods and head wraps. Beneath Bedouin-style robes we spy not shoes or boots but bare feet and worn, open-toed sandals.

We have entered the Bible.

Ahead, Manning's Humvee is honking, trying to clear the throughway. Ben-David shouts down from our cab to one ragged straggler.

> BEN-DAVID
>
> Where is everybody going?

> STRAGGLER
>
> Gehenna.

> BEN-DAVID
>
> Why?

> STRAGGLER
>
> Who knows? People just started moving.
> It's crazy.

I'm recording the spectacle on my phone. The sense is of collective derangement, of mob energy mounting out of control. Threadbare trekkers are hauling themselves up onto our running boards. Others are clambering up the outboard rails.

Ben-David swings out onto the flank of the truck. Giora shouts at him to get back in. Over the comm channel I hear Dana reinforcing this call. Ben-David ignores both of them. He's trying to protect the tech gear in the cargo beds. The tailgates of the trucks are sealed only by canvas.

Already free-riders are tearing their way aboard with pocketknives and bare hands.

I'm on the channel to Manning, reporting the emergency.

MANNING'S VOICE
(from comm channel)
Follow me. We're cutting cross-country.

I'm squinting right and left across the wasteland. The dust bowl as far as I can see is carpeted with tent encampments and hobo jungles. Vans and camper-shell pickups, sedans and mini-buses squat not only along the shoulders of the highway but fan rearward across open country, first in ordered rows, then in chaotic clutches, finally in a mad jumble back, back into the flat, burned-out badlands.

Giora is shouting to Ben-David to get back to the cab. Manning's Humvee is pulling away. Already its taillights are being swallowed amid the multitude.

Around our convoy flows a river of the desperate and the devout— children and ancients, male and female, the hale and the infirm. Aged indigents hobble on crutches and walking sticks, enfeebled crones are being borne in wheelbarrows and towed under blanket wraps in wagons and two-wheel carts. I'm thinking, *These are the church ladies we saw boarding buses on Central Park West. They're the Chasidim from Crown Heights and Borough Park.* Plus tens of thousands from Europe, Asia, Africa. How have they survived in this hell? Where do they get water? The faithful must be perishing by the hundreds every night.

Ben-David returns. He hauls himself inside, dropping hard into the seat beside me.

BEN-DAVID
Go. Go!

Our convoy commander points left, to an unpaved agricultural road. Giora turns onto it. The column picks up speed over open ground, shedding the last of the hangers-on.

An hour passes. We've lost Manning and Rachel. We've lost the road.

DANA

(over comm channel)

Amos, are you watching the needle?

Ben-David checks the EXT TEMP gauge: 121° Fahrenheit.

Another forty minutes. The electrical storm intensifies. Comm signals sizzle and break apart.

Barometric pressure is plunging. I feel it in my ears. The leaden sky turns to ink. The gale rises. The heat has become unimaginable.

Where is Instancer?

Ahead?

Behind?

Is he at Gehenna now?

Where is Manning?

His channel comes through in snatches on the console screen depicting Humvee #1. But his vehicle locator signal has vanished. We have no idea where he is.

The sky crackles with *migdalim*. Gloom devours our headlights. It's not yet six, but our truck creeps forward on a track gone to midnight.

BEN-DAVID

(into comm channel)

Rachel, this is Amos. Where are you?

We can see Rachel and Manning on our console screen (and even hear them in bits and pieces) but they can't hear us. They're not responding.

> BEN-DAVID
>
> Rachel, do you copy? Rachel!
>> (to himself)
> Goddammit, what the fuck's wrong with
> this thing?

Five more minutes pass. On the screen we can see Manning and Rachel. They've stopped.

> MANNING
>
> Amos! Dewey! If you copy . . . don't
> follow us. I say again: stay back. We've
> entered some kind of defile . . . intense
> heat . . . way beyond—

Manning's signal breaks up. Ben-David tries every channel to reach them.

Nothing.

They're blind too in this storm.

Their EXT TEMP gauge reads 134° Fahrenheit.

Video from Manning's Humvee returns. We can see him. He's getting out of the vehicle. Great sheaves of gale-driven sand boom in. Rachel is shouting something to Manning. Something about water bags . . .

> BEN-DAVID
>
> They've boiled over.

The Humvee's forward exterior camera shows Manning struggling to raise the hood. He's wrestling a desert water bag from its rig on the Humvee's grille.

An endless minute passes.

Now Rachel gets out. She too struggles forward into the storm. Another minute.

Suddenly both Manning and Rachel come pounding back to the cab, diving in, in obvious extremis.

They have one water bag between them. Manning presses it into Rachel's hands. He shouts to her to drink it, drink it all. It takes all Manning's strength to get the doors closed. Rachel is upending the flax water bag above her mouth. But the liquid seems to vaporize the instant it gushes forth. Rachel gets only drops. She sucks the tube. The bag is dry.

INT TEMP 141.

Manning's in the driver's seat now. He starts the engine. Rachel shouts something that the channel garbles.

> MANNING
>
> We have to move. We'll die if we stay
> here.

In Ben-David's cab, I'm trying everything I can think of to get a fix on Manning and Rachel's position. But the electrical storm is driving every instrument crazy. The magnetic compass on Ben-David's dash is spinning like a top.

> ME
>
> Amos, we have to find them. Go forward!

> BEN-DAVID
>
> Where? Into a ditch? Over a cliff?

Our driver Giora inches tentatively into the gloom. Three minutes. Five. How long can Manning's engine run at these temperatures without coolant? How long can Manning and Rachel keep functioning before they go into heat shock?

Ben-David and I can see Manning and Rachel in snatches, half depixelated on the dash tablet.

Suddenly Manning's head lurches wildly out of the frame.

The Humvee's cab upends.

MANNING

Quicksand!

Manning and Rachel are lifted out of their seats and pressed against the overhead. The cab rotates ninety degrees onto its side. We hear steel bolts snapping. Manning and Rachel are flung powerfully into the windshield.

The Humvee stops with a violent wrench. Manning and Rachel rebound off the dash and windshield.

In Ben-David's cab, a red light starts to flash on the tablet screen linked to Manning's Humvee. An automated voice repeats:

AUTOMATED VOICE

MAYDAY! MAYDAY! All stations, MAYDAY!

The Humvee has stopped on its side.

ME

Manning! Manning, can you hear me?

I'm bawling into the mike on the convoy system and into my own phone.

No response.

The gun turret behind and above Manning and Rachel bangs open with a thunderous clang. Rachel, hanging on to the steering wheel with both hands, barely keeps herself from being flung rightward over the center console. Manning in the passenger seat is bowled sideways into the armored window of the starboard door.

The Humvee is pinned at the foot of a collapsing dune. The right-hand door is buried against tons of sand, the driver's door submerged beneath the dune caving in from above. Rachel struggles against its subsiding weight.

Manning manages to clamber over the high, boxy console. He squeezes his body between Rachel and the steering wheel, seating his shoulders against the door. Planting both soles against the console's left inboard edge, he pushes upward against the doorframe with all his strength.

A weight of tons presses from above.

No hope.

Manning falls back.

Sand pours into the cabin through the open hatch of the gun turret. For moments Manning and Rachel struggle to climb over the seatbacks, seeking the last avenue of escape—through the opening of the turret.

The collapsing dune seals this.

Darkness. I keep calling Manning's name. A flashlight switches on. The interior of the Humvee's cab is sealed like a tomb. INT TEMP 145°.

RACHEL

We're going to die here.

Manning lets himself topple rightward and down, onto the passenger-side doorframe, which has become the vehicle's floor.

In Ben-David's cab I can see Manning, illuminated by Rachel's flashlight, groping across the instrument panel. At once the Mayday call shuts down.

> MANNING
> (from comm channel)
> Amos . . . Dewey, if you can hear
> me . . . do NOT attempt rescue. I say
> again . . . DO NOT enter this section
> of ground. It's unstable. Our vehicle
> has plunged into a sinkhole. A dune has
> collapsed on top of us.

Manning instructs me, at all costs, to get Ben-David to Gehenna.

> MANNING
> Don't worry about me. I'll get there
> somehow. Amos, can you hear me? Get to
> Gehenna! I'll get there!

Ben-David and I, and Giora, our driver, peer at the screen depicting the overturned interior of the Humvee illuminated only by flashlight. We glance to one another. No one speaks.

The screen continues to flicker and depixelate.

> RACHEL
> (to Manning)
> We've stopped sweating.

Rachel's fingertips probe her forehead.

                    RACHEL
Our bodies' cooling mechanisms have shut
down. We're in heat shock. Our internal
organs are failing.

The Humvee has settled at a ninety-degree angle. Buried, top and bottom. Manning and Rachel are immured. They can no longer hear the gale outside.

Manning's side of the cabin continues filling with sand. He sets himself into the seat and braces against the seatback. Manning kicks with his bootheels violently against the windshield. The forward window glass in a Humvee is in two sections with a steel column between. Manning kicks first at his side, then at Rachel's. The glass is two inches thick, laminated polycarbonate, bulletproof against even a .50-caliber round.

                    RACHEL
     Stop.

Manning looses another volley of kicks.

                    RACHEL
     Leave it.

Manning lets his weight fall against the passenger door, which has become the floor of the compartment in which he and Rachel find themselves entombed. He forces a breath of superheated air. Cascades of sand and grit sheet in through the chassis seals and the ruptures in the overhead. The sand rises like floodwater through the floorboards.

Manning's eyes meet Rachel's.

> MANNING

Tell me one thing.

> RACHEL

What?

> MANNING

And for once don't lie to me.

Rachel waits.

> MANNING

You were with Instancer in Moscow. You
drove the car after he murdered Golokoff.
Tell me the truth. A witness saw you. A
witness who has no reason to lie.

Rachel glances to the temp gauge on the dash: 147°. It takes her long
moments to raise the strength to answer.

> RACHEL

Yeah, I was with him. But only then. Only
that one time. Every other place, every
other minute, I was hunting him. That's
the truth, whether you believe it or not.

Manning makes no response.

> RACHEL

You don't know what it's like.

                    MANNING
What what's like?

                    RACHEL
Him. His power. To be with him. To feel
him . . .

Rachel sets the flashlight down on the console below her. Its beam flickers, illuminating her face with an unearthly, orange glow.

                    RACHEL
Did I know who he was? I didn't want to
know. He was the greatest thing that ever
happened to me.

Rachel's breath comes shallow and spasmodic.

                    RACHEL
His idea to identify the Thirty-Six
was beyond brilliant. I don't care what
happened. He changed everything for me.

Rachel speaks not to Manning or even to herself, but as if to some universal, incorporeal listener.

                    RACHEL
So what if he was the devil? If there's
a devil, there's a God, and if there's a
God, there's meaning. Hell itself can't be
worse than life without meaning.

Rachel's eyes turn back toward Manning.

                    RACHEL
    Did I mention he was the greatest fuck I
    ever had, or any woman ever had?

Rachel's breath comes shallower and more broken. Her lids close. Her chin lolls forward onto her chest.

Manning himself begins to go under.

Then:

A sound like knuckles rapping on metal.

Manning hears it. He tries to open his eyes.

The sound intensifies.

No longer rapping on steel.

Glass now.

The windshield.

Manning forces his lids apart. He turns toward the glass.

Outside, a hand scrapes away sand and grit.

Daylight.

A man's face appears.

Boots mount the overturned hood of the Humvee. Manning stares as lugged soles clamber to the driver's door topside.

With a heave of inhuman strength the man hauls the door open. Sand pours in onto Rachel and down onto Manning.

                    INSTANCER
    Hello, Jim.

Instancer reaches down into the cabin with one hand, seizes Rachel by her shirt collar. He hauls her out.

Manning peers up.

Instancer's hand stretches down a second time.

Manning clasps Instancer, wrist to wrist.

Instancer hauls Manning clear.

Instancer lowers Manning past the heeled-over roof into the sand on the far side. Manning collapses beside the overturned Humvee.

Instancer has already deposited Rachel in this spot.

She struggles to one knee, sucking in great gulps of air. Temperature has dropped dramatically outside the coffin confines of the buried Humvee.

Backed up to the Humvee, tailgate-to-grille, squats Instancer's Chevy Chinook. Taillights, cargo-bed lamps, and the rear-facing red and yellow spot-beams of the light bar blaze into the gale-beaten murk.

> INSTANCER
> (to Manning)
> Help me do this.

Instancer drops the pickup's tailgate. From the cargo bed he hauls two heavy-duty chain-and-hook cables. He spools one clear and passes the other to Manning. Instancer yokes his cable to one of the two D-rings on the prow of the Humvee. Manning does the same with the other. Instancer checks both to be sure they're secure. He starts toward the driver's door of the Chinook.

> INSTANCER
> (to Manning and Rachel)
> Keep clear of the vehicle. This thing's
> gonna come out like a cannonball when it
> pops.

Manning and Rachel obey. From a rack on the pickup's grille, Instancer removes a five-gallon flax sack with DESERT WATER BAG stenciled on the front. He tosses it to Rachel. The bag lands with a full-sounding splat on the sand before her. Rachel seizes it and upends the bag over her face, pouring the liquid, hot as it is, straight down her throat.

In Ben-David's cab, I'm taking in this spectacle in snatches of garbled sound and depixelated video.

Suddenly our truck—Ben-David's and Giora's—brakes hard and plunges frame-down onto a berm of sand. The vehicle stops as if it had hit a wall. I'm flung violently into the dashboard.

                    ME
    What was that?!

I thrash back to upright. Ben-David and Giora are peering forward over the hood.

The view is straight down.

Our truck has nose-dived over the crest of a dune and belly-flopped to a stop on the summit.

Two hundred feet below, we see headlights and taillights, fog lamps, and the red and yellow spot-beams of a pickup truck's light bar. Through breaks in the murk we glimpse two male figures and one female.

                 BEN-DAVID
    It's Rachel! That's Instancer!

I'm out the door and onto the sand. The second male below is Manning.

>   ME
>
> Go down! Drive down!

>   GIORA
>
> I can't. We'll flip like they did.

I'm shouting down the dune to Manning.

With the storm he can't see or hear me.

I start down on foot. Ben-David grabs me. Giora holds me back too.

>   BEN-DAVID
>
> That's quicksand. You'll sink into it like
> water.

I'm struggling against them.

>   BEN-DAVID
>
> Wait!

Ben-David points to the base of the dune. I follow his finger. I'm straining to see through gaps in the murk.

As Ben-David, Giora, and I watch, Instancer mounts to the driver's seat of the Chinook. Even through the storm we can hear the growl of the 7.6-liter Duramax diesel. The pickup bucks forward. Its massive desert tires churn. The buried Humvee won't budge. The diesel screams again. We can see the Humvee twitch, then buck a foot or two forward. Sand spills from its topline. Instancer rocks the pickup, tugging, tugging. The tow chains sing. We can hear them, like human voices, through the gale. Suddenly, with a ferocious heave and pop, the Humvee springs forward and up, shedding sand in great sheaves. The vehicle careens wildly, almost flips, then squirts free, totters for a moment on its rightmost rims, then lurches again and crashes down hard onto its four tires. The Humvee has righted itself. Instancer has righted it.

> BEN-DAVID
> Giora, back off this dune! Get the truck
> moving!

I'm peering through binoculars now. I see Instancer, moving swiftly and efficiently, decouple the tow chains and sling them, clanging, back into the cargo bed of his truck. He lifts the tailgate and shuts it.

Instancer and Manning stand across from each other.

They're speaking.

I'm watching and timing the exchange in my head. Five seconds. Ten. Part of me wants to scramble back to the comm tablet in Ben-David's cab on the chance of catching a phrase or even a word. But I don't dare tear my eyes from the scene below.

Instancer and Manning finish speaking. Instancer returns to his vehicle. Manning boards the Humvee. The pickup grinds forward, out of the two hubcap-deep tracks it had torn up in the earth. I hear the diesel growl as Instancer shifts up. The truck churns away.

> ME
> What direction is he going?

> BEN-DAVID
> Gehenna.

The Humvee's engine starts. Two plumes bark from the stacks. The frame shudders slightly as Manning shifts into gear. The vehicle pulls clear of the dune and accelerates, turning in the same direction as Instancer's Chinook.

BEN-DAVID

Dewey, get back here!

I clamber aboard Ben-David's six-by. Giora has gotten us free of the summit. We take off after Manning and Instancer, keeping clear of the collapsed dune. Ben-David is on the comm channel to the other convoy vehicles, sending our location, warning them of the quicksand hazard, and ordering them to follow as fast as they can and to arm the tunnel weapons.

Later, replaying the audio from Manning's Humvee, I catch the final verbal exchange between him and Instancer at the base of the dune.

INSTANCER

You weren't surprised to see me.

MANNING

Did you expect me to be?

31

GEHENNA

I'M IN THE MIDDLE of the bench seat of Ben-David's six-by, between Giora at the wheel and Ben-David against the passenger door, when the Chevy Chinook emerges from the murk at high speed.

Instancer slams into us, prow-first, directly below Ben-David's door. The army truck skids sideways. The fuel tank on its right flank crushes against the frame. The Chevy brakes in a four-wheel power slide. Instancer's boot propels his driver's door open. So fast that none of us has time to react, Instancer leaps from his truck and flings himself onto the right side of ours.

Instancer hauls the passenger door open. His right hand clasps the frame; his left seizes Ben-David by the waist of his trousers.

Ahead in our headlights: Gehenna.

The dig and its floodlamps loom through the gale-driven grunge.

Ben-David twists violently in the seat, turning both boots, now kicking wildly, toward Instancer. I'm hanging on to Ben-David, right arm around him from behind, left hand clamped like a claw onto the steering column under the dash. Giora stomps the brakes and heaves the wheel hard left, trying to use centrifugal force to fling Instancer out.

No use.

With one hand on Ben-David's belt buckle, Instancer hauls him feet-first out into the storm. I watch the Israeli's body plummet, bang, bang, off the edge of the seat. His skull cracks violently into the running board. Instancer drags him clear. He pulls Ben-David by one ankle across the ground.

My earbud squalls:

MANNING

I'm here.

Through the open truck door I see Manning's Humvee burst out of the gloom, hurtling straight toward Instancer and Ben-David. Manning sees them. He flattens the brakes.

An up-armored Humvee weighs twelve thousand pounds. The vehicle skids wildly, throwing up great breakers of sand and stone. It stops. Manning springs from the cab. I toss him the Zombie Killer. He cocks it and pumps two shells point-blank into Instancer's back.

I see Ben-David crab-scurry clear.

Manning slings the shotgun away.

He flings himself onto Instancer.

The two grapple and merge into a single form. For a moment it seems as if Manning has gained command.

Instancer hurls Manning powerfully off his back.

Something makes me turn toward the Humvee. Rachel emerges from its right-hand door.

She sees her brother.

Ben-David has gotten to his feet. His eyes find Rachel's. I have never seen a look like the one that passes between them in this moment.

Has Rachel come to stand by him or to kill him? Clearly Ben-David can't tell.

His glance seeks Dana and the other paratroopers.

Without a command the soldiers race for their weapons.

Instancer stands, untouched, unhurt.

He turns first to Rachel, then to Manning, then to Ben-David.

> INSTANCER
>
> Thirty-six.

The lugs of Ben-David's boots churn the grit and grime. He bolts for the entry to Gehenna.

We're at the summit of the excavation site. A temporary structure, blown half to shreds by the gale, protects the entrance and the passage-ways to the levels below. Ben-David lurches into this, tottering from heat and fatigue. He vanishes from sight down an incline.

Lightning continues to boom across the valley of Megiddo. A keening sound, from the wind and the thrumming of the underground, makes the marrow vibrate inside my bones.

Instancer, absent all haste, turns toward the summit entry. He starts after Ben-David.

Manning is on his feet. He tugs the 226 from his shoulder holster. The Zombie Killer lies in the dirt beside Ben-David's truck, where Manning had flung it when he leapt to grapple with Instancer.

> MANNING
> (to me)
> Bring the gun.

Manning's face is the color of ash. His arms hang, limp from exhaustion and dehydration. He lingers a moment only, to gather himself and to be sure I have heard him and will do what he said.

MANNING

And bring her.

Manning's last glance is to Rachel. Then he turns and stalks toward the summit entry.

I pick up the shotgun. I grab Rachel.

Manning disappears into the excavation.

Instancer has plunged below, pursuing Ben-David.

I glance back to the army trucks. The soldiers are hastily arming the three tunnel-busters. Dana issues orders.

I feel Rachel resisting me. My right hand holds the shotgun. My left clutches her by the elbow.

ME

Try anything and I'll kill you.

I drag her forward.

Into the archaeological mound.

Diesel generators thrum. High-power construction-type lamps light the interior. The place is like a construction site, only going down instead of up.

LEVEL ONE

I know Rachel knows the layout. I order her to tell me which way to go.

RACHEL

There's only one way, Dewey. Down.

I spot an elevator, open-sided, like in a mine. No way I'm stepping into that coffin. Graded inclines—floored with corrugated tin, shored with timbers—descend beside the shaft. Safety signs plaster every wall. Every slope is roped or fitted with handrails.

I hear Ben-David's boots, echoing from below on the corrugated flooring.

Instancer is calling to him. I recognize his voice but can't make out what he's saying. I hear Manning's voice.

I tow Rachel after me.

Level Two.

Level Three.

Where are Dana and the soldiers? They must have their tunnel weapons by now. I'm trying to visualize how they'll use them.

The dig itself is one giant mound. *Tel* is the archaeological term. It goes down a hundred and seventy feet. The tel is constituted of the layered remains of human habitations dating back five thousand years. Each historic settlement was founded on the ruins of the city, town, or village that went before, as each race of conquerors displaced the one that preceded it and was, in turn, supplanted by the wave to follow.

We have entered the pyramid at the top. Our route is straight down. But the mound can also be accessed at its base. Indeed, three excavation adits, wide and high enough to accommodate borers and other earth-moving equipment, enter the tel horizontally from three different sides, at the base of the pyramid. These tunnels converge at Level Seven around the central descending shaft.

Dana and her weapons crew have entered one tunnel.

Another team advances along a second tunnel.

A third penetrates the final lateral.

LEVEL FOUR

I stumble down the tin-floored incline, propelling Rachel before me. Heat ascends from beneath my soles.

I smell sulfur.

Shouting echoes from below.

CAUTION signs in Hebrew, Arabic, and English plaster the walls. Alarm lamps flash in amber and red. I spot a locker area cut out against one wall. Flame boots sit in neat rows. Heat suits hang beneath visored helmets.

LEVEL FIVE

GEOTHERMAL ACTIVITY

FLAME SUITS MANDATORY BELOW THIS LEVEL

Rachel pulls away from me toward the lockers.

RACHEL
(snatches flame boots)
Grab something.

ME
Keep moving.

RACHEL
Are you stupid?

Level Six.

I force Rachel down before me. Heat has become unfathomable. My bare hands are so hot I feel my fingernails curling. Why didn't I stop and grab a flame suit . . . or at least gloves? My neck and ears are blistering. I press down another corrugated incline.

Suddenly: the central shaft opens—a vaulted atrium where the three equipment tunnels come together.

Instancer stands at the nexus.

Manning stops at the incline entry. I stagger up beside him, dragging Rachel.

                    MANNING
        Stay back!

He catches me and presses me into the wall. He's smart; he has grabbed flame boots and gloves.

                    MANNING
        Cover your face!

Manning makes me take his gloves and boots.

As I'm struggling to don them . . .

The first tunnel-buster fires.

There's a split-second delay. Then the second and third go off.

The shock wave hits like a building collapsing. My feet bowl from under me, even in the lee of the access tunnel. I go deaf and blind. Super-heated dust fills my mouth and nostrils. Overhead panels crash. Alarms blare. The central shaft collapses in sections on all three sides.

I'm clinging to one of Manning's fire boots. He has gone down too. I've forgotten Rachel completely. My only thought is, as during the warrant service, *Hang on to that shotgun!*

The corrugated floor writhes beneath me. It's the back-suck from the initial concussion. I'm being swept. The air that has been pushed in by the tunnel weapons' triple blast now roars back in the opposite direction—out.

                    MANNING
        Dewey! Can you hear me?

Manning pulls me by the collar back into the incline tunnel.

By increments, the central shaft clears.

Instancer stands there.

Soot-black from sole to crown.

But unfazed.

Grinning.

LEVEL EIGHT

A steel stairwell descends from the blasted atrium. Ben-David has plunged down. Instancer follows.

GEOTHERMAL AREA
NO ENTRY

Alarms blare. Emergency sprinklers gush from overhead. Foam fire retardant blasts from wide-mouth nozzles along the walls.

Manning grabs me.

MANNING

The Zombie Killer!

I press it into his hands.

LEVEL NINE

Manning vanishes down the stairwell.

Am I a coward? Every cell is screaming, *Run! Climb! Get outta here!*

I can feel the earth's core beneath me. It rumbles like a nuclear reactor. The soles of my feet, despite the flame boots, burn as if I'm standing on a hot iron.

What is that sound?

Magma?

The geothermal core?

I descend the stairwell. Its bottom is a sheltered cell.

My heart fails me.

I can't take another step.

I peer, shielding my eyes with the oversized, Mylar-faced flame gloves.

Level Nine is a domed arena, the size of a wrestling ring. Its floor is sizzling corrugated tin. You can see the magma glow beneath it.

Ben-David crouches in a defensive stance on the far side. An alcove no bigger than a coffin protects him. He wears a flame suit with boots and gloves. He's holding a helmet up to protect his face.

Instancer stands in the center of the ring, facing Manning, who has stepped from the stairwell. A space of ten feet separates them.

I hear a sound from above.

Rachel.

She half tumbles down the ladder well. In flame boots but with no suit, no gloves, no helmet. I realize I'd lost track of her. I curse my heedlessness. I lunge at her.

She wrestles against me.

RACHEL

Where's the gun?

We both turn toward Manning.

He clutches the Zombie Killer.

Instancer faces him. Smoke rises from his shirt and trousers.

Manning steps forward. His clothes are smoldering too.

                    MANNING
      You can fall.

                    INSTANCER
      What?

                    MANNING
      Motherfucker, you can fall.

Manning pumps three shells, not at Instancer but at the floor he stands on. The surface shreds, opening like a trapdoor.

Instancer plunges into the void.

A fury primeval roars upward from the center of the Earth. Manning's shirt and trousers erupt into flame. He had started toward Ben-David, to drag him clear, but the blast bowls him backward. Then he sees:

Instancer.

One hand clutches the twisted corrugation that Manning's shotgun had torn apart.

A second hand reaches up.

Instancer's head and shoulders appear.

Ben-David squirts from his shelter, dashes along the wall to Rachel and me in the stairwell.

                    BEN-DAVID
      Go! Go!

He grabs us both and pushes us toward the rungs leading up.

Rachel resists.

I do too.

Instancer hauls himself up out of the chasm. He's half clear when Manning bull-rushes at him.

Manning flings himself full-speed, full-weight upon Instancer.

Heat is rising from the void in scarlet waves. Manning clutches Instancer from behind and above. It's some kind of wrestler's hold.

Manning hauls Instancer's left hand off its grip. He pries with all his strength and leverage to free the right.

Instancer jack-knifes himself with impossible power. Both hands recover their grip. He rises, with Manning clinging to his back.

Something pushes me aside.

For a second I think it's Ben-David.

Then I see Rachel, bending to retrieve the Zombie Killer.

She steps from our sheltered cove into the central arena.

She fires as she advances.

One shot.

Two.

Three.

Each successive impact blows Instancer rearward. But his grip on the rim never slackens.

Manning, hanging on to Instancer from behind, struggles to pry Instancer's hands from their hold.

With a cry, Rachel flings the shotgun aside. She lowers her shoulders and charges with all her strength into Instancer.

Instancer's grip fails.

The three, fused in fire, plunge as one into the inferno.

BEN-DAVID

Climb, Dewey! Get out of here!

When I reach the surface, every follicle of hair on my body, including those on my arms and legs, has been seared to the skin. My phone in my pocket has melted. It's not till I recover my laptop from Ben-David's truck that I can enter their cloud codes and retrieve my comrades' status lines:

END RACHEL TRANSMISSION

END MANNING TRANSMISSION

BOOK EIGHT

CYPRUS

32

EARTH'S LAST CHANCE

O UR PARTY, absent Manning and Rachel (and Dana and her soldiers, who have remained in Israel), has crossed to Cyprus by
sea from Haifa. Representatives of a hundred and seventy-four nations,
including forty-seven heads of state, attend this climate conference billed
without overstatement as "Earth's Last Chance."

The harbor at Nicosia has been converted into an exhibition space
for two dozen tidal, sea current, and saltwater energy projects, including Ben-David's SROG, Seawater Re-Oxygenation and Generation technology. Crowds in the thousands swarm the site in a celebratory mood.
The emotion of the climate conference is one of long-awaited, overdue
breakthrough.

Around the globe, atmospheric anomalies have stabilized. Rain is falling in parts of Africa, Australia, and Central Asia where drought conditions
had prevailed for decades. Two Category 5 Atlantic hurricanes have been
downgraded to tropical storms, and even these seem to be abating further.

Is this the hour of salvation at last?

Ben-David has, moments before, delivered his keynote address to the
representatives and heads of state of the assembled nations. I'm descend-

ing the steps to Amity Square. The hall behind me echoes with the ovation for Ben-David's speech.

What had seemed unachievable until this instant has at once become not just practicable but inevitable. The species *can* grasp its own destiny. Humankind's expedient and self-destroying impulses will not win out yet again.

What about Manning? I set his loss alongside the salvation of the planet. It's crazy, I know. But in my mind the two stand equal. What keeps me (so far) from feeling devastated is the thought that Manning in some way *wanted* his fiery end. He felt in that moment, I'm certain, that his life meant something. As for Rachel, all my feelings of protectiveness have come flooding back. She was a vessel broken in a hundred places, who put herself back together for the one moment that meant everything.

I have a message from Dana in Israel, sent forty-eight hours ago. Earthmoving equipment and demolition engineers have arrived at the site of the Gehenna dig. Dana is there. She is witnessing the transformation firsthand. With the blessing of global leaders, the "portal to hell" will be sealed permanently beneath thousands of tons of basalt and sand.

I hear a scream behind me.

For a moment I think, *Ah, a cry of joy.*

Then conference-goers in panic begin streaming past me down the convention hall steps. I turn and look back. Hundreds are fleeing the hall.

"Ben-David!" someone cries. "Ben-David has been murdered!"

My blood goes to ice.

My hands and wrists are still wrapped from burns. My eyebrows, singed to the skin line, are just starting to grow back. My bare skull, salved in oil and antiseptic, is sheathed in a scarf.

I have no weapon.

I swim back up the steps, into the stampede.

"Who?" I'm shouting to anyone who might answer. "Who killed him?"

No one knows.

I find a policeman. The killer got away, he says. "He escaped into the crowd."

I clutch the officer's arm.

>   ME
> How was Ben-David killed? With a gun?

>   POLICE OFFICER
> Strangled. By hand. Choked to death.

I plunge back down the steps amid the throng. I don't know where I'm going. I have no idea what I hope to do.

Am I running?

From what?

To where?

I try to summon Manning. What would he do?

As I'm thinking this, I spot Dana.

What the fuck?

She's below me, on the steps, climbing toward me, toward the hall.

>   ME
> Dana!
>   (rushing down to her)
> What are you doing here? I thought you
> were in Israel.

I stare at Dana. She's dressed in civilian garb—a skirt and a low-cut summer blouse. She's wearing eyeliner and mascara, with her hair free and flowing. She looks feminine and sensual.

When she sees me, her expression turns stricken, even shamefaced.

Then I realize she is here with a lover.

The man is standing next to her, holding her hand. I haven't noticed him, being too startled and surprised by seeing Dana.

> INSTANCER
>
> Hello, Dewey.

I can't breathe. The earth seems to collapse beneath my feet. I stare. It's him. Untouched, unscathed, unaltered.

> INSTANCER
>
> Have you had time to bring your notes up
> to date? Collated? Uploaded to the cloud?

He knows I have.
I know what's coming.

> INSTANCER
>
> You're my chronicler, Dewey. Thank you.
> What we have accomplished shall endure
> forever.

His right arm shoots toward my throat, swift as a striking snake.
I feel my voice box being crushed.
The organ-failure alarm chirps on my indicator. My last thought is to picture my status line as it updates in the cloud.

END DEWEY TRANSMISSION

And God saw that the wickedness of man was great in the earth, and that every imagination of the thoughts of his heart was only evil continually . . . And the Lord said, I will destroy man whom I have created from the face of the earth; both man, and beast, and the creeping thing, and the fowls of the air; for it repenteth me that I have made them.

GENESIS 6:5–7

SPECIAL THANKS

To COLONEL ROBERT GOUGH and to Bill Bagshaw, whose encouragement kept me going when I was inches away from pulling the plug. To Shawn Coyne, who "put the Story Grid on" the narrative when it crashed in midstream and provided the direction to put it back together. To Kate Snow for contributions above and beyond the call of duty. To Officers Gina and Freddie Pineda of the NYPD for their counsel on police procedure; to Amanda Tunnell for matters of tech and media; to Rabbi Mordecai Finley for his wisdom on all things Judaic. To Star Lawrence for his belief in this material and his rigor in pushing it to its most highly realized level. And to Sterling Lord, who put everything together and made this whole damn thing happen.